ALSO BY CLAIRE COOK

Wallflower in Bloom

Best Staged Plans

Seven Year Switch

The Wildwater Walking Club

Summer Blowout

Life's a Beach

Multiple Choice

Must Love Dogs

Ready to Fall

TIME FLIES

Claire Cook

A TOUCHSTONE BOOK
PUBLISHED BY SIMON & SCHUSTER
NEW YORK LONDON TORONTO SYDNEY NEW DELHI

Touchstone
A Division of Simon & Schuster, Inc.
1230 Avenue of the Americas
New York, NY 10020

First Touchstone hardcover edition June 2013

TOUCHSTONE and colophon are registered trademarks of Simon & Schuster, Inc.

For information about special discounts for bulk purchases, please contact Simon & Schuster Special Sales at 1-866-506-1949 or business@simonandschuster.com.

The Simon & Schuster Speakers Bureau can bring authors to your live event. For more information or to book an event, contact the Simon & Schuster Speakers Bureau at 1-866-248-3049 or visit our website at www.simonspeakers.com.

Designed by Claudia Martinez

Manufactured in the United States of America

10 9 8 7 6 5 4 3 2 1

Library of Congress Cataloging-in-Publication Data
Cook, Claire, 1955-
  Time Flies / Claire Cook.—First Touchstone hardcover edition.
     pages cm
  "A Touchstone book."
  1. Separated women—Fiction. 2. Female friendship—Fiction. 3. High-school reunions—Fiction. 4. Self-realization in women—Fiction. 5. Road fiction. I. Title.
  PS3553.O55317T56 2013
  813'.54—dc23
                                      2012045269

ISBN 978-1-4516-7367-8
ISBN 978-1-4516-7369-2 (ebook)

To my high school classmates, and yours.

I

I am

I am writing

I am writing this

I am writing this in

I am writing this in the

I am writing this in the corner

I am writing this in the corner of

I am writing this in the corner of your

I am writing this in the corner of your old

I am writing this in the corner of your old yearbook

TIME FLIES

CHAPTER 1

When my cell phone rang, I'd just finished cutting up my marriage mattress.

I put down my chain saw carefully so it wouldn't scratch the hardwood floor. Then I slid my safety glasses up to the top of my head like a headband and reached for my phone.

"Hel*lo*-oh," I said.

"Hey," B.J. said. "It's me. What's up?"

I puffed a sprinkling of sawdust from the phone. "Not much. Same old, same old."

"So, check your email—the invitation just went out. You *are* coming up for our reunion, right?"

"No way." When I shook my head for emphasis, more sawdust flaked from my hair like dandruff. "Come on, B.J., we've been over this at least eight times already."

B.J. blew a raspberry into the phone line. "*No way* is not an acceptable answer. You're going. No excuses. You're not still mooning around about Kurt, are you?"

"You mean like counting the days till he sends me a Hallmark card for Almost Ex-Wife's Day?"

B.J. still laughed exactly like she had in high school, a series of sharp staccato barks. "See, your sense of humor is back."

"Ha," I said.

"What you need is some fun in the sun. Plus, if you ask me, there aren't nearly enough opportunities to act like a teenager once you get to be our age, so we've got to grab any chance we get. And the good news is we can drink legally this time around."

"Great," I said, "but I'm still not going."

"Jan wants all of us to stay at her beach house for the week—"

"Jan who?"

"Don't give me *Jan who*. Jan Siskin. Actually, I think it's Reeves now. Or maybe it was Reeves but it's now Schroff. Or maybe it's Siskin again. Who cares. Anyway, as you well remember, we kind of hung out with her all four years in high school. And now she has a beach house."

"I don't think she really even liked me," I said.

B.J. aimed a blast of air across seven states and into my ear. "Hey, you haven't heard from Veronica, have you?"

I sighed. "You mean in this millennium?"

"She's not returning my phone calls or emails. But. She. Will."

I let B.J.'s tenacity wash over me like a wave. When I looked down, I saw that my non-cell-phone-holding palm was open, faceup, as if to emphasize my own uncertainty.

B.J. was still talking. "So, you know how I'm on the committee, right? Well, we've decided we're not going to mention either the year we graduated or how many years it's been. We're just going to call it The Marshbury High School Best Class/Best Reunion Evah."

"That's ridiculous." I opened one of the French doors to the deck off the master bedroom to get rid of the gasoline smell. I seriously needed to upgrade to a battery-operated chain saw.

"The committee consensus is that the actual numbers might be a turnoff. It's a lot of years to wrap your brain around, and none of us feels that old, and most of us don't look that old, especially the women, so we just thought it would be more fun if we focused on the positive."

"Which would be?"

B.J. let out a little snort. "That we're still alive?"

I took a quick stab at the math, then gave up. "How many years *has* it been anyway?"

"Don't even think about it," B.J. said. "It's way too depressing. Come on, we haven't seen each other in forever."

"Okay, so how about you go to the reunion, and then you can fly down here and tell me all about it."

"Mel, I'm serious."

"Me, too. I'm seriously not going, B.J., so drop it. Please."

"Give me one good reason you shouldn't go."

I sighed. "Everyone else will dress better, look better, *be* better than I am. High school reunions are like a test for personal success and I'll slide right off the bell curve. I'm not famous, I didn't turn into a knockout, my husband left me. And I stopped wearing heels years ago and now my feet will only tolerate work boots and flip-flops."

"One good reason," B.J. said. "I'm still waiting."

After we hung up, I put my cell phone down and contemplated the savaged chunks of king-size bed before me.

It's not that I was bitter. I mostly just wanted the springs.

Okay, maybe I was a teensy bit bitter.

Our two sons, Trevor and Troy, were seven and six when Kurt had dragged me kicking and screaming to the suburbs of Atlanta. They were thriving on sandy summers boogie-boarding at the beach and snowy winters sledding down the biggest hill in our little seaside Massachusetts town. We lived a tree-lined walk away from the best local elementary school. I had a boring but comfortable part-time job answering phones for a nearby art gallery that let me work my hours around my kids. Mothers' hours.

Life was good.

Kurt said his job offer had come out of the blue. As if it were luck. Or destiny. Kismet. Serendipity. His old boss had taken a job at a big Atlanta corporation a few years before, where he'd been moving up ever since. And now he wanted Kurt to come work for him.

"Out of the blue," I repeated as I stirred a pot of homemade chicken alphabet soup with a wooden spoon. "He just called you out of the blue and said uproot your whole family and take them away from everything they've ever loved because I have a job for you. Even though you already have a perfectly good job."

Trevor ran through the kitchen and out the back door. "Give it *back*," Troy yelled as he ran after him.

"Dinner," I yelled. "Ten minutes."

Kurt shrugged. He loosened the blue-striped tie I'd bought because it reminded me of the way his eyes changed shades in different lights. He unbuttoned the top button of his white shirt. Long-sleeved. Extra starch.

I stared him down. In the fading light of the early evening, his eyes were a dark navy, almost black.

He looked away first.

I flicked on the kitchen lights and turned my attention back to the soup.

"Smells good," he said as I stirred.

I kept stirring.

"Okay, I put out a few feelers," he finally said. "It's time to move on. I think I've taken things as far as I can here."

For a quick, crazy second I thought he was talking about the boys and me.

After I loaded the bed chunks into heavy-duty black plastic contractor bags and dragged them out to the garage, I vacuumed the bedroom. Then I hauled my mattress-flecked self into the bathroom and turned on the water. It sputtered like it always did, then burst forth in a ferocious battle of brushed-nickel showerheads and body jets. I peeled off my clothes and let the wet needles pummel me like a bad marriage.

I towel dried while I contemplated putting on actual pants, the kind that zipped and buttoned at the waist and everything. This seemed extreme, so I went with my regular uniform: yoga pants, baggy T-shirt, flip-flops.

I stood on my stone front steps and blinked against the bright North Georgia sunshine. The sun rose later here, and eventually I'd found out that it was because we were so close to the central time zone line. And just south of the foothills of the Blue Ridge Mountains. Coolish, evergreen-scented mornings gave way to steamy semi-tropical afternoons that stretched into long cook-out-on-the-back-patio evenings. An enormous magnolia held court in the front yard, surrounded by camellias and Lenten roses, as well as a solitary blue hydrangea that reminded me of home. But I'd also planted windmill palms and banana trees, plants I'd thought would only grow as far north as Florida. Surprisingly, they'd thrived here.

As soon as I opened the barn doors on one side of my Honda Element, I leaned in and flipped one of the two backseats forward at the waist. Then I lifted the whole seat up and hooked it to the side of the car with the carabiner that dangled from the ceiling. I circled the car and repeated the steps on the other side. An amazing amount of empty space materialized, anchored by the Element's black nonslip rubber-matted floor, which actually hosed down for easy cleaning. I wanted a house like that.

"All aboard," I said in my cheeriest talking-out-loud-to-yourself voice. "Next stop, Ikea." I'd done my online research. You couldn't beat the design for the price. After all the years of compromise—Kurt's traditional taste trumping my own—I wanted a clean-lined, ultramodern bed. The latex mattress I'd decided on even came rolled, so I'd just get someone at the store to help me shove everything into the back of my Element and then figure out how to get it inside once I got home.

I was fine as I backed out of my driveway. I rolled down the hill in my safe little neighborhood and pretended I was just going to Publix or Whole Foods, or to get my hair done. I was still fine as I navigated the interminable crush of traffic on Roswell Road, with lanes that mysteriously disappeared and tried to trick you into turning right when you didn't want to.

Long rows of burgundy and pink crepe myrtle graced the islands in the center of the road, flanked by mounds of cheery yellow Stella d'Oro daylilies. Enclaves of new brick and stone neighborhoods peeked out between clumps of chain stores and restaurants. If you could shop it or eat it, you could find it within a three-mile radius of my house. Except for Ikea.

The instant I saw the sign for the highway, my mouth went dry. I'd stay to the right, drive as slowly as I needed to. Anybody who didn't like it could just go around me.

My hand shook as I clicked on my blinker.

I could do this.

I willed my foot to stay on the accelerator. I wound my way up the on-ramp slowly, pretending I didn't see the car behind me getting right on my butt.

The feeder lane dumped me out onto the highway. The car behind me screeched past and catapulted into the maze of speeding steel as if it were hurling itself off a cliff. Lane after lane after lane stretched out to my left, cars flying downhill at terrifying speeds.

Anxiety sat on my chest like a baby elephant. The skin on my arms prickled, closing me in, walling off any hope of escape. Impending doom climbed in and took the passenger seat beside me.

My right leg started to shake from working so hard to keep my foot on the gas pedal. I crept along in the slow lane, trying not to feel the angry force of the mammoth vehicles that whizzed by my left shoulder—SUV, tractor-trailer, SUV, car, SUV, SUV, SUV. I risked a quick peek at the speedometer and made myself push it up to fifty-five. That was respectable, wasn't it? I mean, if you could drive fifty-five miles per hour, you were perfectly normal, right?

I just had to drive past four highway exits, take the fifth, and then it was only a hop, skip, and a jump to Ikea.

Breathe.

A sign came into view announcing that the first exit was coming up in three miles. I tried to picture driving past it, but I couldn't even imagine reaching it. For three endless miles I white-knuckled it.

By the time the first exit finally appeared, I knew I had to get off the highway. But it felt as though fear had frozen my arms in place.

I had to get off. I couldn't get off.

I forced myself to lunge for my blinker, my hand shaking as if I had Parkinson's, and managed to turn the wheel and escape the highway four exits too soon. I crawled my way to a semi-deserted fast-food parking lot just down the road from the off-ramp.

I leaned back against the headrest until my sweat chilled and my heartbeat returned almost to normal.

Maybe I'd just sleep in the guest room.

CHAPTER 2

Even before I'd worked the first steel spring free from the mattress foundation, I knew it would be a skirt. A great big Southern hoop skirt that twirled around and around and around. Next would come a parasol with a handle made of steel rebar, or even a splurge of copper pipe. And a hat, a wide, floppy garden hat made from galvanized chicken wire mesh. Ooh, maybe I could line the chicken wire hat with sphagnum moss and fill it with potting soil. The hat would come alive with pansies in the cooler months, and later on with bright yellow dwarf marigolds that would hold their own against the heat of the summer.

When Kurt and I bought our suburban Atlanta house, the previous owners had left behind a garage full of welding equipment. Blowtorches of various sizes and a welding machine. C-clamps and vises. Metal saws and sanders. Heatproof gloves and apron.

A big, heavy helmet with a smoked glass face shield that slipped over your head like a Darth Vader mask.

"And we'll get rid of all *this* crap," Kurt said as he tossed the gloves on the trash pile.

I became a metal sculptor instead. The move had left me feeling isolated and rudderless, especially during the long, lonely hours the boys were in school. Creativity had consoled me my whole life, and conquering a new medium was something I could control. And if I was really, really honest, a part of the draw was that Kurt hated the idea.

My first step was to sign up for a welding class at a local vocational school to learn how to use the equipment. "So, what?" Kurt said. "You and a bunch of plumbers-to-be?"

He was pretty much right, although a few of the guys seemed to have their sights set on auto body shops or industry production lines, and the field of *robotics* was dangled reverentially in front of us by our ruddy-faced instructor, who wore his pants crack-exposingly low, like a cartoon plumber.

I was intimidated—by the heft and force and heat of the equipment, by the fact that I was the only woman in the class—but I hung in there. Arc, or stick, welding was the scariest. The AC electric welder we used, 220 volt with 250-amp output, gave off inferno-like heat, penetrating the barrier of leather apron and flame-retardant long-sleeved shirt I was wearing. And arc welding creates a lot of slag, an ugly name for the flux coating on the weld that can burn right through your clothes or your skin or your eyes. By the time the slag cooled to a solid and I could chip it off, my sweat-drenched body would have chilled, too, and I'd be shivering.

"Here, let me get that for you," one of my classmates would say. "Wouldn't want you to break a nail, ma'am."

The *ma'am* thing was scarier than the welding and the sexism put together. I knew it was just Southern but it still made me feel a million years old.

When the class moved on to the MIG welder, which was the kind I'd inherited with the house, I was in heaven. MIG, or metal inert gas, welding is a lot like using a hot glue gun—the temperatures are lower and you can do it with one hand. And a MIG has a continuous wire feed so you can weld uninterrupted.

"If you can use a lighter without setting yourself on fire, you can weld with a MIG," the instructor said. He meant it to be dismissive, but I was encouraged.

Not that I wasn't terrified the first time I actually pulled the trigger of a MIG welder. Lights flashed, sparks flew, a piercing crackle assaulted my ears. Welding took every ounce of courage I had, but eventually I managed T-welds and edge-welds and butt-welds. It was like learning a new language. I took it weld by weld, and eventually I had the building blocks I needed to attempt my first sculpture.

All these years later, my technique had improved but I still had the same game plan: to make the pieces I'd want to buy myself. And along the way, to do my little part to save the planet by using recycled scrap metal wherever I could.

Trevor called just as I'd finished cutting up some pieces of old tin roof with my titanium-bonded tin snips to form the panels of the parasol. I took off my leather gloves and reached for my cell.

"Hey, Mom, just checking in to see if you need anything."

Since Kurt had moved out, this was Trevor's and my new

ritual. He called once a week from California where he worked long crazy hours editing movie trailers, as if he could just swing by with a half gallon of skim milk or to fix my leaky sink from the other side of the country. As if he'd stepped up to be the new man of the family. It was an oddly soothing routine for both of us.

"Thanks, honey, I'm all set."

"Okay, well, let me know if something comes up."

"Will do," I said. "Working on anything interesting these days?"

Trevor breathed a sigh of relief, and we launched into work talk. The client his team couldn't please no matter how many brilliant ideas they came up with; the blockbuster movie Trevor's boss was sure they'd landed. The juried show that had accepted one of my pieces.

"Have you talked to Dad yet?" I finally asked.

"I don't want to talk about it," he said, and for just a second the hurt in his voice made him sound like a little, little boy.

As if Trevor had summoned him, Kurt was sitting on one of the stools at the kitchen island when I walked into the house from the garage.

I jumped when I saw him and swallowed back a scream. I gave my helmet hair a knee-jerk fluff with one hand, then got mad at myself for bothering.

Kurt stood up. He was wearing jeans with actual creases ironed in them and a baby-blue T-shirt I'd never seen before, kind of tight-fitting. *French cut* popped into my head randomly. And a thick silver chain around one wrist. A man-bracelet?

"I knocked first," he said, "but you didn't answer." The implication being that it was *my* fault he'd scared me.

"For future reference," I said sweetly, "when that happens, the appropriate thing to do is to go away. Oh, wait, actually the even more appropriate thing would be to call first."

Kurt walked over to the kitchen sink and turned it on. Then he opened the cabinet above it and took out a water glass.

"You can't do that anymore," I said.

He put the glass down on the counter. He walked across the kitchen and sat down on the same bar stool again. His bar stool. Former bar stool.

We stared at each other. Neither of us looked away.

"Melanie," he said finally. "I'm thirsty. Can you please get me a glass of water?"

I walked over to the sink and turned on the water. I chose a different glass, one I'd never really liked in the first place. I filled it with water.

I walked slowly over to the man I'd lived with for decades.

With a sharp flick of the wrist I must have seen in an old movie, I threw the water in his face. Then I dropped the glass on the cool, unforgiving tile floor.

When I walked away, the crunch the shards of glass made under my welding boots was crisp and satisfying.

By the time I got back out to the garage, I'd figured out the pose for my second box spring lady. Over her swirling skirt, she'd have one hand on her hip, elbow bent at a jaunty angle. With her other hand she'd be holding her parasol out in front of her. Like a shield. Or maybe more like a weapon.

I'd chosen the steel spring for her skirt and I was reaching for my apron when Kurt pushed the door open from the mudroom to the garage. This was my entrance, my side of the garage, and in all the years we'd both lived here together he almost never came out this way.

Once I'd taken up metal sculpture, it was as if Kurt and I had divided the garage right down the middle with an imaginary line. The side closer to the house was my studio. The side closer to the street belonged to Kurt and held his car, his golf clubs, the lawn mower, the non-metalworking tools. The boys' bikes and sports equipment lined the far wall—neutral territory. Either Kurt opened the garage door with the remote control and entered and exited that way, or he walked across the patio behind the house and in through the back door.

"I think you need to apologize," Kurt said.

"I think you need to apologize more," I said.

The watermark on the front of Kurt's T-shirt looked like an ascot. Or maybe a man-necklace to match his man-bracelet. I flipped the leather apron over my head.

"Is that our bed?" Kurt asked.

I followed his gaze. A carved hardwood spindle was sticking out of one of the heavy-duty contractor bags.

I shrugged.

"Jesus, Melanie, do you remember how much that bed cost? If you didn't want it, Crissy and I would have taken it."

I picked up a steel bar. Kurt took a small step back.

He crossed his arms over his chest. "Listen," he said. "Let me buy you out. You'll be much happier in a town house."

"Right," I said. "I'm sure my town house neighbors would welcome the sound of metal grinding with open arms."

Kurt's steel-blue eyes scanned the garage. Even I had to admit my side looked a little bit like a junkyard.

He shrugged. "So, you'll rent some studio space."

I ignored him. "And those homeowners' associations are really big on letting you try out your works-in-progress in your front yard."

"Maybe even buy one of those live/work units. You know, work space on the ground floor, living space up above it."

"Have you called the boys yet?" I asked, partly to change the subject, but also because I knew he hadn't.

Kurt gave his slow, long-suffering head shake, one of my least favorite moves in his repertoire. "That's not what we're discussing here. Listen, we have three choices. One, I buy you out, which I think makes the most sense all around. Two, you buy me out, though I think it's way too much house for you. And three, we put the house up for sale, take our losses in this abysmal market."

When he reached up to check the wet spot on his T-shirt, I could almost pretend he was putting his hand over his heart. That he'd had a change of heart, even that he *had* a heart. That somehow, against all odds, there was a fourth choice: We could rewind past the last few years back to the days when we'd sit out on the deck with a glass of wine before dinner and watch the hummingbirds drink from the flowers. And we'd talk about our days.

Because if we could go there again I wouldn't have to deal with any of this.

I made myself look at Kurt. There was nothing heartfelt in his eyes. The purse of his lips was cold and dismissive.

"It's time to move on," he said. And then he walked over to the wall and pushed the button for the garage door opener. The heavy double door cranked open slowly and relentlessly.

Without another word, Kurt walked through the opening.

He kept walking, without looking back, leaving my box springs and me exposed for the whole wide world to see.

CHAPTER 3

The guest room mattress had seen better days. Or maybe it had always been this uncomfortable and now I knew why our guests never stayed very long. I tried one more toss and a couple of turns, and then I gave up and kicked off the covers.

I tottered out to the kitchen on legs that didn't wake up quite as quickly as they used to, like an aging Barbie whose arches had fallen into flex position. After I started a pot of coffee, I stood over the sink and ate a breakfast yogurt while I stared out the window at nothing. Nothing. NOTHING.

I turned around to face the kitchen island, thinking maybe a change of scenery might do me some good.

My laptop glittered up at me from the countertop like a beacon of hope.

I picked it up and circled the island in the direction of my bar stool, at the far end of a matching row of four. They were chunky and traditional, oak throwbacks to the eighties stained a shade that suddenly flashed back to me: Burnt Passion.

"Ha," I said.

"So funny I forgot to laugh," I added as I slid onto my stool. Wait. They were all my bar stools now. I moved down the row and tried out the other three stools, one by one.

I cut short the Goldilocks reenactment and went back to my own seat. I sipped some more coffee while my laptop came to life. Then I scrolled through my daily serving of email spam. An invitation to change my life by changing my Internet provider. A recipe for a refreshing summer gazpacho. A Groupon to save up to 53 percent on a helicopter tour.

An email from B.J. sailed into view like a lifeboat.

To: Melanie

From: B.J.

Subject: 5 Reasons To Go To Your High School Reunion

1. You'll laugh like crazy. Who laughs enough these days?
2. You won't have to wish you'd been there when you see all those pictures online.
3. It will give you fresh perspective and make you realize you've come a long way, baby.
4. You won't have to lie about your age. Everyone there will be older than dirt, too.
5. You'll regret not going more than you could possibly regret going.

To: B.J.

From: Melanie

Subject: 5 Reasons NOT To Go To Your High School Reunion

1. I don't want to.
2. I really don't want to.
3. I really, really don't want to.
4. I really, really, really don't want to.
5. I don't want to more than I could possibly want to, which is not at all.

I pushed SEND and went back to scrolling through my email. An excellent opportunity to work at home. An old family friend I'd never heard of mugged in Wales while sightseeing writing to me with tears in his eyes. Substantial savings on a penis enlargement patch. I thought about forwarding that one to Kurt just to get a rise out of him, but managed to restrain myself.

I reached for my coffee cup. Midway to my lips, my hand froze.

To: Melanie

From: Finn Miller

Subject: blast from the past

Melanie,

I found your email address on the Facebook page somebody made for our class. If you don't remember me fake it okay because you only get to break my heart once.

Now that we've got that settled. I'm writing to see if you're going to the reunion. Holy shit time flies. How the hell did we get to be this old huh? The way I look at it we should go to this one. Because by the next time one or both of us could be senile. But even then I'll still remember the way you used to look walking into math class. One hand holding your books and the other yanking down one of those teeny little mini skirts you always used to wear.

To me you were the prettiest girl in the whole school. I bet you still are.

Sorry to hear about your marriage. Mine bit the dust too.

Fond memories from math class and beyond.

Catch ya later,
Finn

Finn Miller. Finn Miller. I could almost picture him. At least I was pretty sure I could.

I read his email again, then closed my eyes. All I managed to see was the Pythagorean theorem, two smaller squares with a bigger one balanced on top, sketched in white chalk on an old oak-framed blackboard. *The area of the square built upon the hypotenuse of a right triangle is equal to the sum of the areas of the squares upon the remaining sides* popped into my head from a gazillion years ago. How bizarre that I could still remember this when lately I had to use the calculator on my phone to add on the tip at a restaurant.

I concentrated. There was a boy at the blackboard. Tall and lean, his baggy flannel shirt making him look like a puppy that hadn't quite grown into its skin. Long brown hair, faded bell-bottoms. One hand resting on the chalk tray, the other slowly writing out the algebraic version of the theorem, as a couple of the boys in the back row gave him the answer and coughed to disguise it at the same time.

$$a^2 + b^2 = c^2$$

"Well done, Mr. Miller," the teacher said. He paused. "And company."

The class burst out laughing and the boys in the back row let out a chorus of apelike grunts. I waited for Finn Miller to turn around so I could see his face.

I scrunched my eyes tighter and conjured up a vague image, more good looking than not good looking, more early Beatles than Rolling Stones, kind of a retro Every Boy.

I read the email again. Finn Miller had liked me, he'd really liked me. Imagine how devastated he'd be that I couldn't exactly remember him. And, not that the bar was high, but it was hard to ignore the fact that his email was quite possibly the most exciting thing that had happened to me in a while. Maybe even in this millennium.

Okay, so I'd fake it.

To: Finn Miller

From: Melanie

Subject: Re: blast from the past

Hi Finn,

Of course I remember you! I remembered you right away, and I'm actually amazed that you remember me. Some days I don't even remember myself.

If I don't make it to the reunion, let me know how it goes, okay?

2 Good 2 B 4 Gotten,

Melanie

CHAPTER 4

I pulled up MapQuest on my computer and typed in my address and the address of Art in the Park, the regional art show that had accepted one of my pieces. I'd emailed them a photo and entered it in the sculpture category months ago. They'd bumped it over to the mixed media category, but at least they'd taken it.

It was a huge show, and with luck it would lead to a sale, and maybe even some commissioned pieces to grace the over-the-top gardens of wealthy Atlantans. I'd once made a ten-foot copper toddler that peed into a preexisting moat stocked with live white swans. You accessed the wannabe mansion by driving over a drawbridge wrapped with miles and miles of white lights, all completely visible from the main road. It looked like a year-round Christmas display, but it also made me remember my grandfather singing "Way Down Upon the Swanee River" to me when I was a child. Years later I realized the river was really the Suwannee, not *Swan*ee, but I still pictured fluffy white swans paddling downstream whenever I thought of it.

The piece that made it into Art in the Park was called *Endless Loop*, an abstract I'd made with rusty metal loops from two dilapidated whiskey barrel planters I'd salvaged at the dump. Circle welded to circle after circle after circle. I'd hidden a fountain pump in the center, attached an old rain showerhead I'd also found at the dump, and snaked a hose up to meet it. Properly installed with the pump turned on, you'd swear you were watching the patter of real rain on halos of rusty metal. And if the sun hit it just right, you could see a rainbow in the watery mist. I'd described all this in detail on my application. I hoped the powers-that-be hadn't placed me under a tent and that I wouldn't have to fight to be moved into the sunlight, near a water source.

There was a small link for driving options on MapQuest that I'd never noticed before. I clicked on it and a series of choices popped up. Wow, you could actually check a box to avoid highways. And not only could you avoid highways, but there were also boxes to avoid country borders, tolls, seasonal roads, ferries, and timed restrictions, whatever they were. Was it possible to be afraid of seasonal roads?

The strangest part about my driving issue was that not long after Kurt left, just to cheer myself up, I made a list of all the things I wouldn't have to do anymore. Mostly petty aggravations like listening to him gargle for what seemed like centuries, lap his ice cream, scrape his teeth on his fork. And watching him yell at the television like a maniac, as if he had the power to influence the outcome of some football game. And trying to ignore the repulsive way he looked at the tissue after he blew his nose—every time—and left his dirty clothes on the floor *beside* the hamper and his disgusting toenail clippings wherever they landed. But at the very top of the list was this: I'll never have to ride in the car with him again.

From our first date, Kurt always had to be in the driver's seat. He was a skilled, decisive driver, but he was also an angry one.

"Right on red, you idiot," he'd yell.

"We have plenty of time," I'd say. "The movie doesn't start for another twenty minutes."

"That's not the point."

It took me years to figure out what the point actually was, but eventually I realized that Kurt simply thought the rest of the world should see driving the way he did: It was a game of skill, and the first one who got there won.

"Slow down," I'd beg. "For me."

"Relax. I just have to get around this bozo playing with his radio."

"Stop playing with your radio, bozo," Trevor would yell from the backseat.

"Yeah, stop pwaying with you wadio, bozo," Troy would parrot.

"See what you're teaching them," I'd hiss.

Kurt would look into the rearview mirror. "Boys, there are a lot of jackasses on the road. And no matter what your mother says, when you drive, you will not be one of them."

I'd bring it up after the boys were in bed. About presenting a united front and treating each other with respect in front of them. And that even if Kurt looked at things differently, he should want to drive in a way that would make me comfortable riding in the car with him.

"Sometimes I'm really afraid," I'd say.

"Jesus, Mel. I mean, how many accidents have I been in since you've known me? I'm an excellent driver."

"That's not the point. You can't control the other drivers on the road. And you're so full of rage I don't want to be in the same car with you."

"That's not rage. That's how I drive."

Sometimes I'd just give up. I'd look for excuses to take separate cars or offer to drive the boys to their sports clinics on the other side of the city myself. I'd feel footloose and fancy-free as I drove off to a master sculpture class at SCAD, the Savannah College of Art and Design.

Other times I'd keep pushing until I got Kurt to promise to take it easy the next time. But by the next time he'd have forgotten. It was the endless loop of a long-term marriage—the same fights playing over and over again, until one of you broke free.

And when Kurt finally did, I thought, well, at least I'll never have to ride in the car with him again.

But in one of the biggest ironies of my life, that's when my own driving problems began.

Art in the Park wasn't far from the hospital where Troy worked, so the plan was that he'd help me install *Endless Loop* at the show and then we'd have lunch. He had a great job in the apparently hot field of Health Internet Technology, and did something with databases that made him a lot of money. Beyond that, I hadn't a clue what my younger son did for a living.

The whole way here I hadn't been able to shake a kind of low-grade worry that MapQuest might be wrong about being able to avoid highways. And even if it could avoid them, what if there were roads that looked liked highways and felt like highways but weren't technically highways? But the directions had taken me first down Powers Ferry, and then I'd followed Northside Drive practically the whole way here. Now I felt relieved and empowered that I'd found a workaround. I mean, so what if it had taken me an extra half hour, mostly waiting at red lights, to get where I was going. At least I got here.

Troy was already waiting just outside the entrance tent, wearing jeans and a deep teal short-sleeved buttondown shirt. He ran one hand through his hair and grinned when he saw me. I hurried over to him and we gave each other a big hug. Then I pulled back for a quick mom-check: no smell of smoke, no bloodshot eyes, healthy weight, good hygiene, clean clothes, recent haircut, direct eye contact.

"It's so good to see you, honey."

"Yeah, you too, but it's only been a week."

We retraced my steps, and Troy opened the back door of the Element.

"Wow. Cool piece, Mom."

"Thanks, honey. Okay, you grab that side and then we'll wiggle it out like this."

The installation went pretty smoothly once we found the water spigot behind the arts pavilion on the outside wall of the restrooms. Troy and I set up my trusty old collapsible wooden display stand that looked like an oversize easel. Fortunately I'd brought an extra hundred-foot hose, too, which we snaked discreetly through one of the tents. A few people gave us dirty looks, but we both ignored them. Troy had his father's quick, decisive confidence. And his eyes. How could you ever shake off a husband when every time you looked at your kids, he was right there looking back at you?

I hammered in one more nail and tucked a couple of squares of heavy-duty stick-on Velcro behind the bottom circles just to be sure they wouldn't shift.

We both took a few steps back to get a better look.

Troy gave me a thumbs-up.

"Thanks." I tucked a clump of hair behind my ears. "Okay, you stay here and keep an eye on it, and I'll run over and turn on the water."

His phone made the triple beep of a text landing. He pulled it out of his pocket and smiled. Not that I was counting, but it was the third smile-producing text in the last five minutes.

"Is that Ashley?" I asked.

"Mo-*om*," Troy said without looking up. It was the same answer he'd been giving me since his first girlfriend, Katie Dougherty, in sixth grade.

I watched for a minute, happy to see Troy so happy, even if I might never get any details. Possibly until the wedding. I was fairly sure my younger son would at least give me a heads-up before my invitation arrived in the mail. I had a sudden vision of the wedding, big and Southern, at a manor called Lady Something. Everyone would be blond and call me ma'am. And they'd all be named *Crissy*.

And the real *Crissy* would be there. She'd be blond and Southern and her family would have owned Lady Something Manor
since before the Civil War. And she'd have offered to let Troy and
Ashley use it for the wedding, along with the servants and the
caterer. So as much as Trevor and Troy didn't want me to see them
being nice to her, I mean, who could blame them. Kurt would be
in his glory, and even though I knew, *I knew*, I was so much better
off without him, I still wanted to punch his lights out for taking
the beautiful day this could have been away from me.

Troy looked up from his cell. "Mom? Are you all right?"

I blinked my way back to reality and smiled. "Of course I am.
Be right back, honey."

I traced the hose through the other exhibits to the restrooms,
making sure there weren't any loops that might trip somebody or,
worse, impede the flow of water to my sculpture.

Once I turned on the faucet, I retraced my steps as quickly as
I could. Artists and show organizers and food concession people
were milling around everywhere now, and I could taste the pre-
show electricity in the air, as if it were scorched steel.

The excitement of fully imagining something in my head and
then translating it into metal just never got old. But as incredible
as that process was, it was as if one of my pieces didn't fully exist
until it was on display and other people could see it, too.

As I cut through the tent, I took the time to check once more
for kinks in the hose, and to make sure it was tucked as far out
of the way as it could be. Back when my first pieces had started
getting accepted for exhibit, it was all I could do not to camp
out and babysit them round the clock for the duration, just in
case something went wrong. But I'd since learned to check and

double-check and even triple-check during the installation, and then let it go.

I walked out of the tent and turned the corner.

A split second later the hose detached from the sculpture. It started spraying water everywhere, a vinyl boa constrictor gone wild.

A few people yelped as the cold water hit them. Troy lunged for the hose. It danced away, spraying two women and a display of dolls with carved and wrinkled dried apple faces.

The women screamed.

"Do something," a man roared. He jumped in front of an assortment of ornate doghouses and spread his arms wide.

I dove.

CHAPTER 5

I took a sip of iced tea. "Sorry about that, honey."

"No problem." Troy grinned and reached for his napkin and gave his forehead another wipe. His gelled hair had gone flat on the top and was sticking out in little points on one side.

"Next time I promise I'll bring you an umbrella." I leaned forward in the booth, hoping to camouflage the dried mud, laced heavily with red Georgia clay, on the front of my T-shirt. At least it was black and not white. "I can't believe you talked me into coming into a restaurant looking like this."

Troy shrugged and reached for his sweet tea. "I gotta hand it to you, Mom, that was some save you made."

I shook my head. "The high stakes of using sprinklers found at the dump. And I know better—one more turn of the wrench on that hose would have done it. Do you believe that doghouse guy tried to get them to cut off my water supply?"

"What a jerk," he said as he put his glass down. "The apple doll ladies were cool, though. Don't worry, I'll walk over after work and make sure everything's copacetic."

"Thanks, honey. Between the extra wrench action and the duct tape, I think we're okay, but that would be great if you wouldn't mind double-checking."

Troy's cell triple-beeped. He looked at it quickly, smiled, and then put it back in his pocket.

"Well, that's a relief," I said. "At least your cell phone didn't drown."

Troy grinned. "Always tuck your phone under your armpit before you attempt a water rescue. I learned that back in college."

"Good to know all that tuition money wasn't wasted."

The waiter placed Troy's bison burger and my turkey wrap in front of us. We ate in comfortable silence as if we were back at the family dinner table. Even with my muddy clothes and damp, grass-flecked feet, I wished I could freeze my life right here: my incredible son across from me, a piece in an art show down the street, a beautiful day, an uneventful drive over. Or maybe I could call Trevor first and have him fly out and sit down at the table with us. And then I'd freeze my life.

Troy took a long sip through his straw, and I flashed back to him drinking out of a Juicy Juice box as a toddler. When I looked at my kids now, I sometimes saw the whole trajectory of their lives, as if they had time capsules encased just under their adult skin.

"Remember," I said, "when we used to spend a month in

Marshbury every summer and you and Trevor practically lived at the beach? Grammy and Grandpa used to say if you got any wetter you'd start to grow moss between your ears."

Troy nodded and stabbed a french fry. "Yeah, that was fun. I hated leaving my friends at home though, so I was kind of glad when we stopped going."

"Remember when you and Trevor built that pirate float for the Labor Day parade? That was so amazing."

"Mom, I think you basically built it for us."

"And you threw chocolate gold coins off it as Dad drove you along the parade route? And that huge crowd of kids followed you?"

"Yeah, and the chocolate melted all over the place and Trevor got stung by a bee."

"Really?" I said. "I don't remember that part."

"You always do that."

"Do what?"

Troy shrugged. "You know, turn your trips down memory lane into a Disney movie."

I considered this. I took another bite of my turkey wrap and sipped my unsweetened iced tea. As long as I'd lived here, I still hadn't acquired a taste for Southern sweet tea. And I'd had only a handful of decent iced coffees that didn't come from Starbucks. People in this neck of the woods didn't seem to know you can't just pour a pot of hot coffee over some ice cubes. You have to brew it extra-strong and then refrigerate it.

Troy took his phone out of his pocket and screen-tapped a message.

I waited until he finished. "So," I said. "Have you talked to Dad?"

He shrugged. "I never talked to him that much before."

"But he's your father," I said, as if this might be new information.

My younger son took another bite of his burger. I'd never really thought about it before, but he even chewed like Kurt.

Troy looked up. "What?" he said.

"Never mind," I said. "It's just—"

"Mom, it doesn't matter whether I've talked to him or not. Either way, I'll deal."

"Sorry," I said. "I was just trying to help."

Troy focused on his remaining french fries. I focused on keeping my mouth shut, the biggest mom-challenge of them all. I picked up a sweet potato fry, took a bite, put the rest of it back down on my plate.

Troy cleared his throat. "What matters . . ."

I waited. Troy shook his head.

"Say it," I said.

Troy tried to run his fingers through his hair, then pulled them out when they got stuck halfway. "What matters is that you stop worrying about whether me and Trevor have talked to Dad."

"But—"

My younger son looked me right in the eyes. "Mom, you've gotta move on with your life."

My eyes teared up. I reached across the booth and rested my hand on his. "Thanks, honey. But I'm f—"

Troy pulled his hand out and placed it on top of mine. "I mean it, Mom. You need to get over Dad. Go somewhere. Have an adventure. Or whatever people your age do."

The waiter came over and asked if we wanted dessert. I bit

my tongue while we waited for Troy's peach cobbler so I didn't ruin our lunch. I mean, thanks a lot. What did he think I was, a dinosaur? The funny thing about your kids as they grew up was you'd start thinking you were on the same wavelength, that they really got it, got *you*, and suddenly they'd come out with a zinger like that.

Although come to think of it, what *were* people my age supposed to do?

I'd reversed the MapQuest directions and printed them out, which I knew defeated the tree-saving aspect of using the Internet, but I didn't want to take any chances. Things were going so well that I could even imagine making it to Ikea one of these days. There had to be a non-highway that would take me there.

I braked at a light and looked around. The growth was so incredibly lush here, and the gardens so beautifully maintained. There were many things to love about the South—the mild winters, the friendliness of strangers—and I'd learned to love it here, in a way, even if I hadn't fully committed to it.

So why did I have to be the one to leave? Why couldn't Kurt and *Crissy* have an adventure? Or whatever people their age did.

Finally, the light changed and the eternal traffic started to move. I poked along and then picked up speed, my favorite Atlanta classic rock station, 97.1 The River, keeping me company. When "Stairway to Heaven" came on, I reached over to turn it up, casually, as if I'd never been afraid to take my hand off the steering wheel. Once in high school, we'd decided to stay up all night at a pajama party to see how many times in a row we could listen to all eight minutes and two seconds of the long version. I dozed off somewhere around number 30, and when I woke up, B.J., who was still Barb back then, swore up and down she hadn't missed a note and that "Stairway to Heaven" was now on its 387th spin on the turntable.

The road widened suddenly, which I didn't remember at all from my earlier ride today. Up ahead, I could just see a sign for Interstate 285, the highway loop that encircles Atlanta, creating what Atlantans call the Perimeter. In some parts it was six lanes wide in each direction, and I'd read that it was one of the most heavily traveled roads in the entire country. For me, it was the scariest highway of them all.

Just the thought of that highway made my mouth go dry. "Relax," I whispered. "Good thing you don't have to go there."

Still, my hands and arms started to prickle. The baby elephant sat down on my chest.

The car behind me beeped the Southern way, short and polite, but unmistakably telling me to pick up the pace. I forced my shaking right foot down harder on the gas pedal.

I wasn't even on the highway and my whole body was telling me I had to get off.

I tried to lift my hand up to turn on the blinker, but it wouldn't go. The car behind me beeped again, sounding a lot more Northern this time.

There was a scream in my ears, but I couldn't tell if it was real or imagined. I tried to breathe but I couldn't seem to remember how.

I jerked the wheel and pulled off the road. The car behind me beeped, long and loud.

"Sorry," I whispered. "Sorry, sorry, sorry."

I started to cry then, long raspy sobs. Hot tears rolled under my sunglasses and down my cheeks, mixing with the sweat that had broken out across my face like a rash. I bumped my way to yet another half-deserted parking lot at yet another fast-food restaurant. I cried until my breathing slowed down and the baby elephant got off my chest and went back to wherever it was that it lurked, waiting for the next time.

I just wanted to go home. I wanted to go home more than I'd ever wanted anything. And the worst thing about it was that I didn't even know where home was anymore. I wanted to click my heels together and be magically transported to wherever it was that might make me feel like whoever I was supposed to be now. Instead of an empty shell that had followed all the rules only to have her husband pull her life out from under her.

I picked up my cell phone. I sorted through the short list of people I could call to ask them to come get me—my older sister in Marshbury, who would probably find a way to get me out of here, but first she'd have to inform me that she'd never had driving issues herself, or any issues for that matter—and she'd have to slip in a mom-brag, too, in her endless quest to prove that her kids were better than my kids. As for B.J., sympathy wasn't her strong suit, so I wasn't sure what she'd say if I called her, but whatever it was, I didn't think I could handle it right now.

Troy would be here in a heartbeat, and Trevor would jump on a plane immediately if he thought I needed him, but I didn't want them to worry. Even Kurt would probably come, too, eventually, but I wasn't going to give him the ego boost of needing anything from him ever again. My closest Atlanta friend had moved away about a year ago. I thought about my other local friends, but it seemed like too big a litmus test for friendship to ask any of them to drop everything and come get me. Maybe I could call AAA and just pretend my car had broken down?

I dropped my phone on the passenger seat. I'd only tried explaining my driving thing once, just weeks after Kurt left, to my primary care physician at my already scheduled yearly physical. He'd nodded a few times, then dashed off a prescription for a beta-blocker.

I took it for a few days. I didn't feel any worse, but I didn't feel like driving on any highways, either. Then I dropped a piece of metal on the garage floor while I was welding. When I bent over to pick it up, the whole world started to spin.

May cause dizziness jumped out on the list of side effects when I Googled the beta-blocker later that day. In my profession, dizziness could mean a really bad burn, or worse. I kept reading. *May cause weight gain* clinched it. Kurt might have left me, but I certainly wasn't going to give him the satisfaction of thinking it made me get fat. I threw the pills away.

I looked around the fast-food parking lot, wondering how I was ever going to get out of here. The smell of fried pickles was making me nauseous. I knew it was a Southern thing, but I mean, really, why the hell would anyone want to fry a pickle?

Rationally, I recognized that all I had to do was drive past the entrance of Route 285, get to the other side of it, and I'd be fine for the rest of the ride home.

But it took me four tries, and every ounce of willpower I had, to make myself do it.

Finally, finally, some twenty-five long minutes later, I was able to put on my blinker and turn onto my own street. As I pulled into my driveway, a voice whispered in my ear: *Get out. Get out. Get out while you still can.*

CHAPTER 6

To: Melanie

From: B.J.

Subject: Spin-the-Bottle Reunion Centerpieces

Save your empty wine bottles until you have one for each table at your reunion-to-be. Using a paintbrush, cover bottles thoroughly with black chalkboard paint. Let dry and write "Spin the Bottle" in white chalk on each bottle. Guaranteed to get the party started!

Super cute, huh?

P.S. Did you book your flights yet?

To: Melanie

From: Finn Miller

Subject: sweet dreams of you

Do you remember that Leon Russell concert a bunch of us went to at the old Music Hall in Boston? The one where LR stood up from his piano and told the audience of screaming stoned-out kids that he wasn't going to start playing again unless they shut the f up. Well last night I dreamed we were back there again and he made everybody else leave and then he played a set just for us. We held hands and then we started making out and then Leon Russell told us he wouldn't keep playing unless we knocked it off. Great dream.

Sadly, I couldn't recall ever going to a Leon Russell concert. I Googled up a song sampler of *Leon Live* and listened to "It's Been a Long Time Baby." It was a good song, though I had to admit I didn't quite remember it, either.

Spin the Bottle, on the other hand, I could remember. I pushed my laptop away and slid down from my bar stool. I walked across the kitchen and opened the refrigerator. Bottled water, yogurt, walnuts, mixed salad greens, baby carrots, individually wrapped one-hundred-calorie dark chocolate bars. A four-pack of individual servings of hummus almost made me cry. Somehow my refrigerator had turned single again before I'd fully accepted it myself.

I considered the ketchup bottle and a bottle of shrimp cocktail sauce briefly, but kept looking. Way in the back, I found a half-empty bottle of dessert wine that someone at work had given Kurt last Christmas. Even though we'd both hated it, we'd never thrown it away because Kurt had been convinced it was crazy expensive.

I held my nose in case it smelled like a science experiment by now and chugged the whole thing.

I shivered and wiped my mouth with the back of my hand. I held the bottle up to my mouth. "Now that, ladies and gentlemen, was one bad bottle of wine," I said into my wine bottle microphone. I blew into it a few times, unsuccessfully trying to get the melody of "Red, Red Wine."

"And I am one cheap date," I added as the wine rushed to my head.

I gave the bottle a quick rinse and turned it upside down on the top rack of the dishwasher to finish drying. It wobbled and started to fall.

"Uh-uh-uh," I said as I grabbed it. "I'm not through with you yet, little bottle."

I giggled. I definitely had a bit of a buzz on and was quite possibly having a midlife meltdown at the same time. I considered a quick WebMD search so I could compare symptoms, but decided this was no time to get sidetracked.

I knew I'd seen the recipe online, and sure enough, when I Googled it, all sorts of links popped up. I clicked on one randomly.

MAKE YOUR OWN CHALKBOARD PAINT

½ cup latex paint, any color

2 tablespoons unsanded grout

bowl

paint stirrer

paintbrush

white chalk

Stir grout into latex paint until lump-free. Paint surface
of chalkboard-to-be. Let dry. Rub chalk over entire surface and wipe off before using it for the first time.

I found an old bag of unsanded grout in the garage and some
black paint called "Beluga" I'd once used to freshen up an old
table. I mixed the paint and grout together in one of the old coffee cans I used for collecting metal scraps.

I layered some long strips of paper towel on the kitchen island and painted the empty wine bottle carefully, stopping once
to double-check that the front door was locked. I mean, how embarrassing to be caught decorating a Spin-the-Bottle bottle at my
age. Although maybe I could pass it off as a menu vase I was making to write the day's pathetic offerings. *Tuesday: single serving
probiotic plus fiber yogurt, single serving hummus with stale crackers,
microwaved single serving frozen Healthy Choice entrée.*

While the bottle dried, I pulled down the creaky attic stairs
in the hallway and climbed up. I hadn't saved much from high
school, but I was pretty sure my yearbook was still packed away
somewhere. I found boxes and boxes of Trevor and Troy's old
things, everything from Matchbox cars to Halloween costumes to
Sesame Street stuffed animals to report cards to retired refrigerator drawings. Spiderwebs stuck to my face and arms like strands
of sticky hair. I brushed them away and tried not to think about
what other creepy-crawly things might be up here.

Tucked in a corner under an old grapevine wreath I found a cardboard box with MELANIE'S STUFF written on it in loopy letters with faded purple marker, the I in MELANIE dotted with a red heart. The first thing I found was an eight-track tape of Carly Simon's *No Secrets*. Yellowed paperbacks followed—*Fear of Flying, Love Story, Everything You Always Wanted to Know About Sex But Were Afraid to Ask, The Great Gatsby*. A pet rock in a crate, a chocolate leatherette backgammon case, a ticket stub from *The Sting*, a picture postcard of the waves at Hampton Beach, New Hampshire, with a five-cent stamp. *Having a great time! Wish you were here!*

Alone in my attic, I giggled across the decades. "Who the hell were you, Finn Miller? Wish I remembered!"

I could have sworn my high school yearbook was blue and white, our school colors, but it turned out to be bright yellow with MARSHBURY HIGH SCHOOL written in orange psychedelic swirls.

I backed my way down the attic stairs, holding the yearbook in one hand as if it were a Magic 8 Ball that might reveal my future: *Signs point to yes. Outlook good. You may rely on it.*

I found my bar stool and placed my yearbook carefully on the kitchen counter. It was in pretty good shape for its age, but who knew, one wrong move and it might crumble into dust. I thought about looking for my own picture, but I couldn't quite bring myself to do it. What if it was even more embarrassing than I imagined? The remnants of my dwindling self-esteem might just crumble into dust, too.

"Will I remember Finn Miller?" I asked my empty kitchen as I flipped to the *M*'s.

I found him in the middle of a page. The yearbook pages were black and white, which softened the clash of his plaid suit jacket and striped tie. He had a serious side part going on, his long, wavy hair obscuring most of one eyebrow before it tucked behind his ear. But his chin was strong and his eyes were dark and borderline sexy. His smile was a bit forced, but he was probably just camera-shy. I scanned down to his quote: *School's out. Memories past. Don't ever doubt. The fun will last.*

I carried the yearbook into the little office we'd made in one corner of the guest room. I scanned Finn's picture and the pictures of some other fairly cute male classmates. I enlarged them until their heads were big enough to fill a page of computer paper, then I printed them and cut them out like paper dolls.

I left them on the kitchen island while I searched the garage, finally settling on two relatively clean brooms and a long-haired mop that had never been used. I carried them into the kitchen, turned them upside down, and taped the paper faces onto their business ends.

Music. Poor Carly Simon's eight-track tape was never going to find its match in a tape player again, so to make it up to her I downloaded *No Secrets* onto my laptop. "You're So Vain" filled my kitchen with retro longing.

"You bet I think this song is about you," I said to Finn Miller.

His mop hair was a good look for him, a step up from that old side-part swoop, almost like white dreadlocks. We danced around the kitchen together, his hair tickling my neck, his paper face crinkling when he leaned close. He dipped me, and I smiled up at him as Carly sang her approval.

The two broom boys leaning back against their bar stools never took their eyes off us. "Sorry, guys," I said in my sexiest, slightly wine-soaked voice. "I'm taken." It came out low and scratchy, almost like a croak, the voice of a woman spending way too much time alone.

When the song ended, I wedged Finn Miller through the spindles of a stool and dragged him around the island until he was diagonally across from me.

I reached for the bottle and wrote SPIN THE BOTTLE on it in white chalk in my old loopy letters.

"So, who's up for a little fun?" I was getting better at the sexy-voice thing. I looked from chair to chair, pretending my former husband and sons had never sat in them and that this was a high school party: lights out except for a single lava lamp off in one corner, "Born to Be Wild" pulsing in the background, hormones raging, hearts beating.

I gave the bottle a generous spin and leaned back to let fate have its way with me.

The bottle skittered across the shiny granite to the edge of the counter. I lunged and caught it just before it fell off.

The mouth of the bottle was pointing between two bar stools, so I spun it again.

It pointed right at Finn Miller.

It's not easy to fake a make-out session with a long-haired mop, but I gave it everything I had. I closed my eyes and stroked the long, scraggly mop-locks and tried to remember the smell of Brut, the Pepto-Bismol taste of a hastily chewed and then spit-out piece of Clark's Teaberry gum, the heat of an unremembered boy pressing up against me.

To: Finn Miller

From: Melanie

Subject: Re: sweet dreams of you

I remember that Leon Russell concert like it was yesterday. I couldn't take my eyes off you. Was I a good kisser? (In the dream, I mean!)

To: B.J.

From: Melanie

Subject: Re: Spin-the-Bottle Reunion Centerpieces

Oh, grow up. (No offense.) And no, I haven't booked my flights. I've moved beyond high school.

CHAPTER 7

The next morning I tucked a branch of flowering crepe myrtle into the chalkboard bottle sitting on the kitchen island to make it less conspicuous. Every time I looked at the bottle, I practically blushed, but I still couldn't make myself put it out with the recyclables. I mean, acting out a harmless little fantasy was progress, wasn't it? Before I knew it I'd have a sparkle in my eye and a spring in my step.

Either that or I was totally losing it.

I added some water to keep the branch alive, possible evidence that I was both lucid and compassionate. Then I woke up my laptop to check my email. I'd gone from checking it once or twice a week to checking it fairly often. Okay, a lot.

My cell phone rang, distracting me from the disappointing absence of a new message from Finn Miller. I didn't recognize the number.

"This is Melanie," I said.

"And this is Ted Brody, who bought a sculpture of yours at the Art in the Park show."

"Oh, right," I said. "Hi. And, well, thank you." I'd been thrilled to hear *Endless Loop* had sold, on the first day of the show, no less. As much as I loved my work, I only made money when somebody bought something. The house was paid off and the property taxes weren't high, but since Kurt had left, I was paying the utility bills myself. And crazy food and gas prices on top of that. I was okay for now, but I was really feeling the lack of a paycheck I could count on. The sale of *Endless Loop* gave me a little bit of breathing room while I figured out what the hell I was going to do next.

"Don't thank me yet," Ted Brody said. "I've got a restaurant to run here, and when a hose breaks loose on a busy night and sprays a courtyard full of diners, and their *food*, I think you've got to find a way to make that up to me."

"Oh, shit."

"My sentiments exactly." Ted Brody's voice was rich and deep, and totally pissed off.

I closed my eyes. "I am so, so sorry. If you tell me where you're located, I'll come over and weld the hose on permanently for you. And in the meantime, if you take two wrenches and turn one in each direction, really hard, it'll hold. And maybe wrap some duct tape around it for extra reinforcement, not that I think you'll need it. Wait, maybe you shouldn't turn it on again until I make sure it's okay."

"Ya think?"

I scrunched my eyes shut as if it might ward off some of his anger. "Again, I'm really, really sorry," I said.

"I'll text you the address of the restaurant."

"Okay, and well, I'll get there as soon as I can, but if anything else happens in the meantime, not that it will, feel free to call me back."

"Count on it," Ted Brody said.

When I powered off my MIG welder, I noticed Ted Brody standing behind me with his arms crossed over his chest, probably keeping an eye on me to make sure I didn't cause any more damage. Lunch was over and dinner hadn't started yet, so up until now I'd had the restaurant courtyard all to myself.

I put the MIG down carefully on a low brick wall, tucked one of my heavy AngelFire gloves under my armpit, and pulled out my sweaty hand. I flipped up the visor on my helmet. Over Ted Brody's shoulder, I could just make out the restaurant's bright-green-and-white sign through the glare of the merciless late-afternoon sun.

"Sprout," I read. I wiped some sweat off my forehead with the sleeve of my T-shirt. "Great name for a restaurant, by the way." More proof that I was a brilliant conversationalist, but at least it was better than adding another babbling apology to the stream. I had to be approaching double digits by now.

I'd white-knuckled it the whole way here, winding along the back roads and hoping the MapQuest directions I'd printed out as backup to my GPS hadn't lied to me and I really could avoid Interstate 75, which I could just *feel* snaking along beside me as I drove. While I sat in my Element waiting for red light upon red light to change, I promised myself that if I could fix *Endless Loop* without Ted Brody asking for any money back, money I hadn't even received yet since the check would come from the art show minus their commission, then I'd use the proceeds to break free from my own endless loop. Somehow.

"Thanks," Ted Brody said. "Glad you like the name. What does it make you think of?"

I took my time pulling off my helmet while I rewound our limited conversation far enough to remember what he was talking about. I gave what had to be a serious case of helmet hair a fluff, not that it mattered. He'd been polite but cool when I arrived, but so far he hadn't handed me a bill for water damages. I gave him the friendliest smile I could muster in a trillion percent humidity.

"Let's see," I said. "Sprout. Green and tender and really, really fresh. Like a baby beanstalk. And healthy and maybe a little bit trendy. Not that I'm an expert, but I really do think it's a great name. It would make me want to eat here in a second."

I closed my eyes as soon as I said it. Now he was probably going to expect me to hang around and buy some food. The last thing I needed right now was a solo meal in a restaurant to remind me how alone I was. All I wanted to do was get the hell out of here.

"My father used to call me Sprout."

"Aww," I said. *Aww? Really?*

When Ted Brody grinned, the light hit his eyes just so and I could see that they were hazel, not brown. He had a nice smile when he wasn't glaring at me. "There were six of us, three boys and three girls, and he actually called all of us Sprout because he could never get our names straight. And he also used to say,

'If you kids keep sproutin' up like that you're going to eat your mother and me out of house and home.'"

His accent shifted when he said the last part. "Where did you grow up?" I asked.

He tilted his head and ran one hand through his salt-and-pepper hair. "A little town on Lake Michigan. Great place to live until winter hits."

"Do you still have family there?"

"One brother. One sister. How about you?"

"I grew up in a little beach town near Boston. My sister's still there, not that I ever see her. I'm working up to visiting one of these days. When I can find the time . . ."

"Hmm, I think I might have a brother like that."

"Ha," I said. "I mean, she's not that bad."

"Every time I hang up the phone with him I feel like I just got sucker-punched. The money he made last year, his new vacation house, his seven-hundred-and-twenty-two-inch 3-D TV—"

"Wow, seven hundred and twenty-two inches. They make them that big?"

"Apparently so. Unless you think he might be exaggerating?"

I laughed and Ted Brody joined me. I tried to remember the last time Kurt and I had laughed at something the other one said, but I couldn't. I could remember us laughing at things the boys said, and even things our couple friends said. But I couldn't recall us laughing when it was just the two of us. Had we ever? We must have, but I honestly couldn't summon up a single example.

Ted was still talking. "And let's not forget his fancy Cuban cigars, and the fact that his kids—"

"—are better than your kids."

"Exactly. The thing is, I wouldn't change lives, or kids for that matter, with him for all the 3-D TVs in China, so it's not that."

I nodded. "I hear you."

Ted Brody smiled again, just as a big white truck rolled past the courtyard toward the back of the restaurant.

He followed it with his eyes. "Can you hang on for a second? I've got a delivery."

Despite myself, I checked him out as he walked away. He was in good shape for a guy his age, especially one who owned a restaurant.

I waited for a few minutes, baking in the sun, before I realized how ridiculous it was to just stand there. It took me two trips to carry my stuff out to the Element. On my way back from the second trip it occurred to me that maybe I should have done a leak check first.

Belatedly, I traced the hose from the back of *Endless Loop* behind some wooden latticework stained a rich shade of terra-cotta, and used the opportunity to finally take a good look around. Three courtyard walls were covered in rough latticework and dotted randomly with clay pots overflowing with succulents and herbs. About a dozen iron tables with mismatched chairs dotted the paved courtyard, each one shaded by a bright red market umbrella. Even though it was tucked behind a row of stores just a stone's throw from a busy road, once the candles were lit, I could imagine the courtyard feeling off the beaten path and practically romantic.

I shook my head and bent down to turn on the spigot. My knees cracked as I stood up again. I pulled my T-shirt away from my sweat-soaked body and watched the old rain showerhead I'd found at the dump begin to spit. As it built up to a patter, I actually shivered. It really did look as if a summer rain was falling on the rusty circles of metal.

A rainbow appeared in the watery mist like a vision.

"Wow," I heard Ted Brody say behind me.

He stepped up beside me, and we watched together in silence. He smelled like rosemary, or maybe it was one of the pots on the wall.

"Amazing," he said.

"You picked the right wall," I said.

"You're really talented."

"Thanks," I said. "You have a nice courtyard."

He laughed. "That's right. You haven't even seen the restaurant yet. Let me give you a tour. Do you have anyone you need to get home to, or can you stay and have a bite to eat with me?"

I looked at him.

He looked at me, waiting for an answer.

"No," I said finally.

We looked at each other some more.

"Which part?" he said.

I could feel my face going from red to redder to reddest. It had to be about a million degrees out here. A blob of sweat broke free from my bra strap and rolled down my back.

"No," I heard myself say. "No, I don't have anybody to get home to. And it really, really sucks."

I was halfway to my Element before I realized I hadn't even said good-bye. I kept walking, horrified by the way I'd acted, too horrified to turn around and go back. I mean, what could I say? *Excuse me, but can I try that answer again?*

It wasn't until I pushed GO HOME on my GPS that I started to cry. Ted Brody had hit the nail on the head: What was the point of going home when there was nobody waiting to notice if you got there or not? Out of the blue and with a force that tore me apart, I missed Kurt, the old Kurt, the one I used to come home to.

I wiped my eyes with an old take-out napkin I found in the glove compartment and put on my sunglasses for camouflage. As I rolled slowly out to the road, I suddenly remembered sitting in the courtyard of a different restaurant with Kurt a long time ago. We'd splurged on a hotel room with a water view on St. Simons Island for our anniversary. Even though they'd argued that they were old enough to stay home alone, Troy had a tendency to get so engrossed in a game of Nintendo that he'd miss the smell of a burning bag of microwave popcorn, and Trevor had a new girlfriend. So we'd left the boys with a babysitter.

It was a five-hour trek, but we were both on our best behavior. Kurt tried to tone down his driving, and when he forgot I distracted myself by scrolling past the surplus of country music stations to find songs from our own personal memory lane. Van Morrison's "Moondance" from our wedding. Nancy Sinatra's "These Boots Are Made for Walkin'," which I played nonstop for two whole melodramatic days after our first big fight. Jimmy Buffett's "Margaritaville" from our favorite vacation. Joni Mitchell's "The Circle Game," which always made me cry when I was pregnant.

We checked into our hotel, made love, walked the beach. We found an old gas station that had been converted into a restaurant, complete with a big gas tank out front turned into a wood-smoke barbecue.

"What'll it be, sugah?" the waitress asked Kurt, completely ignoring me.

Over the red-and-white-checked oilcloth-covered table, Kurt grinned at me to acknowledge the waitress's slight.

Then he smiled up at her. "Two glasses of Chardonnay, please."

She turned and yelled over her shoulder. "Two glasses of the white stuff. Make sure it's the good jug. They're from *Bahston*."

We laughed and laughed until the whole restaurant was looking at us. When one of us would start to wind down, the other one would get us going again. I leaned across the table and wiped a tear from the corner of Kurt's eye.

Kurt reached for my hand and held it between both of his. "And here I thought we were starting to pass."

We cracked up all over again.

CHAPTER 8

To: Melanie

From: Finn Miller

Subject: Re: Re: sweet dreams of you

Were you a good kisser in my dream? The best. Bet you still are in real life too.

To: Finn Miller

From: Melanie

Subject: Re: Re: sweet dreams of you

Guess you'll have to wait and see, won't you?

Finn Miller and I were actually flirting. Flirting. FLIRTING.

I loved wings—butterfly wings, angel wings, even the Brownie wings I got when I flew up to Girl Scouts, which I was pretty sure I still had tucked away in an old jewelry box somewhere. But wings had been done and done again in metal sculpture. So I went with a small boat propeller I'd found picking through the metal section at a junkyard for my third box spring lady.

As a hat, it wasn't very Southern. To make it work with the box spring hoop skirt, I welded strand after strand of thin curly wire to it, and then tied them all together under the chin of my third box spring lady in a jaunty little bow.

I added a parasol, of course, because repetition of elements brings cohesiveness to a series, and because the other box spring ladies had them and I didn't want the third one to feel left out. Her parasol was extended over her head, back up to her propeller.

I gave her long, sexy eyelashes from the same curly wire, just because I could. They made her look happy, even glamorous. I could picture her saying, *Beam me up, Scotty.* And her propeller bonnet would whir and rev up and she'd raise her umbrella higher. And then a fresh, cool breeze would come along. And she'd flutter her eyelashes as she floated up, up—and away from it all.

If only I could hitch a ride with her. I'd have her drop me off at the reunion. I'd float down from the sky—strong, fearless, *alive* for the first time in years. Finn Miller would be waiting for me outside in the parking lot, sitting on an old New England park bench underneath a sky full of stars, the faint strains of "Stairway to Heaven" drifting out from the building. And the minute I set eyes on him it would all come back.

Because nobody knows you better than somebody who knew you way back when.

I'd buried the other paper boys in the bottom of the trash, but Finn's face was now tucked into my yearbook, marking his page. I was curled up under the covers in the guest room, letting my thoughts wander as I held the yearbook. Thinking maybe I'd even sleep with it under my pillow and see if it might trigger a long, sexy dream.

My cell phone rang and I jumped. My heart went into over-drive, as if someone had caught me. Doing what? Acting like a lovesick high school girl? I reached for my phone and my read-ing glasses on the bedside table, saw that it was an 800 number I didn't recognize, somebody trying to sell me something.

I got rid of the call, but my heart had triggered a full-blown flashback, bringing all those old feelings back. *Oh, no, it's him! Did he see me looking? Is he looking at me? Uh-oh, here he comes. How am I going to handle this?*

And that's when I finally remembered Finn Miller.

B.J., Veronica, and I met, like we did every day in high school, in the crowded girls' room before the first bell rang.

"Are you sure it's not too short?" I said. I stood on tiptoe and peered at myself in the mirror through the swirls of cigarette smoke rising from the stalls behind me. The waistband of my brown-and-ivory diamond-plaid A-line skirt had to be rolled down just right so the skirt didn't poof out at the hips. I contemplated my lackluster thighs in the mirror. Was it possible they didn't quite match? It was too gross to consider.

We still had a dress code and Mr. Bernardi, the assistant principal, was not above asking his secretary, Miss Knowles, to measure the distance between the middle of a kneecap and the hem of a skirt with a yardstick. B.J. said they were both perverts and she'd fight them all the way to the Supreme Court if they tried anything with her. I was hoping I'd have time to roll my skirt back down before we got to the office.

"Get over it," B.J. said. "It's not even close to wicked short."

B.J. was wearing a denim skirt she'd made by cutting off a pair of dungarees, opening the crotch seam with a stitch ripper she'd stolen from Home Ec, then overlapping the pieces and sewing them up again. When she elbowed her way in to claim some mirror space, her new creation rode up to within inches of her underpants.

She pulled the pink-and-orange-striped cover off a tube of Yardley Slicker, waving it around as much as possible to make sure nobody missed it. Then she added a topcoat of Frosted Slicker over her Yardley Pink Frost lipstick. B.J. had Basic Slicker, Frosted Slicker, Surf Slicker, Sunny Slicker, and Tan-Tan Slicker, plus Uptown, Downtown, Good Night, and Good Morning. On the days she wore most of them at once, her lips took on the consistency of frosted Jell-O.

I reached into my fringed macramé bag and pulled out my own Yardley Liplighter case. One end held a Frosted Slicker and the other a London Look Lipstick in Pinkadilly, one of six new man-trapping colors. It even had a mirror attached to it that the Yardley magazine ads said were for peeking behind me to make sure I was being followed.

The Liplighter combo had only cost me $2.50 even though it was a $3.60 value. The Slicker came free with the purchase of the lipstick, saving me just over two hours of babysitting for the bratty kids down the street.

Beside me, Veronica dug her index finger into a Yardley Pot o'Gloss tinted lip gloss in an unfortunate bright coral color her mother had picked out. B.J. and I offered her our Frosted Slickers at the exact same moment.

"Jinx," we all said at once. Then we passed around B.J.'s creamy blue Cover Girl eye shadow, the exact same kind that Cybill Shepherd wore in *Seventeen*.

The bell rang and we walked down the crowded hallway together and then separated for our classes. Without my friends as bookends, my self-esteem took an immediate nosedive. My mouth went dry and I had to force myself to keep putting one foot in front of the other so I didn't get stuck in the hallway alone forever.

I ducked into the doorway of my math class and dropped my head as I headed to my seat at the back of the room.

When I sat down in the beige Formica chair, I tried to yank some of my skirt under me so the back of my possibly mismatched thighs wouldn't stick to the chair and have red marks on them when I stood up again. I moved my math book to the top of my pile and opened my five-section spiral notebook to the math section. Mr. Jackman was standing at the front of the room writing on the blackboard. He had a smudge of chalk shaped like a handprint on the back of his suit jacket. Last week it had been a jagged piece of masking tape that said TELL ME I HAVE A NICE ASS.

Beside me, Finn Miller looked over and smiled.

By the time I figured out he was smiling at me and I smiled back, he'd looked away again.

Then I looked away.

When the bell finally rang at the end of class, I squeezed my thighs together so my underpants wouldn't show when I swung my legs out from under the desk. My skin peeled away from the chair painfully, like a Band-Aid.

Once again, Finn Miller and I looked at each other.

Then we both looked away.

B.J. and Veronica were waiting for me in the hallway, retouching their lips.

"So," Veronica said. "Did you talk to him?"

My heart skipped a beat. "*Shhh.*"

"Ch-ch-*chiiiicken,*" B.J. said. "Where is he?"

"Shut. Up." I scrunched my shoulders up around my ears and reached back to make sure my waistband hadn't started to unroll. "Come on, you guys, let's get out of here."

All these years later, sitting on the guest room bed clutching my high school yearbook, I tried to imagine this lifelong ch-ch-chicken finally turning into a red-hot hen.

CHAPTER 9

When I came back inside from a sweaty session in my studio, two whole messages were waiting on my voicemail, like smoke signals from civilization.

My initial excitement turned into a dull dread when I saw one was from Kurt and the other from Ted Brody. A broken marriage and a broken hose did not bode well in the voicemail department. Anxiety bubbled up and I considered just deleting them.

I changed into a dry T-shirt and guzzled a glass of water. Deleting unlistened-to messages was probably a little bit crazy, but maybe it would be well within the realm of normal if I merely avoided listening to them until I was having a better day.

Wait. Now I'd be afraid of highways *and* voicemail. Pretty soon I'd add spiders and vacuum cleaners and maybe frozen pizza to the list, and one day I'd wake up and realize I hadn't left my house in a decade.

I took a deep breath and tapped Kurt's message.

It's me. Listen, call me as soon as you get this. We both know we need to talk. So let's just cut to the chase and do it. And FYI, this time I'll expect you to dial down the hysterics.

"Dial down the hysterics?" I yelled. I started to throw my phone across the room. I reconsidered and walked over and kicked Kurt's recliner with one of my welding boots instead.

"Dial down the hysterics?" I yelled again. And again. And probably a few times after that.

When I finally stopped kicking, my big toe really hurt and Kurt's recliner looked exactly the same. "And *FYI*, you have crappy taste in furniture, you bastard," I yelled.

I found my phone again and tapped Ted Brody's message just to get it over with.

Hi, Melanie? This is Ted Brody. I wanted to let you know that no innocent bystanders have been watered by your sculpture since you fixed it, and I thank you kindly for that. And, uh, I seem to have said exactly the wrong thing when you were here and, well, I'm just check- ing in to make sure you're okay. And to tell you that, pun intended, you have a rain check to be my guest for a bite to eat whenever and if ever it works for you. And finally, I agree, a house with no one at home waiting for you does suck. Big-time. Trust me, I know.

I thought about calling Ted Brody back, I really did. It was a sweet message, and chances were he was even a nice guy. But the thought of having to sit across a restaurant table from a perfect stranger and say all the right things while you tried to get to know each other all the way from scratch was just exhausting. Bone wearying. No shared frame of reference, no guarantee that you'd have anything at all in common. All that baggage to unlock and open and all those quirky little bits and pieces to sort through.

If Finn Miller and I were sitting across from each other in a restaurant courtyard, we'd both be wearing rose-colored glasses. A retro haze would surround us like soft lighting, taking away all the rough edges. If the conversation started to lag, we could tell old stories from high school, about things and people we'd both known.

Halfway through math class, I twisted in my seat and angled my Yardley Liplighter mirror so I could see Finn Miller. I watched him put his elbow on his desk and rest his chin on the palm of his hand. He tapped his fingers on his jaw over and over again as if he were playing the piano. I sighed.

When class was over, I pushed myself out of my chair and reached behind me to yank my skirt down casually and, with luck, dislodge a slight wedgie at the same time.

I picked up the stack of books on my desk. B.J. had borrowed some purple dye from the biology room and we'd all painted our fingernails and toenails with multiple coats last night and then Veronica and I had helped her sneak it back into the classroom before first period this morning. I wiggled my fingers and watched my nails under the flicker-y fluorescent classroom lights.

"A purple people eater, huh?" Finn Miller suddenly said beside me.

I jumped. My face burned a million shades of red, and I squeezed my hands into fists.

He grabbed one hand and unfurled a purple-tipped finger. "Psychedelic."

A tiny laugh that sounded like the bark of a seal pup came out of my mouth. My heart skipped a beat.

Finn reached over, took my books from me, and piled them on top of his own. He turned and walked up the aisle. He waited for me at the doorway and let me go through first.

Then he walked over to B.J. and Veronica and handed B.J. my books.

"Take good care of her," he said.

I finished the last of my breakfast yogurt, scraping the edge of the spoon around and around the plastic container as I tried to remember the rest of our story. It was sometime in the fall of senior year when Finn Miller finally asked me out. We went to the movies with two of his friends and their dates. Was it *American Graffiti*? Whatever it was, the guys hooted through the whole thing, loud and obnoxious. I'd found the movie beneath my level of maturity and wished we'd gone to see something more sophisticated instead, maybe *The Way We Were* or *Scenes From a Marriage*. Whenever I reached for our shared popcorn, Finn reached in, too, and our hands brushed. When he put his arm around me, all I could think of was that if he got butter on my sister's sweater, she'd know I'd borrowed it while she was away at college, and she'd kill me.

We'd ridden together in Finn's friend's family's boatlike, wood-paneled station wagon, and after the movie all six of us cruised around for a while in a pale imitation of the movie. "Hi, neighbor, have a Gansett!" Finn's friends said over and over, as if it had been funny the first time, while we passed around two stolen-from-home cans of Narragansett Tall that tasted like watered-down skunk. The rest of the group waited in the car while Finn walked me to the door. When he kissed me, somebody leaned on the horn.

On Monday, Finn carried my books to my classes. He called me after school. And the next weekend, he ditched his friends and borrowed his own family car and let me pick the movie. He was nice. Attentive. A little bit boring maybe, but who was I to talk?

I threw my yogurt into the trash. So hard to remember: Did this go on for a few weeks? Longer? At one point I broke his heart, but how?

Yikes. By telling him I wanted to spend more time with my friends. I cringed as I remembered delivering this, the lamest of brush-offs. On the phone, no less, holding the receiver to my ear and stretching the long curly black telephone cord until it reached the privacy of the bathroom, because I didn't have the guts to say it in person.

Looking back, the truth might have been that he'd never stood a chance. From the start I'd thought there must be something wrong with him because he seemed to like me so much. Maybe steady kindness was too subtle for a young girl to appreciate. But now, all these long years later, it sure as hell looked like some kind of wonderful.

How lucky I was that Finn Miller had emailed his way into my life again. How incredible that our worlds had imploded simultaneously, that the universe was giving us this opportunity to rise from the rubble and build something better together.

Everybody knew that old magnetism never died. You could walk into a room decades later and still feel the pull. Physical attraction was chemistry, science. The shape of a face, the pitch of a voice, the scent of your perfect match.

I'd been such a little fool all those years ago. But I was older and wiser now, and I knew what was important in a relationship—kindness, stability, invulnerability to women named *Crissy*.

I'd appreciate Finn Miller the second time around. And when we saw each other again, this would be our chance to finally get it right.

The only thing standing between us was getting from Point A to Point B. Anxiety gripped my chest as I tried to picture making it all the way from the suburbs of Atlanta to the suburbs of Boston. I could only hope that love really did conquer all—including fear of highways.

To: Melanie

From: Finn Miller

Subject: Re: Re: Reunion

♫ ♪ ♫ ♪ Save the last dance for me. ♫ ♪ ♫ ♪

To: Melanie

From: B.J.

Subject: It's Never Too Late to Make a Reunion Time Capsule!

Do inform your classmates in advance so they can bring an item that represents an important memory. Think: never-returned textbooks, old report cards, record albums and 8-track tapes, as well as condoms (unused only, please) and other prom memorabilia.

Don't overlook the importance of choosing the right container for your time capsule. Even you and (most of) your aging classmates will hold up longer than a flimsy cardboard box. Should one of you have a professional connection, a simple casket works perfectly. Leave open and place in a prominent location at the reunion.

Instead of dreaming about Finn Miller, I dreamed about art-ist and former nun Corita Kent, who created the famous LOVE postage stamp. In high school, or maybe it was junior high, she became my hero when she designed the rainbow of swashes that was painted on one of the enormous storage tanks along the Southeast Expressway and changed the commute to Boston forever. Not only was it pop art and the coolest thing *evah*, but rumor had it that she'd snuck the profile of Ho Chi Minh into the blue swash as a protest against the Vietnam War.

She died when Trevor and Troy were still little, but in my dream she showed up at my house in Georgia and asked me to touch up the tank for her.

She was wearing her nun's habit again. I wondered if it was a last-minute religious reconversion before she died, but I didn't ask in case it might be rude. Her headpiece was too wide to fit through our front door, so I stepped out on the stone front steps to talk to her.

"Thank you for thinking of me," I said. "But I couldn't pos-sibly touch your work."

She smiled a beautiful smile and I wished she weren't a nun because then maybe she could be my mother. "Don't be ridicu-lous," she said. "It's a storage tank."

"But I'm not a painter."

A gust of wind caught her rosary beads and she smiled again. "We'll give you a metal paintbrush and metal paint, and you'll be just fine."

"But I'm afraid."

"Of course you're afraid. We're all afraid. There are only two choices: afraid and boring."

"Really?" I said. "I didn't know that."

"That's okay. If you knew it, I would have asked someone else." She reached into the pocket of her habit and pulled out a child's eight-color watercolor paint set.

I held out one hand and she placed it on my palm. It was lighter than air. "That's it? That's all I need?"

She was starting to levitate. "Yes, there's a metal ladder built onto the side of the tank, so hold on tight and just don't look down. And make sure you get Ho Chi Minh's nose right. It's the blue one."

My heart did a double beat and the baby elephant sat down on my chest. "But I'm afraid of heights. I can't even drive over a bridge. And how am I going to get to the tank anyway? It's right on the edge of a *highway*."

Corita Kent was fully airborne now, and for the first time I realized that Sister Bertrille from *The Flying Nun* had been up in the sky waiting for her all along.

"Boring," they both yelled. And then they giggled and flew off together.

When *The Flying Nun* came out, my sister, Marion, and I watched it religiously every Thursday night at eight. We even talked our mother into cutting our bangs so we'd look like Sally Field.

It was all fun and games until Marion decided to make me

fly. She was four years older so she should have known better, but one day she wrapped me in a sheet and helped me climb up and stand on my bed. It was an iron cottage bed that had belonged to some old dead relative, and it was painted a shiny white. Marion stood on the bed and gave me ten fingers to stand on the slippery footboard, which seemed a hundred feet high.

I was trying really hard not to cry. "I don't think I can fly," I whispered. I twisted around to keep from falling forward and ended up mostly on the bed. My head hit the edge of the metal frame. When Marion dabbed at my face with a corner of the sheet, it turned really, really red.

"Don't tell Mom," she hissed, so I started to scream. Then Marion started to scream as if she were the one bleeding, so I screamed louder. When our mother came running in, she screamed, too, then ordered us both out to the car. My mother hated blood and she hated to drive and money didn't grow on trees. By the time we found the hospital, the six stitches and one lollipop I got from the doctor was practically the best part of the day.

I ran one finger along the tiny raised scar near the top of my forehead. It had started out just above my eyebrow, but as my face grew it had moved up, just like the doctor promised.

In honor of my dream I was watching an episode of *The Flying Nun* that I'd found on my laptop and sent to the family room TV via the wireless thingee Trevor and Troy had configured for us last Christmas. I was stretched out in Kurt's former recliner that I'd sprayed with Febreze so it wouldn't smell like him.

The episode was called "The Candid Commercial." The gist of it seemed to be that the convent washing machine breaks down, forcing Sister Bertrille to take all the nuns' laundry to a Laundromat. In a pretty big coincidence, a producer and cameraman just happen to be there filming a candid commercial for a laundry detergent called Delight.

I sighed. Back when Kurt and I were living in our first little rental apartment, we used to go to the Laundromat every Monday, since it was the slowest night. I'd bring our economy-size jug of Wisk detergent and pour it carefully around the neck of each of Kurt's and my shirts, hoping to avoid the "collar soil" that would result in the heinous "Ring Around the Collar" described in the Wisk commercials.

Kurt would have taken over the entire length of a folding counter to sort the change we'd saved all week, pocketing the quarters for the evening's dinner, filling the coin-operated washers and dryers with the nickels and dimes, and rolling the pennies in orange wrappers we'd store in a shoe box until we had enough to take to the bank.

As soon as we got our two jam-packed washing machines going, one for colors and one for whites, we'd stop in at the local pizza place, put in a to-go order, take a walk, then circle back to pick up the single cheese pizza we could afford. On nights when the timing worked out just right, we'd walk into the Laundromat with our dinner as the spin cycle was winding down.

We couldn't wait until we could afford to buy our own washer and dryer. When Kurt's parents finally upgraded and handed down their old Harvest Gold Kenmore set, we christened them with a champagne toast as if we'd won the lottery.

Who knew those laundry-and-pizza dates would turn out to be some of the best times of our marriage.

To: Melanie

From: B.J.

Subject: Why Not to Go to Your Reunion on an Empty Stomach

GOLDFISH GET-TO-KNOW-YOU REUNION ICEBREAKER: Ask class officers, cheerleaders, potheads, and other formerly prominent classmates to carry a large bowl of Goldfish snack crackers to each table, instructing everybody to take as many as they wish but not to eat a single one yet. After everybody has a handful, pause a dramatic moment, then inform the crowd that they have to take turns sharing one personal fact with their tablemates for each Goldfish they took.

To: Melanie

From: B.J.

Subject: 5 Reunion Don'ts

1. Junior sizes (even if you can still fit into them)
2. Pantyhose
3. Matching spousefits (outfits for spouses)
4. Mirrored sunglasses
5. A case of water bottles labeled with your business logo that just happened to be in the trunk of your car

"Have I worn you down yet?" B.J. asked when I answered my cell.

"Mirrored sunglasses are a reunion don't?" I said. "Really?"

B.J. barked a laugh into my ear. "Absolutely. Well, unless you're Dog the Bounty Hunter. And I think even he's on borrowed time with the sunglasses indoors look. Anyway, what's new?"

"Let's see. I just finished watching an episode of *The Flying Nun*, and last night I had a dream that Corita Kent asked me to paint something for her."

"Ha, the *Flying Nun* part better be a joke. Okay, enough small talk. I'm not hanging up until your flights are booked. And I don't want to hear any whining about how much the tickets cost. It's your own damn fault for waiting so long."

"Okay," I said. "I'll go."

There was dead silence on the other end. I used the time to scroll through my email, just in case something else had come in from Finn in the last three minutes.

B.J. cleared her throat. "Really?"

"I just said I would, didn't I?"

"What's going on?"

"Nothing. You talked me into it, that's all. You're very persuasive."

B.J. blew a gust of wind into my ear. "Spill it."

"There's nothing to spill." I took a quick breath. "Hey, do you remember Finn Miller?" I asked, the lure of saying his name out loud impossible to resist.

"Of course I do. You drooled all over him in Algebra *and* Geometry. Didn't you two even go out, or almost go out, or something like that?"

I did my best imitation of nonchalant. "I'll have to check my diary and get back to you."

"Well, he's single again, too, you know. *And* he's going to the reunion."

"Gee, what *don't* you know?"

"What can I say, I'm on the committee. His profile is a ten, too, or at least a nine-point-five. Divides his time between Malibu and Chicago, or maybe it was Maui and Cleveland."

"Ha," I said. "And he has a private plane. And he invented a daily vitamin that reverses gray hair."

"No, no," B.J. said. "Actually it not only gets rid of the gray, it turns your hair any color you want it to be."

"Cool. Like Flintstones for grown-ups. You just pick a vitamin and, presto, ten minutes later your hair turns Wilma White or Frosted Fred."

"Or Bamm-Bamm Blue or Pebbles Pink. And it's time-released, so it lasts all day and most of the night."

"All day and most of the night," we both sang.

"Jinx," we both said.

"I think we may have botched the lyrics," B.J. said. "But who was that anyway?"

"The Kinks, I think. I used to love that line about believing that you and me will last forever. Ha."

B.J. laughed. "You and me *will* last forever—it's the rest of the stupid world we have to be concerned about."

"This is true." I closed my eyes to picture the metal sculpture—a big steel vitamin bottle with Flintstone-like figures climbing out and spilling over the sides. Maybe for a playground or a children's museum, although it would have to be installed out of climbing range to protect it, and possibly sandwiched between big sheets of Plexiglas.

Or maybe Finn Miller would commission me to make it for his Maui estate.

"Okay, let's get your flights booked," B.J. said. "And, for the record, I still think there's something you're not telling me. Oh, and don't forget to call your sister and let her know you'll be in Marshbury. She'll kill you if someone else tells her first."

I pulled myself away from my email screen and found the Delta site. B.J. already had it up at her end, and in no time we'd figured out the best flights and I'd punched in my credit card number.

Delta took me to another screen and gave me one last chance to bail. I hesitated, then shut my eyes and pushed CONFIRM RESERVATION.

"Done?" B.J. asked.

"Done. And thank you. I think." It took me every ounce of willpower I had not to add, *So, guess what? Finn Miller emailed me. And we've been, well, emailing.*

I loved B.J., but she wasn't exactly subtle and she did have a slight tendency to take things over. One mention of Finn Miller and she'd probably be planning the wedding. Or at least booking us the honeymoon suite.

We weren't in high school anymore, and I didn't have to tell my best friend everything. Finn Miller was my delicious secret.

To: Finn Miller

From: Melanie

Subject: Reunion

I'm in! Flights booked and everything. So that means now you HAVE to go. What song do you think will be playing when we finally see each other again after all these years?

To: Melanie

From: B.J.

Subject: 5 Reunion Do's

1. **Do** move beyond once a loser, always a loser. The dorks

are the ones who have it all going on now. The popular kids peaked in high school.

2. As opposed to "OMG, OMG, OMG! You look SO much better than you did in high school," **do** go with a simple "You look great."

3. **Do** step out of your comfort zone and be the first one to say hello and start the conversation.

4. **Do** bury the hatchet. No matter how horribly you were dissed by a classmate all those years ago, you will look a lot better if you at least appear to let it go.

5. **Do** make sure you reserve plenty of time for a catty après-reunion postmortem with your real friends to balance out all this good behavior.

P.S. Call me.

B.J. answered on the first ring. "All I wanna do," she sang.

"Is have more fun," I sang back.

B.J. sighed. "Bummer, we still can't sing. Or remember lyrics. I hate that."

"Oh, well," I said. "If the music is loud enough, we can fake it. Remember when we used to think Queen was singing 'another one likes to dust'?"

B.J. sighed again.

"What's wrong?"

"Do you think it's too late to go on a diet?"

"You mean in terms of our life expectancy?"

B.J. snorted. "No, I mean in terms of Derrick Donohue. He never once, in all four years of high school, gave me the time of day."

"Whoa, where is this coming from? You've never even mentioned him."

"I just remembered it."

"So now Derrick Donohue is going to be your midlife crisis crush?"

"No way. He missed his chance. I just want to look so amazing he eats his heart out."

I walked over to the freezer and opened the door. "Come on, Beej. We both know diets don't work. You lose a few pounds, and a year later you've gained it all back plus six more."

"I don't care about a year later. I only care about the reunion. Listen, I think we should both get a copy of that high school reunion diet book ASAP. How bad can it be—there's a glass of red wine on the cover."

I switched my phone over to my other ear. Buried way in the back of the freezer, behind two bags of coffee beans, I was pretty sure I could see a chocolate chip cookie ice cream sandwich that had formerly belonged to Kurt. "Or we could just buy the red wine and read a good novel instead," I said as I reached for it.

"No, really, I'm not kidding. You're supposed to lose twenty pounds in thirty days on it."

"I think it's twenty *years* in thirty days."

B.J. blew a puff of air across the miles. "Oh, puh-lease. Like that's going to happen. Maybe we can just find a drive-through that does liposuction."

I tucked the phone into the crook of my neck and tore an

opening in the plastic wrapper that covered the ice cream. A freezer-burned mini iceberg glistened up at me, irrefutable evidence that my freezer was now officially single, too. And that Kurt was really gone.

But it was okay. *I* was okay. Because I had somewhere to go now, too. Where Finn Miller would be waiting for me.

I blew a puff of air back at B.J. "Don't be ridiculous. The only diet we need is dying to have some fun. We are sooooo going to rock that reunion."

I brought my three box spring ladies into the kitchen and lined them up side by side across the length of the granite island. Then I opened the liquor cabinet and eyed what was left in there after Kurt had absconded with most of it. I rooted around until I found three shot glasses and placed one in front of each box spring lady. I filled them all with a dollop of red wine, and then poured a human-size glass of wine for myself.

I held up my glass. "Wish me luck, ladies."

I touched my big glass to each of their tiny ones.

"Wait," I said. "Why can't you come, too? It might be a good thing to have some extra moral support. Plus, when everybody at the reunion starts bragging about how important they are, I can just happen to have you with me."

They seemed to think this was a genius idea, so after I acknowledged the fact that I was not only talking to box spring ladies but answering for them, too, I finished my wine and helped them polish off theirs. I mean, the whole thing was barely crazy if you factored in that it wasn't just a pleasure trip for them—I'd be looking for a possible consignment sale, too.

I headed up to the attic to look for the biggest suitcase I could find. I dragged it down the creaky attic stairs, then went back for my carry-on.

"Damn," I said a few minutes later. I'd managed to fit all three of the box spring ladies into the big suitcase, but there was no way in hell I could zip it closed, unless I turned their big hooped skirts into hot pants.

I sighed. To be honest, the whole good-bye toast and suitcase thing had started out as an elaborate stall to put off calling my sister, Marion, which I'd been trying to make myself do ever since B.J. had nudged me, but now I really wanted to take them with me.

Dread turned over in my stomach like sour milk. I stared at my phone, as if I could somehow get points for *thinking* about calling my sister, as opposed to actually calling her. Even without B.J. reminding me, I knew I had to do it. With all the amazing advances in technology over the years, there was still no more reliable form of communication than a small-town grapevine. By now someone Marion had run into at Marshbury's only grocery store had probably already told her I'd bought a ticket for my class reunion.

The longer I waited the worse it would be. Marion was only going to get more and more pissed off that she hadn't heard from me. What else was new. Even as kids, I'd never been able to please her. She was always bossing me around, telling me what to do, what to wear, what to say, as if I was somehow a reflection of *her*.

And when I'd finally had enough, and who could blame me, and yelled "I hate you" or threw a hairbrush at her, she'd sigh and say, "Oh, grow up," as if she hadn't been the one to start the whole thing.

Our mother lumped us both together like we were joined at the hip, which didn't help. *Girls, can you set the table? Girls, can you peel the potatoes and put them on to boil? Girls, clean your rooms— now.*

I found the way to my father's heart by helping him wash the cars, shovel the driveway when it snowed, and load up the trunk with trash for a trip to the dump on Saturday mornings.

"Great," Marion would say as she flapped her hands like an idiot to make her nails dry faster. "Turn yourself into a boy so he'll like you better than me. Be the son he never had."

"I hate you," I'd say.

"I hate you more," she'd say. Then she'd shake her hands harder. "You're such a *child*."

When Marion finally went off to college the year I started high school, I was delirious with happiness. B.J., who was still Barb then, and I waited until my parents were out and then rifled through every square inch of her room, the scent of our Coty Wild Musk oil overpowering the powdery residue of her Love's Baby Soft perfume.

I stood in front of the mirror on the back of Marion's closet door and held up a preppy, navy-blue wraparound skirt. The ties ran through double metal loops at the sides and it had large hip pockets and a bouquet of three big tulips, two red and one yellow, appliquéd over the left thigh.

"Far freakin' out," B.J. said sarcastically. "Come on, even Marion had the sense to leave that nowhere skirt behind." She adjusted her own chocolate-brown shawl over her black Danskin leotard, then reached down to make sure the long fringe on her suede belt was splayed evenly over the right thigh of her perfectly patched dungarees.

I ditched the skirt and threw my chevron-striped pom-pom poncho onto Marion's bed so I had full use of both hands. I found her stash of cotton balls and dabbed my face with Bonne Bell 10-0-6 lotion from an almost empty bottle, then helped myself to a forgotten strawberry Lip Smacker. I slid her white vanity chair over to her closet and climbed up. Way in the back corner I found her old pink jewelry box tucked behind some stuffed animals.

After I climbed back down with it, I couldn't resist winding it up. When I opened the lid, the tiny ballerina circled to the tinkling notes of "When You Wish Upon a Star." I hated that her jewelry box still worked and my identical one, possibly a casualty of overwinding, no longer did. I wondered if I could get away with switching them.

I shook my head and reminded myself that Marion hadn't been all bad. When I was a little, little girl and my mother wasn't feeling well, sometimes she'd help me unpack my book bag after school. "Good job," she'd say as she attached my best paper of the day to the refrigerator with one of our two identical Bozo the Clown kazoos that doubled as magnets. And then she'd get us cookies and milk and actually sit with me at the little kitchen table until we finished them.

My eyes teared up at the memory. I went out to the garage and found a cardboard box. I gave each box spring lady a hug and a loud smack of a kiss and then I rolled her up in a blanket of bubble wrap and rested her gently in the box on a soft bed of tissue paper. I added more tissue paper on top, like a white down comforter. Then I scheduled a UPS pickup.

"Okay, here's the plan," I said before I taped up the box. "I'm going to ship you to Marion's house to break the ice for me. She'll be so busy oohing and aahing about how beautiful you are and how talented I am, she won't have time to yell at me for not living up to her sister standards. And then, after the cookies and milk, we'll get the hell out of there and you can cruise around town with B.J. and me."

B.J. had been after me for years to find a place up north to carry my work and give me an excuse to visit more often, so we could check out some shops and galleries while we were out and about. And of course, Finn would want to see the box spring ladies, too, because everything I did would be endlessly fascinating to him.

As a plan, it wasn't half bad.

CHAPTER 12

My next-door neighbor was pruning her Knock Out roses when the car arrived to take me to the airport. I thought briefly about asking her to keep an eye on the house. But it would certainly tie up loose ends if it managed to burn down while I was gone, so I decided I'd take my chances.

She was wearing crisp white capris and a sleeveless pink blouse, and even from this distance I could see that her roots were freshly dyed and she was fully made up. I couldn't tell from here, but under her strappy sandals I just knew her toenail polish matched her blouse.

I took a moment to regret my own lack of polish, both literal and figurative. Then I double-checked the timer on my lights and locked my front door. I bumped my carry-on down my stone front steps.

The driver popped the trunk open and got out of the car. He took a moment to slide his black suit coat over his white button-down shirt and to don his black chauffeur cap.

Then he wished me a "Good morning, ma'am" and we agreed it was going to be a hot one. He took my carry-on with one hand and opened the rear door of the car for me with the other. Once my luggage and I had been safely stowed away, he stood in the blazing sun and took off the jacket and hat again and climbed back into the car, something I'd never seen before. Maybe his boss had told him he had to wear them, but forgot to specify for how long. In any case, there was something both silly and chivalrous about his minute or two of dressing up for me.

I'd never called a car service for a ride to the airport before, or to anywhere else for that matter, and I was pleased with myself for coming up with the option. It was expensive, but not all that expensive in the scheme of things. Maybe not quite cheaper than paying for parking at the airport, but definitely cheaper than therapy. I felt relaxed and independent, as if I were a woman with things to do and places to go. Perhaps there was even an air of mystery about me. I liked that.

As the driver backed out of my driveway, I rolled down the window to say something to my neighbor. I considered an ironic *Don't mind my town car* or even a generic *Have a nice day*.

Our eyes met for an instant and then she turned her back as if she hadn't seen me.

There are true friends and then there are couples friends. Up until that moment, this particular neighbor hadn't declared herself, so it stung. She and her husband had shown up on our doorstep with a loaf of banana bread when we'd moved in all those years ago. I'd been so overwhelmed at that point that it was all I could do not to burst into tears at their generosity.

Kurt invited them into the foyer, boxes piled everywhere behind us, and we chatted for a bit. "Oh, you're so nice," the woman said. "Now I'm really glad we didn't help ourselves to your plants."

Her husband gave her a look.

"Um," she said, "it's just that the old owners were big gardeners and they told us to feel free to take whatever we wanted before you got here."

The conversation bumped along for a while, and then we thanked them again for the banana bread. Later that day, Kurt and I toured our yard and noticed the conspicuous holes for the first time. Two evenly spaced identical bushes, then a big gap like a missing tooth, then two more. A half circle minus one of identical clumps of daylilies, irises, and plants we didn't recognize.

"Wouldn't you think they would have at least filled the holes back in?" Kurt asked.

Sure enough, whenever something in our yard bloomed, an identical plant bloomed next door. Kurt loved nothing more than to wave at our new neighbors with a big grin on his face while he was mowing the lawn. "Those yellow flowers of yours are looking great," he'd yell. "And how about the blooms on those pink things."

Eventually we decided we liked them anyway. As two couples, MelanieandKurt and TiffanyandHunter, we'd seek each other out at neighborhood functions and occasionally have each other over for a laid-back cookout, and our collective kids had free rein in both yards.

Kurt golfed with Hunter regularly, so maybe the almost

friendship hadn't really ended. KurtandMelanie had just morphed into Kurtand*Crissy*. Maybe my next-door neighbors were even relieved that I'd been replaced in our foursome. Maybe Tiffany had only put up with me because Hunter had liked Kurt so much.

Come to think of it, she'd never once, in all these years, acknowledged my work in any way, even though I asked about her job at a local boutique all the time. Did she not like the rusted metal calla lily fountain nestled in the shady corner of our front yard? Was she jealous of the local press I'd received? Or was I just somehow beneath her interest? Maybe I was simply the crazy welding lady to all my neighbors, the one who they reluctantly let into their lives because her husband was such a nice guy. Ha.

The driver's voice broke in. "Which airline, ma'am?"

"Delta, please," I said.

Delta was based in Atlanta, and a Delta flight left Atlanta for Boston practically every hour on the hour. For the first few years after we moved down here, way back before you could just go online for these things, I'd called Delta reservations and written down the schedule in the spiral address book I used for directions. Some nights, when Kurt was working late and the boys were doing their homework, I'd flip through until I found the page and think: *If I took Flight 1100 at 7:15, I'd be in Boston at 10:02. If I waited until 9:50 and left on Flight 412, I'd be there at 12:33.*

I held my breath as the driver pulled onto I-75 South. I waited for my early warning symptoms—dry mouth, racing heart—but they didn't arrive. Maybe it was riding in the backseat? I wondered if I could rig up a way to drive my own car from there—maybe an extension pole with metals claws welded to it that would grasp the steering wheel.

I leaned my head back and closed my eyes.

Atlanta's Hartsfield-Jackson International Airport is the busiest airport in the world, with close to ninety million passengers traveling through it a year, so the security lines were crazy long as usual. They moved fairly quickly and efficiently, though, and before I knew it my carry-on rolled under the scanner and back into sight and I was sliding into my flip-flops again.

Instead of taking the airport tram, I walked along the center corridor next to the moving staircase all the way to Terminal C so I could stretch my legs and shake off my post-nap grogginess. I couldn't believe I'd fallen asleep in the town car. I hoped I hadn't snored or talked in my sleep. Or drooled. I pictured the driver looking in his rearview mirror and rolling his eyes at the middle-aged woman sprawled untidily across the seat. I didn't think I'd ever fallen asleep in a car before, at least as an adult. I was always keeping a watch on whoever was driving, a second set of eyes, alert for potential disaster.

Maybe I'd crank it up a notch or twelve, and try to earn enough money as a metal sculptor to hire a driver. Or more likely an intern who had her driver's license.

Once I found my gate, I hit the nearest bathroom and then bought a bottle of water, the yin and yang of the quest for hydration, before I sat down to wait for my flight to be called. A woman about my age was standing sideways and holding on to one arm of a black leatherette chair at the end of a long, bolted-together row. Her knees were bent and her feet were flat on the floor. She bent her elbows and lowered her butt almost to the floor, then straightened her arms again.

So that's how you got rid of flabby upper arms at the airport. I smiled at her to show my solidarity, but she was lost in her endorphins. I took out my cell phone, simply because everyone around me but the triceps-dipping woman seemed to be interacting with theirs. I tried to remember what non-exercising people used to do at airports while they waited for a flight. Read a book? Flip through a magazine? People-watch? It was so strange how we were never alone now—our cells connected us to anyone we wanted to be connected to, like two tin cans with a wireless string between them.

Oh, I could see the sculpture already. Two little metal boys—or hints of boys—dashes of metal, really. One with corkscrew metal curls and the other would have short metal spikes for hair. Two recycled tin cans, something vintage if I could find it—the splurge would be worth it if I could track down original Planters Peanuts or Rodeo coffee tins at a flea market or even online, but Campbell's tomato soup cans would work, too. I'd cover the labels with several coats of polyurethane to keep them safe from the elements. A long coil of eighth-inch steel rod would stretch between the boys as they talked into their makeshift walkie-talkies.

I could see it so clearly I was dying to roll up my sleeves and get to work right away, but I had to settle for rooting around in my purse for a receipt and jotting down a few notes on the back of it so I wouldn't forget anything.

When first-class passengers began boarding, I stood up and stretched and found my ticket. Eventually my section of the plane was called, and I fell into line with the crush of passengers. The covered jetway was no match for the Atlanta humidity. The temperature inside the plane wasn't much better. I found my seat, hoisted my carry-on up to the overhead bin, and reached up for the air dial the moment I sat down. A pitiful puff of warm air greeted me.

My phone rang just as a man finished stowing his carry-on and then waved his ticket toward the seat next to mine.

I checked the name on the display.

"What," I whispered into my phone.

"That's my seat," the man said.

"Not you," I said to the man. I stepped out into the aisle.

"You didn't call me back," Kurt said on the phone.

One of the flight attendants was shutting the door to the plane and another was speaking into the microphone and telling us it was time to turn off our cell phones. "Not now," I said as I plopped into the empty seat next to the man. "I'm busy."

"What else is new," Kurt said.

"What's that supposed to mean?" I said.

"You know, it might not be a bad idea for you to get out of that studio of yours once in a while."

"Excuse me?"

"You're right. That's not the point here. I've put together a list of things I'd like to go over. How about we meet for a drink tonight, like civilized people. Say six thirty at that pub on Johnson's Ferry I like?"

One of the flight attendants was looking right at me, shaking his head.

I pushed the END CALL button. I pretended I was turning off the phone while I opened a call-blocking app that Troy had installed on my phone, which I hadn't thought I needed. Until now.

I typed in Kurt's cell number and pushed SAVE.

CHAPTER 13

To: Melanie

From: B.J.

Subject: Itinerary

1. I pick you up at Logan, then we stash our stuff at Jan's beach house, staking our claim on the best available room ASAP so we don't end up on the floor. Then we walk the beach and eat. Or eat and walk the beach.

2. We party with the masses at Jan's until we hear from Veronica.

3. If we don't hear from Veronica within a reasonable period of time, we drive to the Cape to get her so she can party with us, too.

4. We fit in primping, shopping, tattoos, and seafood as time allows.

5. As our grand finale, we party like it's 19-whatever at . . . drum-

roll . . . The Marshbury High School Best Class/Best Reunion Evah.

To: Melanie
From: Finn Miller
Subject: forgot to say

What song will be playing when we finally see each other after all these years? Nights in White Satin by The Moody Blues of course. I can hear it already.

To: Finn Miller
From: Melanie
Subject: Re: forgot to say

Breast song ever.

To: Finn Miller
From: Melanie
Subject: Re: Re: forgot to say

Oops. I meant best. Sorry, just linked email to phone and still getting goosed to autocorrect. I mean used to.

I couldn't wait to see B.J. and give her a great big hug, to feel her dogged determination wash over me like a cool salty breeze.

I'd fallen asleep on the flight, too, something I'd never done before. At takeoff, the guy next to me gripped his armrest as well as the one we were theoretically supposed to be sharing. I watched the woman diagonally in front of me close her eyes and then mouth some words that looked like a prayer.

Despite the fact that I was surrounded by nervous wrecks, I was just so relaxed, more relaxed than I'd been since I started sleeping on that awful guest room mattress, not that that was saying much. I wasn't really sure why. Maybe it was because I wasn't in the pilot's seat, and there was no hope of even backseat-driving this mammoth chunk of metal. We'd make it or we wouldn't, and there wasn't a thing I could do to influence the outcome. So I had to let it go.

As we landed, I stared past my armrest-gripping seatmate and out the window at one of the most beautiful landing strips in the world. Inlets edged with sea grass twisted and turned, and it looked as if we were going to land with a plop right into the water. I imagined the smell of salt air. I could almost taste the briny water and feel the way it would dry on my arms and legs under the hot summer sun. Once the ocean gets under your skin and into your heart, it never lets you go.

"Nights in White Satin" was stuck in my head, playing over and over again, my new endless loop. I was still a sucker for that melancholy flute. And all these years later, just what the truth was, I sure as hell still didn't know anymore.

I sighed. Anticipation was better than chocolate, rich and dreamy, but also like a shot of adrenaline, snapping me out of the coma I'd let myself fall into over the past few months. I wanted to savor every minute of this week, to walk the beach, to splash in the ocean, to imagine the exact moment of seeing Finn at the reunion over and over again, in every possible variation.

I pulled my carry-on along, following the signs for baggage, slowing my pace so I could count the Red Sox hats on the heads of the people I passed. I thought about stopping at Legal Sea Foods Test Kitchen to have live lobsters shipped to Trevor and Troy, but I was afraid Trevor had been in California long enough that he might try to turn his into a pet, and Troy's would be long dead before he got around to cooking it.

My cell phone rang and I stopped to pull it out of my purse. "Sixteen," I said.

"Candles?"

"Nope."

"Okay, I'll bite," B.J. said. "Sixteen what?"

I smiled. "Red Sox hats since I landed."

"That's nothing. The Hubster has more than that in his closet."

"Impressive," I said. "I didn't realize Tom was that big a fan."

"I think it's more about covering his bald spot."

"By the way, is he okay with you spending all this time with me?"

"He didn't get a vote. That's why we're still married."

"Got it," I said. "How about work? Did you get the time off-off, or just sort of off?"

"Off-off. Someone's covering for me, and I'm not going to check messages once. Shit, shit, shit. This cop is trying to tell me I have to go wait in the live parking lot, which for your information has been moved to Timbuktu in the eternal quest to keep everyone entering or exiting Logan Airport totally confused."

"But at least they finally finished the Big Dig. Didn't they? Can you just circle around and I'll wait at the curb till you get back?"

"How about you run and I'll play dumb till you get here? Hurry, my acting range is limited."

I jumped into Mustang Sally, B.J.'s red vintage Mustang convertible and longtime companion, and gave B.J. a quick hug. After B.J. put on her blinker, she turned to look at me. Her hair was long this time and blond—actually more like calico, with highlights and lowlights that ranged from platinum to a deep warm brown. There was gray in there, too, if you looked carefully, but somehow it just added dimension to the whole effect instead of making her look old.

"Your hair looks great," I said.

"Thanks. Yours looks like shit," B.J. said. "I knew it would, so I got a referral from my stylist to Salon TAJ, which he assures me is *the* cutting-edge Marshbury salon, and made you an appointment for later today."

"I didn't see that on the itinerary."

"Sure you did. It falls under primping."

"Thanks so much for asking first," I said. "And for insulting my hair. Oh, and I'm starving, so at the risk of throwing off our schedule I think we should eat first."

As hungry as I was, I also couldn't wait to get to the beach. Maybe we could stop first at Maria's Sub Shop and bring our lunch with us to eat by the water. Maria's was one of those quirky little local places that you appreciated more with every year you spent living in the Land of Subway. In your memory, the sub rolls became softer, the meatballs grew more tender, and the fact that Maria's had refused for generations to add lettuce, chopped or otherwise, to their subs because they considered it "filler" became less ridiculous and more charming with the passage of time.

As we paid the toll coming out of the airport and followed the signs for the Southeast Expressway, I held my breath and waited for my heart to start doing its highway dance. B.J. was an aggressive driver, and a little bit erratic, too, using one hand to drive and flinging the other one around as she talked or hunted down her lip gloss. But with her, I was remarkably symptom-free. Maybe I'd left my driving issues behind in Atlanta. Maybe it was just one of those fluky things that happened, like a sniffle that you keep waiting to turn into something bigger, but instead you wake up one day and find that it has simply disappeared and you're all better again.

I breathed a sigh of relief and leaned back into Mustang Sally's worn leather seat. We stayed left at the Braintree split and headed south on Route 3. A few exits later we got off and followed the back roads through Norwell. It had been at least four years, maybe five, since my last visit, and it felt both like coming home and visiting a strange new planet for me.

I couldn't take my eyes off the houses, shingled and weathered and shuttered, and I felt a pang as I remembered that to qualify for old-house status here they had to be at least a hundred years old instead of Atlanta's maybe ten or twenty. The Georgia trees were lush and gorgeous, but seeing my New England sugar maples and sycamores again, with their frayed rope swings, next to old stone wells with water buckets attached gave me another twinge. And the hydrangeas. Hydrangeas, hydrangeas everywhere.

"Déjà vu all over again," I said.

B.J. tilted her head in my direction. "Coldplay?"

I laughed. "Yogi Berra. And that's all the sports talk you'll ever get out of me."

"They're big in the South, huh?"

"Not so much baseball, but they're crazy for football down there. If I never see another tailgate party, it'll be too soon."

"Bless your little pseudo-Southern heart," B.J. said. "Y'all come back now, ya hear," she added in a really bad Southern accent.

"Hey, knock it off," I said. "That's my *abode* you're making fun of."

"I thought you hated it there."

"Where did you get that idea? I hated that Kurt made the decision to move there, not me. And I hate it when people who don't live there think they know what it's like."

"Got it." B.J. put on her blinker and pulled over to the side of the road. She unbolted two metal latches above the windshield, then jumped out and shoved the convertible top into submission. It finally folded, then nestled into the space behind the backseat.

She jumped back in, reached past me to the glove compartment, and pulled a silky red scarf out like a magician. "Here. Not that I think that hairdo of yours is worth saving."

"Thanks," I said. "My self-esteem is soaring already. In another minute you're going to have to start being mean to me so I don't get all conceited."

B.J. laughed. "Ha. I forgot about conceited. Maybe we can add it to the awards at the reunion. Who was the most conceited girl in our class?"

"I'm pretty sure it was you," I said.

"Of course it was. And I'd still blow those wannabes out of the water." She turned the rearview mirror in her direction while she tied an animal print scarf over her hair. "Okay, now you're Thelma and I'm Louise."

"Why do I have to be Thelma?"

"Because you're more naive and vulnerable."

"I am not."

B.J. rubbed her index fingers under her eyes, not quite touching her concealer. "I. Am. Not," she said in a pouty little voice.

"Screw you," I said, "and your stupid dress-up scarves, too."

"Okay, you can be Louise, but just this once."

Our scarves rattled in the wind as we drove through the tree-lined streets.

B.J. plugged her iPod into an adaptor. Billy Joel broke into a spirited rendition of "Only the Good Die Young."

"I think we missed last call for dying young," I said. "But how cute that you made a reunion mix tape."

She turned up the volume. "It's called a playlist now."

"I know that."

As soon as Billy Joel finished singing, Cyndi Lauper jumped

right in with "Girls Just Wanna Have Fun." B.J. started singing along at the top of her lungs. I held out as long as I could, but I couldn't resist joining in on the chorus.

We were still singing, way off key and really loud, especially considering we had the top down, when we pulled into the parking lot in front of Maria's Sub Shop.

"Wow," I said. "Great minds think alike."

B.J. barked her crazy laugh, and I couldn't imagine anywhere in the world I'd rather be.

We carried our subs over to the town bandstand and sat on the steps overlooking the water.

Across from us, boats bobbed up and down at their slips and I breathed in the decomposing smell of low tide as if it were perfume. The poured concrete between the bandstand steps and the inner harbor sparkled with colored flecks, like fairy dust.

"When did they put sea glass in the sidewalks back here?" I asked.

"A while ago—isn't it awesome? I tried to talk The Hubernator into having it done at our house, but he wouldn't go for it."

"Wow, I'd love to try doing that. I think you'd just sprinkle the sea glass in with the aggregate while the cement is still wet, and then smooth it out with a board or something."

B.J. took a bite of her Maria's Special: a domestic ham and American cheese sub with yellow mustard. "You always were so artsy fartsy."

"Really?" I pushed a meatball that was trying to escape back into my sub with one finger. "I didn't think I had any street cred at all as an artist. The art teachers only liked the kids who knew how to draw. You know, if it came out looking like it was done with paint-by-numbers, they must have talent."

"Ugh," B.J. said. "That's how I felt about the English teachers. Remember, you couldn't even get into a Creative Writing elective unless you were in Honors English? I had a lot to say—who the hell cared if I knew where the fuck to put my commas?"

I reached for my iced coffee. "They should have at least been impressed by your vocabulary."

"Exactly," B.J. said. "And Home Ec, don't get me started on Home Ec. I had this purple jumpsuit I was dying to make. But nooooo, Miss McWhoosiface made me rip out the stitches on my apron three times until they fully satisfied her anal tendencies."

"Miss McNally," I said, "or maybe it was McNulty. I petitioned to take Shop instead, and they totally shot me down. And then the very next year, all the boys and girls had to take half a year of each. I couldn't believe they took away my one chance for a Norma Rae moment. Wait, did *Norma Rae* come out before or after we graduated?"

B.J. shrugged. "Who knows. You have to admit, Home Ec got a lot more fun then. Remember when Michael Giacomo added a quarter of a cup of pot to those brownies and left them in the teachers' lounge?"

I leaned back on my elbows and turned my face up to catch the sun. "I don't think he ever got in trouble for that. I think the teachers were hoping if they let it go he might do it again. Remember how we all used to think Mr. Oswell looked like Davy Jones?"

A seagull hovered over us until I threw a piece of sub roll a few feet out. The gull nose-dived and caught it before it hit the ground.

"Ohmigod, how the hell did we get to be so freakin' old?" B.J. yelled.

CHAPTER 14

B.J. shook her head to make sure her animal print scarf was tied on tight. "Okay, your choice. Do you want to be Romy or do you want to be Michele?"

"Do we have to?"

"Of course we have to. *Romy and Michele's High School Reunion* is a classic chick flick."

I rolled my red scarf into the shape of a headband and tied it in a knot on top of my head. The ends stuck out like little wings. I did have fashion flair when I focused.

I sighed. "I hate that term. And I think we're too old for it anyway—it's high time we moved on to hen flicks."

"If we were men at least we could have dick flicks. It sounds a lot edgier." B.J. put the Mustang into reverse and backed out of the parking space. "Okay, I'll be Michele."

"Was that Lisa Kudrow's character or Mira Sorvino's?"

"Lisa Kudrow's."

"See, you always do that. Why do I always have to be the sweet, innocent one?"

"Fine, you can be Michele. But I think we need to come up with something better for our reunion elevator speech than inventing Post-its."

I reached for a tin of mints in my purse. "Ooh, I love that part. Do you think it's human nature to be so insecure that we want people we haven't seen in years and have no real interest in to believe we're more successful than we really are?"

I took a mint and then held the tin out to B.J.

"Don't be ridiculous," she said, taking one. "We have nothing to prove. But just in case, I filled out your profile form for the reunion booklet, the one you never emailed back to the committee. I said you're an internationally renowned sculptor currently working on an abstract series for an independent collector in Dubai."

"You did not," I said.

The traffic light ahead turned yellow. B.J. floored it. Once we'd made it through the intersection in one piece, B.J. turned to look at me. "And don't worry, under Personal, I just said that after years of standing by Kurt through his many and myriad personal issues, and much soul-searching, you've finally moved on and you're now actively but not exclusively dating again."

"If you're not kidding, you are so dead meat."

B.J. laughed. We drove along the bumpy streets close to the water, the ones that flooded in practically every hurricane. Most of the houses had been lifted up on top of tall pilings, like stilts, with money from the same federal grants that rebuilt the seawalls every time the ocean knocked them down. The people who lived here joked about opening all their doors in a storm and just letting the waves go in the back door and out the front.

Growing up, we'd lived in a safer part of town, and I both envied these more adventurous families and wondered how they could decide which of their precious things to take when they evacuated for a storm. The diary with the heart-shaped lock or the autograph book from eighth grade? The 45s or the albums? Their favorite bell-bottom jumpsuit or the long hippie skirt made from thrift shop ties?

B.J. pulled into the driveway of an old gray-shingled beach house with a big wraparound porch covered in flaked white paint. She put the car into park and we jumped out. The crushed mussel shell driveway crunched under our feet.

"Just wondering," I said, "but what did *your* profile say?"

B.J. shrugged. "That I was in the process of inventing a second generation of virtual Post-its, but it was top secret and I couldn't talk openly about it yet."

"Genius. Hey, are you sure this is the right place?"

"Of course I am." B.J. walked up to one of the salt-sprayed windows to get a better look inside.

There was no sign of life at Jan's beach house. No cars in the driveway, no answer to our repeated knocking. Both the front and the back door, which B.J. insisted on trying, turned out to be locked.

"I used to have dreams about living in a beach house like this when we first moved to Atlanta," I said. "Did you tell Jan what time we'd be here?"

"Of course I did. At least I think I did. Let me try her cell."

I sat on the porch swing while B.J. dug through her purse and found her phone.

"She's not answering." B.J. tucked the phone in the crook of her neck and bent down and picked up a corner of the weathered sisal welcome mat. "You'd think she would have at least left us a key under here."

"Like we would have just walked right in," I said.

"We could try the windows," B.J. said, "but you'll have to be the one who climbs in. These jeans are brand new."

"Sorry," I said. "But I don't do breaking and entering. Let's just leave the car here and take a walk on the beach."

We crossed over to the water side of the street and walked until we found a beach entrance.

I leaned forward to smell the beach roses in front of a dilapidated wooden fence that flanked the path. "I spent years trying to find a perfume that smelled like the beach—you know, a little bit of beach rose, a splash of salt air, a dash of suntan lotion. Bobbi Brown's 'Beach' is pretty close, but I don't think you can ever completely duplicate the real thing."

"So, move back," B.J. said. "I mean, think of how much money you'll save on perfume."

"Ha," I said. "You make it sound so simple."

B.J. dropped her head and looked over the top of her sunglasses. "Your kids are grown, you're self-employed, and your husband left you. It doesn't get much simpler than that."

"Leave me alone," I said. "I'm not ready to think about it." I loved B.J., but boundaries were not her strong suit.

"I can't leave you alone," B.J. said. "I'm your best friend and I think it might be time to start pushing yourself a little bit."

I shook my head. "Why should I, when I have you for that?"

B.J. grinned. "Love you, too."

I kicked off the flip-flops I'd been wearing since Atlanta and bent down to pick them up. "You know, flip-flops are truly the world's best invention, much better than Post-its. I think you should change your profile to say that you invented flip-flops and have been living off the proceeds at an undisclosed location on a private island in the Caribbean."

B.J. held on to my shoulder as she stepped out of her jute espadrilles. "Ooh, good one. Do me a favor and remember that so I can write it down when we get back to the car."

"Whoa," I said, finally noticing. "What happened to the beach?"

The ocean came right up to the seawall. A few huge rocks broke through the surface. The sandy beach I remembered had completely disappeared.

"Erosion," B.J. said. "I guess you have to wait for low tide to walk the beach now."

"Oh, that's so sad."

We climbed a ladder and walked along the top of the seawall for a while, then turned around and walked back the other way. A young couple in bathing suits was out walking the seawall, too. They stepped way off to one side and teetered on the edge to let us pass.

"Did you see that?" B.J. hissed. "It was like they thought they were helping two little old ladies cross the street."

"Shh," I said. "They'll hear you. And they were just being polite."

"My point exactly," B.J. said. "If they thought we were still in our prime, they would have staked their claim and made us walk around them."

My cell phone rang as we were climbing back down the ladder. I fished it out of my shoulder bag as soon as I hit the ground. Kurt's name smirked up at me.

"Nooooo," I said.

B.J. looked over. "What's wrong?"

I pushed the IGNORE button. "Unbelievable. I thought I'd blocked Kurt's number, but apparently not."

B.J. shrugged. "Roaches are like that, too. You think they're gone and then one day you open a cupboard—"

"Wait," I said. "I need to concentrate." I opened up the block app *again*. B.J. shrugged and reached for her own cell.

I triple-checked when I tapped Kurt's number in this time, then pushed the SAVE button.

"Damn, she's still not answering." B.J. looked up from her phone. "What was that all about anyway? Can't you just answer, tell Kurt to go screw himself, and then hang up?"

"Like I haven't done that before," I said.

"Give it time. Maybe you were married so long he's temporarily forgotten *how* to screw himself."

CHAPTER 15

B.J.'s stylist's former boyfriend, Sam, lifted two handfuls of my hair up over my head and then let them fall. I assumed this was part of his process—maybe he was trying to get a glimpse of the hairstyle within the way I could sometimes see a fully formed sculpture in a hunk of rusty metal.

We looked at each other in the mirror. His eyebrows were perfectly arched and his black hair was short and spiky with a long burgundy piece on one side that reminded me of a raccoon-tail hat on sideways.

He shrugged. "So, what were you thinking?"

"Actually," I said as I checked out my boring brown hair, "I wasn't. To tell you the truth, I don't really spend a lot of time on my hair. I usually just pull it back into a ponytail, so as long as you leave me enough for—"

"Don't listen to her." B.J. popped up from her pedicure chair. "Short and perky. Get rid of those wiry gray stragglers and add some highlights. We're going for *youthful*."

"Youthful?" I said. When I looked in the mirror, my expression reminded me a little bit of Linda Blair in *The Exorcist*, right before her head started to spin around. Or maybe Macaulay Culkin after he slapped on the aftershave in *Home Alone*.

B.J. got the rest of her pedicure, followed by a manicure. After her nails finished drying, she came over and coached Sam while my color cooked. Then she paced around outside in front of the plate-glass window and talked on her cell phone.

Two and a half hours later, I was pronounced youthful.

"Really?" I said. "You don't think it looks too much like the pixie I had in third grade?"

"Bingo," B.J. said. "That's the whole point. It's very Ellen Burstyn in *Alice Doesn't Live Here Anymore*."

I squinted at the mirror.

Sam tilted his head. "I'm getting a flash of Linda Ronstadt on the *Heart Like a Wheel* album cover. With a better haircut, of course."

"There's some Twiggy in that side part, too," B.J. said, "plus or minus a few pounds. We'll go with lots of black eyeliner for the reunion, and some false eyelashes."

"Speak for yourself," I said. "I don't do false eyelashes."

"Of course you do," B.J. said. "You're youthful now."

She insisted on paying and tipping Sam for me.

"Are you sure?" I asked as she handed over her credit card.

She gave what was left of my hair a little fluff with one hand. "Absolutely. You can pick up the tab for our tattoos."

"Ha," I said. "Very funny."

Back at the car, B.J. actually let me choose the song this time. I scrolled through her iPod until I found Grand Funk Railroad's "Some Kind of Wonderful."

Before Grand Funk even got to the first chorus, I reached over and turned it down fast. "Ugh. I just remembered Kurt used to sing this to me. I think we even danced to it at our wedding."

"You were always too good for him," B.J. said.

"Thank you. Spoken like a best friend."

"It's true." B. J. reached over and hit the SHUFFLE button and Maria Muldaur's "Midnight at the Oasis" filled the car.

"Ooh," I said. "I loved this song."

"I'm pretty sure I got pregnant to it," B.J. said.

"Thank you so much for that image."

"You're welcome."

"So, what else is new?" I said, mostly to keep B.J. from over-sharing her conception details.

"Well, when I was flipping through a magazine in the salon I found out someone is developing these new contact lenses that measure the blood sugar of diabetics so they don't have to draw blood. Apparently tiny particles in the lenses react with the glucose molecules in tears and change the color of your eyes based on how high your sugar levels are."

"Fascinating," I said.

B.J. nodded. "My first thought was that I wanted to get a pair, but it's probably a lot easier and definitely more figure-friendly to just buy tinted contacts than to try to eat enough sugar to get them to react. But then I started thinking maybe we could say we invented a new twist on the mood ring. You know, contact lenses that change the color of your eyes based on your mood."

Despite myself, I flashed on an image of Kurt's ever-changing eyes.

I shook my head to clear it away. "You're certifiable," I said. "But I have to admit I do miss my mood ring."

"How about Kurt—do you miss him, too?" B.J. took one hand off the wheel and stretched it up over her head.

"Whoa," I said. "Where did that come from?"

"Hey, you're the one who brought him up."

"No, I didn't. Grand Funk Railroad brought him up."

B.J. switched hands and stretched the other arm up over her head. I hoped she wasn't about to launch into a full series of yoga poses while she was driving.

"I don't know," I finally said. "I think I mostly miss the idea of Kurt, if that makes sense."

"I get that. A husband is a pretty good safety net, even when the marriage has a few holes in it."

"Oh, he had a few holes, all right. Actually, I guess we both did. You know, it was kind of like I could see us drifting away from each other, but I just couldn't muster the energy to do anything about it. I suppose I thought we'd both keep drifting, but we'd be, I don't know, polite about it."

"Like he'd just politely screw around on you?"

"Thanks. I guess I really didn't think about that part. Do you know Kurt made this huge point about claiming that nothing had really happened between *Crissy* and him before he moved out? As if it was some kind of badge of honor."

"Oh, puh-lease, they always say that. Like he would have

moved in with her if he hadn't slept with her first. I mean, what if she was truly pathetic in bed?"

"I cut up our bed with a chain saw," I said.

B.J. reached over and patted my knee. "That's my girl. I hope he was in it."

"Ha," I said. "I didn't think of that."

"Next husband, call me first." B. J. turned down the music. "You know, it's really starting to bother me that Veronica isn't answering my calls or calling me back."

"Hmm," I said. "Jan isn't, either. We might have a theme here."

"They didn't let me into Honors English, so I don't acknowledge themes."

"If a theme falls in the forest and no one acknowledges it, is it still a . . ."

B.J. reached for her lip gloss. "Not being able to get through to our friends is a colossal drag. Have our lives gotten that out of control? Once your kids are grown and you get to our place in life, you're not supposed to be too busy to pick up your phone. You're supposed to be able to relax and enjoy and do exactly what you want to do, when you want to do it. Where is our chance to be selfish again? Where is our second childhood?"

I'd managed to sneak in an unproductive email check during B.J.'s soliloquy. "You're not going to rant all week, are you?" I asked as I tucked my phone back into my purse.

"I never rant. Okay, let's get serious here. Next up: tattoos."

"Very funny."

"It's not a joke. It's on the itinerary, which means it's essentially etched in stone. Remember that time we almost got them when we were seniors in high school? And, I might add, it was even your idea. We took that endless bus ride all the way to up-state New York to stay in your sister Marion's dorm because she said she'd take us. I can't remember if you only had to be eighteen to get them legally there at the time, or if it was a sketchy place that did underage tattoos. Either way, it puts tattoos squarely in the category of lifelong-dream-about-to-come-true."

"I'd completely forgotten about that. I couldn't believe she ratted us out, and when we got there my father was waiting for us and made us ride back with him."

B.J. shook her head. "Marion, Marion, Marion. Have you called her yet, by the way?"

"I'm working up to it."

"Anyway, the tattoo parlor is near Plymouth Center, so we stop there first, then we head over the bridge to the Cape and make sure Veronica's okay. Unless you think we should pick up Veronica first so she can get a tattoo with us?"

"I think it's safe to assume that if Veronica isn't answering your calls, she's probably not up for getting a tattoo with you."

"I don't know where you're getting that. But fine, we'll stop for our tattoos first."

"*Your* tattoo," I said. "I'll go with you, but no way am I getting one."

"Oh, yes you are," B.J. said.

"Not in a million years."

"Exactly." B.J. put on her blinker. "That's the whole point. Not in a million years will any of our boring old high school class-mates think of getting tattoos." She turned and smiled at me. "We'll be the hit of the reunion, Romy."

"Michele," I said. "I mean, Melanie."

CHAPTER 16

Mustang Sally climbed the entrance ramp like a geriatric thoroughbred and then jumped into the herd of traffic heading south. My heart did a funny little extra beat, and I wondered if my highway thing was escalating again even with B.J. driving.

It was complicated. Sometimes I was convinced that driving with Kurt—his anger, his aggressiveness—had started the whole thing. And then when he left, some self-destructive part of me had transferred all those years of pent-up anxiety to my own driving. But if I looked back honestly, I'd never been a relaxed driver, and being a passenger with Trevor and Troy driving when they had their learner's permits had freaked me out to the point that I'd turned the whole thing over to Kurt. Maybe my highway anxiety had always been there, like a cold sore, waiting for the next random outbreak, and the more I thought about it the more likely it was to happen.

I held my breath and waited for more symptoms. Nothing. We'd put Mustang Sally's top back up outside the salon before we headed for the highway, and now she felt shady and safe inside, almost like a cocoon.

I breathed a long sigh of relief.

"I knew you'd come around." B.J. took one hand off the steering wheel and turned up the music again. Rod Stewart broke into "Maggie May," and we sang backup on the first chorus.

"So, basically," B.J. said as Rod launched into the next verse without us, "I think the *where* of the tattoos might be even more important than the *what*, so I've done some research."

"On body parts? Gee, I would have thought that you, of all people, would have those down by now."

"Cute."

I ran a hand through what was left of my hair. It was freeing, in a Peter Pan kind of way. B.J. put on the blinker and reined Sally into a faster lane. We passed the sign for the exit to the pool where Trevor and Troy used to go for swimming lessons, a long, long time ago. I could still smell the chlorine and remember the way their fingertips wrinkled like raisins by the end of the class.

"Okay, guess," B.J. said. "Where is the last place that sags?"

"Your head?"

"Lower."

"Your feet?"

"Higher."

"I give up. Okay, where *is* the last place that sags?"

B.J. flipped her hair out of the way and pulled her white, boat-neck top down over one shoulder.

"Upper arms?" I said. "Are you out of your mind?"

"*Shoulders*," B.J. said, "are the last to go." She took her hands off the steering wheel and gave hers a quick shimmy.

The Mustang veered over the line. The car next to us beeped, loud and long.

I waited until we were back in our lane and I was sure we were still alive, then I closed my eyes. "Please don't do that again," I whispered.

"It wasn't me," B.J. said. "That guy's an idiot. Okay, so we get the tattoos high up on the backs of our shoulders, safely away from upper-arm territory. And then we wear off-the-shoulder peasant blouses—you know, the ones with that big ruffle that goes all the way around the top. A whole lot of sexy with a little bit of retro thrown in."

I opened my eyes. "Not that I'm even considering this, but where would we even find blouses like that?"

B.J. laughed. "I've got them on hold at Macy's. Two different sizes, just in case. And three colors—I didn't want you to think I was hogging all the control here."

One of my favorite things about B.J. was that she was easily distractible. I found the lukewarm water bottle that had been in my purse since Atlanta, screwed open the top, and drank it dry.

"Boyohboy, am I thirsty," I said. "You know what I could really go for, with all this talk about high school?"

B.J. kept her eyes on the road. "A tattoo?"

I waited a beat to let the suspense build. "A Tab."

"Tab!" B.J. let out a loud scream, completely drowning out the Ramones, who were busy singing "I Wanna Be Sedated."

I smiled.

"Tab," B.J. whispered. "I lived on Tab. I had my first one of the day for breakfast and brought one into my bedroom with me at night. All chemicals, no calories. And if you added a slice of lemon, it was practically a meal in itself."

I didn't say anything.

B.J. launched into full rant. "Why the hell did everyone have to get so healthy? I can understand not smoking and using condoms and eating dark chocolate and switching from white to red wine. But what in the name of all that's retro is so wrong with having a simple *Tab* every now and then? I don't know about you, but I am so seltzered out."

She turned to look at me. "Do you think they still make it? I haven't been in the soda aisle for years."

"I'm pretty sure," I said, even though I had absolutely no idea. It was the quest for Tab I was going for here, not the actual Tab.

"Wait. There's an Ocean State Job Lot at the next exit. Do you mind making a pit stop?"

"Pit stop," I said. "Aww, I completely forgot about that expression."

Ten minutes later we were loading four cases of Tab into the trunk of the Mustang.

"Can you believe how expensive this stuff was?" B.J. said. "Who knew it was a collector's item. I think we seriously lucked out to even find it."

"We sure did." I reached up and got ready to close the hood of the trunk. "And now I really think we need to head straight over to Veronica's house so we can get some on ice right away."

B.J. ducked under my hand and freed two Tabs from their plastic collars.

"Surely you jest," she said as she handed one to me. "Warm Tab is the only way to go."

B.J. shrugged. "It was either this or Do Me Too at the next exit. I figured the flagship would have the more experienced tattoo artists. Only the best for you, Romy."

We were parked outside Do Me Tattoos looking at the posters taped on the storefront window. I had some serious Tab aftertaste in my mouth, almost as if I had licked a piece of metal. I reached for a mint.

"You're certifiable," I said.

"There was nothing in *Consumer Reports*—"

"You've got to be kidding. *Consumer Reports* doesn't rate tattoos? I am so canceling my subscription."

"Don't be fresh."

"Aww, that's right, fresh once meant mouthy. My mother used to say that."

"Mine did, too. Pretty much all day long." B.J. pulled some sheets of paper from her purse and handed them to me. "I printed off everything I could find on Kudzu and Angie's List. This place definitely hit the sweet spot between good reviews and right off the highway."

I glanced down. "'Yo, best tattoo place ever. I've gotten four of my last six tats there—two by Ariel, one by Lenny, one by a dude who I don't remember the name of.'"

B.J. pointed. "Not that one. This one."

"'Really clean in the scheme of things'? Or 'I would definitely recommend them if you're looking for some good if not great artwork.'"

B.J. snatched the papers away. I looked up at one of the posters in the window—a heavily airbrushed woman with a Cleopatra necklace tattooed from collarbone to collarbone. And completely covering the area from the base of her neck to the top of her breasts.

"I don't get it," I said. "I mean I can appreciate the depth and symmetry of the design, but for me it conflicts with the natural beauty of the human body."

B.J. sighed. "Jeez Louise, let's not get all Picasso here. Our natural beauty is practically gone anyway. And we're not talking about an I-want-to-date-Jesse-James kind of tattoo. We're talking tiny. And tasteful."

"Like what?" I couldn't resist asking. I mean, no way in hell was I getting a tattoo, but it was fun to think about what I would get if I did get one. Not that I was going to.

B.J. reached for a mint, too. "Well, when it comes to tattoos, words are the new black . . ."

"Should I be worried that I had no trouble following that?"

"So if we could find the perfect short phrase . . ."

"How about 'No'?"

"How about 'Never Say Never'?"

"Ha," I said. "What about 'Work in Progress'?"

"Hey, that's not half bad." B.J. opened her car door. "Another Tab?"

"No thanks. One's my limit."

She closed her door again and sighed. "I should pace myself, too. What about 'Well-Behaved Women Rarely Make History' or 'It's Never Too Late to Be What You Might Have Been'?"

"Way too many letters," I said.

"We could have them start at one shoulder and go right across our back to the other one."

"'Midlife Rocks'?"

"Too perky. 'Living Well Is the Best Revenge'?"

"Overused." Despite myself I was kind of getting into this. "What about an expression from high school? Maybe 'Lighten Up'?"

"People might think we've joined a diet cult. What about a song title? Carole King's 'You've Got a Friend'?"

"Bette Midler's 'Friends' would hurt a lot less."

"How about you get 'Alone Again' and I get—"

"'Naturally'?"

B.J. laughed her crazy laugh. "'Ball of Confusion'?"

"'Comfortably Numb'?"

"Who *was* that?"

"I'm pretty sure it was Pink Floyd."

"'Because the Night'?" B.J. sighed. "God, I wanted to *be* Patti Smith. She had such balls. Madonna and everyone who followed would be nowhere today without her."

A young couple holding hands came out of the tattoo parlor and stopped to kiss on the front steps.

"Wouldn't you think their piercings would get all tangled up?"

B.J. said, watching them. Then she giggled. "Do you remember when Mack Drummond got his lip caught on Julie Waxelbaum's braces at that dance and his parents had to come get him and take him to the hospital for stitches?"

"Not really." My back was starting to hurt from too much sitting, so I put one foot up on the dashboard to adjust the angle. A dusting of sand covered my toes. I started to wipe it off, then decided to keep it as a souvenir. "Well, this is fun. But maybe we should just keep pondering until the perfect tattoo comes to mind. I mean, we can always do it for the next reunion, right?"

"Don't be ridiculous. Okay, moving on to images. Do you think peace signs have been overtattooed?"

"Wow," I said, "that Tab goes right through you. I'll be back in a minute."

"Nice try," B.J. said. "Like I'm going to leave you alone for a nanosecond." She turned to the tattooed receptionist at the desk. "Do we need to take a number or anything?"

"You mean like at the deli counter?" I laughed a little too loudly.

A mother and daughter reading magazines on the waiting room sofa looked up at me.

"Don't mind my friend," B.J. said. "She only acts this way when she's nervous."

The restroom was clean, which seemed like a good sign. Sometime between getting out of the Mustang and walking through the front door of Do Me, I'd decided I just might get done after all. I mean, my kids were grown, I was self-employed, and my husband had left me. What the hell was stopping me? It would be daring and hip, the perfect symbol of a new life, a new me.

I waited till we were standing side by side at the bathroom sinks, washing our hands.

"Hey," I said. "Do you remember those dorky necklaces we gave each other for high school graduation? You know, the little silver heart cut into two jagged pieces. You gave me one half and I—"

"AAAAHHH!" B.J. yelled. "Brilliant!"

By the time our names were called, we had our broken heart sketched out on the back of a receipt.

B.J. jumped up. Ariel introduced herself to us.

I stayed where I was. "I don't know. Maybe you should just get the whole heart."

"Come on," B.J. said, "suck it up, buttercup."

Ariel tapped the toe of one of her knee-high gladiator sandals as if it might make us pick up our pace. She was about Trevor or Troy's age, with long shiny hair and a sweet face, and she was wearing a tank top and short shorts. An entire paragraph had been tattooed on her left thigh. I wondered if it would be rude to put on my reading glasses so I could make out the words. A series of dates looped around both of her wrists like bracelets. There was an intricate design on one side of her neck, maybe some kind of Celtic thing, and she had a bright green shamrock on the upper arm facing me. I tried to imagine what her tattoos would look like when she got to be our age. Would her shamrock have sagged into a pool of green slime?

B.J. reached for my hand and pulled.

We followed Ariel into a tattoo room and signed our release forms.

The room was small. A chaise-like thing that looked like a cross between a massage table and a dentist's chair was taking up most of the limited space. A fresh sheet of white paper had been pulled out from a roll and stretched across the length of it. A box of non-latex disposable gloves sat on the counter next to an autoclave that looked like a small microwave oven. There was antibacterial soap on the sink, and next to that a bottle of antiseptic spray, a box of sterile pads, and a tube of maximum-strength Dr. Numb. Tiny disposable bottles of ink were displayed artfully on a shelf above the counter adjacent to a box of Skin Skribe sterile surgical markers.

I squinted at some boxes of disposable needles: round liners, round shaders, flat needles, mag stack needles, curved mag needles. What appeared to be a tattoo machine was sitting on the floor, tucked partially out of sight behind the tattoo chaise. The walls were painted a soothing sage and the trim a crisp, clean white.

I couldn't find a single germy excuse to get us out of here.

Ariel gestured to two chairs pushed up against the wall. B.J. and I sat down, our hands folded in our laps, as if we'd been called into the principal's office.

When Ariel stood directly in front of us, the room was so small our knees almost touched hers.

"The word *tattoo*," she began, "comes from the Tahitian *tattau*, which means 'to mark.'"

My hand shot up of its own free will.

"Yes?" Ariel said.

"Is there going to be a test on this?" I asked.

Nobody laughed. When I sneaked a peek at B.J., under the bright fluorescent lights she looked like a poster child for the old Procol Harum song "A Whiter Shade of Pale."

"Tattoos," Ariel continued, "have also been found on Egyptian mummies dating as far back as 2000 BC."

I elbowed B.J. "See, we won't be the oldest tattooed mummies in the world after all."

B.J. didn't even look over at me. She was staring straight ahead and making a funny dry-mouth sound as she separated her tongue from the roof of her mouth repeatedly.

Ariel cleared her throat. "According to Harris Interactive via Wikipedia, thirty-four percent of Americans with tattoos feel sexier, and twenty-six percent feel more attractive. However, forty-two percent of people who don't have tattoos think people who *do* have them are less attractive, fifty-seven percent think they're more rebellious, and thirty-one percent think they're less intelligent."

I was starting to get a math headache so I kept my mouth shut.

"And finally, seventeen percent of Americans with tattoos regret them, most often because they include a person's name."

I took a moment to appreciate the fact that even though I'd made a lot of mistakes in my marriage, at least I hadn't had Kurt's name tattooed on my butt. Not that I expected to sleep with anyone in the near future, but just in case things went really, really well with Finn, there'd be one less thing to have to explain. Out of nowhere, sadness washed over me like a hot flash. How did people find the energy to pick up the pieces of their lives and try again?

Ariel handed us each a shiny brochure titled *How Tattoo Removal Works*. "I'll give you a minute to look these over."

B.J. was still strangely silent. I skimmed the first few lines of the brochure but didn't bother reading the whole thing because, honestly, if the tattoo didn't work out, I'd probably just pretend it wasn't there. I'd gotten through most of my adult life that way.

We gave the brochures back to Ariel. B.J. was still clutching our receipt drawing, so I peeled it away from her sweaty hand and gave that to Ariel, too.

Ariel looked at it carefully, as if our broken heart doodle were a blueprint by Frank Lloyd Wright.

Ariel looked up. "Half for each?"

I nodded.

"Where?"

I pointed to the back of my right shoulder.

"Okay, let's do this." Ariel made a practice drawing on a sheet of paper, then held it up for our approval.

"Wow," I said. "You're good."

She smiled and pulled two Skin Skribe sterile surgical markers out of a box. "Okay, shirts off. You can leave them dangling around your neck and hanging in the front if you want. And slide one bra strap off your shoulder and take your arm out."

I got a little bit confused the way I always did at the doctor's office. Did the nurse say to take off my underwear, too? Was the johnny supposed to be tied in the front or the back? Once, back in high school gym class, we were doing the climbing ropes and tumbling unit. I was hanging by all fours from big wooden rings attached to the ceiling, terrified to be up so high and trying not to let it show, when the gym teacher told me to let go of a leg and an arm. Maybe directions under pressure are always confusing, or maybe I'm one of those people who can't think upside down, or maybe it was my fear of heights, but I let go of both arms and both legs and hit the blue vinyl mat below with a loud and painful thud.

I was older and wiser now, but just to be on the safe side I looked over at B.J. to make sure I was doing it right. Her upper lip was covered with tiny polka dots of sweat and she was staring at the boxes of disposable needles. Her white boat-neck top was hanging around her neck like a bib awaiting drool.

"Hey, Beej, are you okay?" I whispered.

She took a jagged breath between each word. "You. Go. First."

I looked at Ariel and she patted the table. I climbed up on it, paper crinkling, and sat with my back facing her. She drew my half of the heart on the back of my shoulder and then I twisted my head while she held up a hand mirror for approval.

"Some artists use transfer paper, but I like to go freehand," Ariel said.

I checked out the purple broken heart. "Perfect," I said. "But do you have anything you can show me in red?"

"No worries, this is just the outline." She held out the marker. "Keep it. We can't use them again so we give them as souvenirs."

"Thanks," I said. I figured if things got bad I could always put the marker between my teeth and bite down on it like a bullet.

I heard the antiseptic spray and then Ariel rubbed something cool and wet over the whole back of my shoulder. When Dr. Numb had worked his magic, Ariel reached down for the arm of the tattoo machine. She tore the protective paper off a disposable needle. B.J. gasped.

It hurt, but not like childbirth, not like when Kurt left, not even as much as a bee sting. It felt like a long slow oven burn. The noise was a lot like a dentist's drill, but a little bit buzzier.

The sound started and stopped, started and stopped. Ariel dabbed on some cool gel, like putting aloe on a sunburn.

"Antibacterial ointment," Ariel explained. She ripped open a Band-Aid and put it on so gently I barely felt it.

"That's it?" I said.

She walked around to the other side of the table. "That's it."

"Wow," I said. "I feel like I should get a lollipop. Or a sticker."

"I gave you a marker," she said.

"Never mind," I said. "It's a lovely marker." I slid down from the table.

Ariel and I both looked at B.J.

B.J.'s hands were on her knees and she was leaning forward as if she might faint. Or throw up.

"Hey," I said. "Come on, your turn. Don't worry, it was a piece of cake."

B.J. looked up. Her perfectly foiled hair had started to frizz, and one long hunk was sticking to the right side of her face. Her eyes were flat.

"Do. Me. Right. Here," my best friend said.

To Ariel's credit, she agreed. We managed to get B.J. turned sideways in the chair, and I held her hand.

Ariel rolled the tattoo machine over and reached for a new needle. B.J. started to sob.

Ariel looked at me. "I can't do it unless you can get her to hold still."

I put my hands on B.J.'s shoulders. "I've got her."

I pressed my chin down on B.J.'s head just to be sure. "It's okay to cry, just don't move."

Ariel turned on the machine.

B.J. let out a loud, piercing scream.

"Stop that right now," I said. "If you leave me with the only half of a broken heart, I will never, *ever* forgive you."

CHAPTER 18

Ariel held a shaky B.J. by the elbow while I gave the receptionist my credit card. She ran it through the scanner and handed me a pen.

A moment later the receptionist looked up. "Do you have another card? This one's been declined."

"It must be a mistake," I said. "I have plenty of credit. Can you try again?"

On the second slide through, I felt a funny little flutter in my stomach, like a first baby's first kick, when you're so inexperienced you're not really sure what's going on with your body.

On the third slide through, it hit me: Kurt.

I could feel myself blushing—my cheeks were actually burning hotter than my new tattoo. I dug through my wallet for the business-expenses credit card I used for tax purposes, the only card I had that was solely in my name. It had a tiny credit limit, but I paid it off every month.

The receptionist scanned the card and it went right through. I added on a big tip for Ariel, who certainly deserved it after all B.J. had put her through, even if I would probably only be able to afford to eat cat food by the end of the week.

B.J. was still whimpering softly as I helped her into the driver's seat of the Mustang. She pointed to her seat belt, so I reached past her, pulled it around her, and buckled her in.

"Snug as a bug in a rug," I said in my perkiest voice.

She kept crying.

"How about a Tab for the road?" I said. "I think it's just what the doctor ordered."

She let out a wail.

"Okay," I said, "I'll take that as a no."

B.J. managed to put the key in the ignition. She hunched forward over the wheel like a little old lady.

I jumped in on my side and buckled up. A sobbing B.J. pulled out of the parking lot and headed slowly for the highway. This crying thing was getting old, but I figured my best strategy was to ignore it. B.J. would get bored with it soon enough. Or she'd start worrying about her eyes getting puffy. Either way, I'd have my spunky old friend back before I knew it.

B.J. put on her blinker for the entrance to Route 3. I waited until we were safely on the highway, creeping along in the slow lane, and then I reached over to turn on some music. I hit the SHUFFLE button.

The Bee Gees started singing "How Can You Mend a Broken Heart."

B.J. let out a scream.

I hit SHUFFLE again. The Eagles broke into "Heartache To-night."

B.J. screamed louder.

I pushed the OFF button fast. "Sorry," I said, "but you're the one who made the playlist. Just saying."

B.J. pulled into the breakdown lane and we started bumping along so slowly I could have gotten out and jogged along beside the Mustang, maybe even challenged it to a race, and won. There might be highways you can get away with doing this on, but late afternoon on the only fast road that can take you from Boston to Cape Cod is not one of them. Especially when it's actually legal to drive in the breakdown lane of this highway between the hours of four and seven PM.

I looked out the window and into the rearview mirror on my side. A line of traffic was backed up behind us. The Mustang's speedometer was wavering between twenty-three and twenty-five. At this rate, we'd both be another year older before we got to the Cape.

"Beej?" I said. "You might want to push down on the gas pedal a little bit more."

She shook her head. She sniveled some more.

Without any warning, she jerked the wheel hard. We rolled off the highway and into an open field at the edge of the road.

A guy in a big white truck, who'd been directly behind us, leaned on his horn and then sped away. The woman behind him gave us the finger as she passed us.

"Come back here and try that again, you morons," I yelled.

The old Mustang rocked as car after car whizzed by in the

breakdown lane. There were probably far more dangerous places to be in the world, but at the moment I couldn't think of any. All it would take was a single rubbernecking driver to look our way and get hit from behind to then hit us. Mustang Sally would be toast and we'd be whatever was worse than toast.

B.J. was staring straight ahead, whimpering rhythmically. I reached into my purse and handed her a tissue. She clutched it in one hand and sniffed.

There was a loud squeal of brakes to our left as one crazy driver cut off another crazy driver. My heart kicked into overdrive.

"Okay, that's it," I said. "We can't stay here. Let's just get to Veronica's in one piece and then you can cry for as long as you want to. Or we can talk about it. Your choice."

B.J. let out a long ragged breath. "You. Drive."

By Atlanta standards, it was barely a highway. Just a couple of lanes going in each direction. No steep hills or death-defying drop-offs. A soft buffer of scrub pines on both sides. Not the least bit panic-worthy.

We were too close to the road to risk opening the door on the driver's side, so I made B.J. crawl over me. We managed to switch bucket seats without either of us getting impaled on the gearshift or rupturing our tattoos.

"Ouch," I said. "That would have been funny a few decades ago when I didn't bruise so easily."

B.J. moaned and reached for her new seat belt. I saw it as a sign of progress that she was buckling herself in this time.

I fastened the belt on the driver's side. When I adjusted the rearview mirror, the person looking back at me took me totally by surprise. Big, scared eyes stared out from under pixie bangs, as if to say, *How did a nice, formerly young girl like you end up in a ridiculous place like this?*

I took a deep breath.

I cleared my throat.

I took another deep breath.

I stretched my hands out in front of me, like a concert pianist getting ready to play, then rested my hands on the steering wheel. The cracked leather covering stuck to my sweaty palms.

A loud snore made me jump. When I looked over, B.J. was sprawled across the passenger seat with her eyes closed, and her head was resting against the window as if it were a pillow. She snored again, long and loud, through her open mouth.

"Great," I said. "There goes my copilot."

I tried to remember which town Veronica lived in. Sandwich? Harwich? I closed my eyes and attempted to picture the return address on the last card she'd sent me, maybe a few years ago, maybe half a decade. I'd been such a poor correspondent to my old friends as my world shrank down to the size of a small family. I'd send back a Christmas card if I received one, and once that custom waned, I fell out of the loop even more.

Okay, so I'd just get us onto the Cape, then I'd wake up B.J. and we'd take it from there.

I made myself look at the traffic whizzing by. I watched cars and trucks and SUVs and flashy sports cars, surfboards strapped to the top of a jeep, a bicycle trailer bumping behind a mini van packed to the gills with kids and beach paraphernalia, a golden retriever with its head out the window, tongue hanging out and a smile on its face.

"Lions and tigers and bears, oh my," I heard myself say. I made myself laugh, as if I'd said it to be funny, but the high pitch of my laughter sounded crazy, even to me. I'd once read that only non-crazy people think they're crazy, because genuinely crazy people always think they're just fine. So maybe there was still hope for me.

I decided I'd count ten cars passing, and then I'd put on my blinker.

I turned the key in the ignition and gave Mustang Sally some gas. She started right up. I moved my foot to the brake and slid the gearshift into drive.

I counted ten cars. Then I counted ten more.

My hand shook as I clicked on the blinker.

A gap appeared in the breakdown lane traffic. A white SUV flashed its lights and slowed down a little, telling me to go for it.

"Give me a minute," I said. "I'm not quite ready."

The SUV beeped.

"Fine," I said. "Be like that." I hit the gas and yanked the steering wheel to the left.

As soon as I started driving, the SUV bore down on me, getting right on my butt. I tightened my grip on the wheel and tried to push the gas pedal harder.

The SUV gave up on me and nosed into an impossibly small space in the next lane. The traffic adjusted itself to let it in. Nobody crashed. Nobody died. Nobody's kids had to attend her funeral, the casket closed because seeing her mangled body would be too traumatic.

Yet.

I made my foot ignore my shaking thigh and stay on the accelerator. I opened my dry mouth to let more air in, and when my tongue came away from the roof of my mouth it felt like separating two strips of Velcro. I kept my eyes on the road and focused on the slow, even burn of my tattoo like a talisman, a lucky charm. It was a pain that made sense, that I could understand, one that had a direct cause and effect.

"Cross your heart and hope to die, stick a needle in your eye," I whispered a few times in a chant that came to me from the depths of my childhood.

"But I have promises to keep and miles to go before I sleep," I chanted next, over and over, from a mostly forgotten Robert Frost poem I'd had to memorize once. Sixth grade? Seventh?

I switched to "If I have only one life, let me live it as a blonde." It had a nice rhythm to it. I said it straight. Then I gave it a big dramatic flourish. Then I added a funny little twist at the end. It was a commercial for a hair color, but which one? Clairol?

Despite my best efforts to recite it away, the baby elephant was back. It climbed up on my chest and sat down. The skin on my arms prickled and swelled, closing me in, making it impossible to get away from whatever it was that I had to get away from. Myself? Impending doom climbed in and squeezed into the passenger seat next to B.J.

B.J. let out another big snore.

I had to get off. I couldn't get off.

A sign came into view announcing the next exit. I gripped the steering wheel tighter and willed myself to drive right past it, to stay in the breakdown lane all the way to Cape Cod, whatever it took.

Almost before I realized it was happening, the straightaway disappeared as the breakdown lane in front of me turned into an exit.

"Shit, shit, shit," I said as, despite all my fierce resolve, the highway spit me out.

I rolled off the exit ramp and then took my first left into a parking lot.

I locked the Mustang, took the keys out of the ignition, and fell asleep to the smell of McDonald's french fries.

CHAPTER 19

The ring of my cell phone woke me.

I rummaged blindly in my purse, rage coursing through my veins. I couldn't believe Kurt had the nerve, the *balls*, to call me again. An image of my canceled credit card flashed before my eyes like a big blinking billboard.

I found my phone, pushed the button, and jumped right in. "FYI, it will take more than canceling my credit card to get me to talk to you, Mr. Dial Down the Hysterics. You're blocked, even if I can't get this stupid app to work. You're still blocked because I say you're blocked, which, *FYI*, means you officially can't call me until I say you can."

"Okay," a strange male voice said.

"Wait." I shook off my post-nap fog and tried to put the pieces together. "Who *is* this?"

I tried to remember how to pull up the Caller ID without disconnecting the person I was talking to. I took a stab at it and tapped the screen once. I reached for my reading glasses: Ted Brody.

"Shit," I said. "I thought you were my husband. Former husband."

"Sounds like now's not a good time."

"Ha. Sorry about that." My cheeks were so red they were burning. I pushed the door open to get some more air, then pulled it shut as a mosquito tried to invade the car.

Ted Brody cleared his throat. "There aren't any nearby cliffs around you're about to jump off or anything, are there?"

I smiled. "Ha. Trust me, that'll never happen. I'm too afraid of heights." Two screaming toddlers ran across the parking lot, mothers in hot pursuit. A pickup truck backfired.

"Where *are* you, anyway?"

On the west side of the McDonald's parking lot, the setting sun was throwing off a dazzling display of Technicolor stripes. It was a beautiful parking lot, symmetrically landscaped and well maintained, with an abundance of freshly painted parking spaces. The Mustang even had its own little private subdivision off in one corner, under the shade of a row of Bradford pears.

"Massachusetts," I said. "On the way to Cape Cod."

"Business or pleasure?"

"Is there a third option?"

Ted Brody let out a booming laugh. "Now, that's funny."

Beside me, B.J. made a funny little sound, almost like a kitten mewing. I opened the car door again and slid out as quietly as I could. "Actually, I'm up here for a high school class reunion."

"Brave soul."

"Not really." I pushed the car door gently until it clicked, then walked around to the front of the car and leaned back against the hood. Highway traffic rumbled from the other side of a windscreen of tall trees. "Have you gone to any of yours?"

"Hmm, only one, maybe my tenth. I'd just finished graduate school and wanted to show all my former buddies and the girls who had been unimpressed by my charms how well I turned out."

"There were girls who were unimpressed by your charms?" I heard a flirty voice say.

"Hard to believe, huh?" Ted Brody roared out a laugh. "The cool art girls like you walked right past me like I didn't exist."

I walked around to the outside mirror on the driver's side and bent over to check out my haircut. "I was so not a cool art girl. I couldn't even draw."

"What's that got to do with anything? That sculpture of yours blows me away every time I look at it."

"Really?"

"Really. And I've been collecting for years."

"Metal sculpture?"

"Nope. You're the first. Mostly paintings. Abstracts by up-and-coming artists, and some hill country folk art, the real deal, not those kitschy tourist pieces. It's how I survived twenty-three years in corporate middle management with my soul intact. I didn't even have a place to display most of them. I just stacked them up against the wall in the playroom once the kids stopped using it—my twisted version of a man cave, I guess. The goal was to collect one hundred pieces before I died, or cashed in on my retirement, whichever came first."

"Wow," I said. "How many kids do you have?" I scrunched my eyes closed as soon as I said it. It was the wrong question. I had a million better questions than that, fascinating questions, artsy questions, questions that wouldn't make me sound like a total loser.

"Two grown daughters. You?"

"Two sons. All grown up. Maybe even more grown up than I am." I laughed an odd, misshapen laugh.

There was dead silence. A siren started screaming out on the highway, like a buzzer on a game show announcing that I'd managed to kill our conversation.

"Well," he said. "It's pretty nuts in here and I'm starting to get the evil eye from the hostess."

"Oh, I'm so sorry. I should have realized you were at the restaurant, especially since it's, you know, dinnertime. Okay, well, have a nice night. Bye."

"Wait, the reason I called—" I heard Ted Brody say just before I hit the END CALL button.

Across from me in the booth, B.J. checked the time on her cell phone. "Wow, that must have been some traffic. I thought we would have made it to the Cape ages ago. But good thinking— I'm famished."

When she looked up, her mascara was smudged but her eyes were barely puffy. Maybe the trick to crying as you age is to stay in an upright position so the tears can drain.

B.J. looked over one shoulder at the McDonald's employees

and then pulled a can of Tab out of her purse. When she opened it under the booth, the metal ring made a click followed by a little whoosh of pressure releasing. She reached for her paper McDonald's cup.

"I can't believe they don't have sweet tea here," I said.

B.J. made a face. "Yuck. How can you possibly like sweet tea anyway? You don't even put sugar in your coffee."

"I don't have to drink it to think it's a civilized custom." I waited until she finished pouring her Tab under the booth table, then handed her my cup. "And I really don't think you have to be that sneaky. We paid for small sodas to get the cups."

B.J. filled my cup under the table. "I know, but it's more fun this way. Remember when we used to sneak nips of Kahlúa into the dances?"

I reached for a french fry. "I think we only did that once. And we chickened out and threw them away before we had to walk by the chaperones."

B.J. reached for a fry, too. "I don't think so. I think we did it at all the dances. Ohmigod, this is the best dinner I've had in decades. I think we should have only french fries for every single meal the whole time you're here. I mean, why the hell not?"

I slid the plastic tray to the exact center of the booth. I leaned the two bright red super-size cardboard containers of french fries against each other until they were standing up. I arranged a few fries up in our little paper cups of ketchup, like flowers in tiny vases, and then I tied the straw wrappers around two straws like little scarves and placed the straws in our cups of smuggled soda.

B.J. eyed my masterpiece. "Do all metal sculptors play with their food?"

"I'm pretty sure that's how it starts. Though I also remember getting in trouble for wrapping our cat with my Slinky when I was about six." I reached for another fry. "So, are you okay now?"

B.J. twirled her straw around in her drink and made the ends of the paper scarf flutter. "Of course I am. Why wouldn't I be?"

I didn't say anything.

She shrugged and tried to smooth out her frizzy hair at the same time. "I'm probably just coming down with the flu or something."

"Never mind," I said. "I was just asking."

I reached for a fry and dragged it around in the ketchup until it was fully loaded. I pictured Ted Brody hanging up his phone and shaking his head as madly-in-love couples holding hands thronged onto his romantically lit courtyard. Right now he was probably wiping his brow dramatically and thinking, *Whew, whatever I wanted to talk to that crazy sculpture lady about, uh, never mind.*

Kurt and *Crissy* might even be eating there at this very moment, for all I knew. Kurt probably wouldn't even recognize my work when he saw it hanging on the courtyard wall.

I couldn't believe Kurt had canceled that card. Maybe he'd simply called the credit card company and said the cards had been stolen, which would mean they'd merely cancel the old cards and send new ones. Maybe he did it just to make me call him so I'd have to listen to all the things I didn't want to listen to. Or maybe he'd actually closed out the account. I wasn't stupid—I'd seen enough talk shows to know I needed to check our bank account balances and insurance policies. I needed to call a lawyer or a legal advocate or a legal something. Maybe I could find one who made house calls so I wouldn't have to drive to the office. Or maybe I could just climb under this booth and hide.

So much better for me to leave the past behind and focus on the future, even if it was a future that started with the past and built from there. Maybe that was what The Moody Blues meant by *Days of Future Passed*. I'd have to remember to bring that up when I finally saw Finn. *Ooh, heavy*, he'd probably say with a twinkle in his eyes. What color *were* his eyes anyway? Black-and-white yearbook pictures had serious shortcomings.

Maybe I'd just stay right here and get a job at McDonald's. I could find an apartment within walking distance. The work was probably pretty repetitive but I bet they had decent benefits. Health insurance and maybe even dental, all the things you're about to lose when you're a self-employed artist whose husband has left you. I'd have to let Trevor and Troy know I was okay, but Kurt would never hear another word from me. He'd eat his heart out with worry while I ate my weight in McDonald's french fries.

"It started back in high school," B.J. whispered.

I shook my head to make room for her words.

B.J.'s eyes didn't quite meet mine. "Remember when pierced ears first came into style?"

"My dentist pierced mine," I said. "Can you believe there was a time when they actually did that? And it's also pretty amazing to remember that there was a time you couldn't just walk into a mall and get your ears pierced. Ha, maybe because there weren't any malls yet. Wow, if you think about it, we were practically pioneers."

B.J. closed her eyes. "My older sister and her friend were piercing each other's ears up in her room, and I talked them into doing mine. So they held all these ice cubes on my earlobes and took this huge, huge, darning nee . . ."

She paused and made that funny dry-mouth sound.

"Needle?" I said.

"Ugh, I can't even say the word." B.J. reached for a fry, then put it down. "If I even see a picture of one, I freak out. I had natural childbirth just to avoid the epidural—I mean, how messed up is that? And I couldn't even stay in the examining room when my kids got their vaccinations. If it weren't for laughing gas, my teeth would probably be falling out of my head by now. And if you gave me a choice between lockjaw and a tetanus sh . . ."

She put her forearms on the booth and flopped her head down on them.

"That's awful," I said. "You poor thing. I mean, it must really get in the way of your life sometimes."

She lifted up her head just enough so that her eyes met mine. "It *dictates* my life. I will do anything to avoid nee . . . well, you know. And it's so embarrassing, I never talk about it."

My mouth was suddenly dry. When I reached for my Tab, my hand trembled just a little. I faked a smile. "So exactly why was it that you wanted us to get tattoos then?"

B.J. pushed herself away from the booth and looked at me. "I just hate to let it control me. And I've always wanted a tattoo, basically my whole life, since we were kids. And I guess I thought I might be braver if you were with me."

I faked another smile. "Hey, Beej, we did it. We got our tattoos. Which can only mean we are both wicked, wicked brave."

······················· CHAPTER 20

·············

"I can't believe we finished all those french fries," B.J. said as we walked back out to the Mustang. "I feel like I'm going to throw up."

"I feel fine," I said.

"Great," B.J. said, "then you drive."

Across from us in the truck section of the parking lot, a scruffy-looking guy wearing a baseball cap was parked directly under the bright floodlights. He leaned out the open window of his eighteen-wheeler and licked his lips at us.

"Yuck," B.J. said. "Now I really feel like I'm going to throw up. Did he just lick his lips at us?"

"Don't look," I said. "It will only encourage him."

B.J. stopped walking and fluffed her hair. "Well, I suppose in a way it's a compliment. I don't know about you but sometimes I feel practically invisible. I mean, you walk past a bunch of construction workers and nobody even glances your way anymore. Not that you want them to, but when they don't it's kind of a rude awakening. And at least you have sons—try walking down the street with your beautiful daughter if you want to feel like you don't exist anymore."

I grabbed B.J. by the arm. "Keep moving. And don't look over."

B.J. looked. "Ick. What the hell is *that* supposed to mean?"

"Uh, I think he's simulating what he'd like you to do to him. Or us to do to him. Or maybe he just wants to do it to himself."

"Really? I always wondered what that meant."

I gave B.J.'s arm another yank. "Come *on*."

She shook my hand off. "I don't know. If you stop to think about it, this is bullying, plain and simple. And the only way to deal with a bully is to stand right up to him. Otherwise he'll just keep doing it, and the next person he picks on might not be able to take it in stride the way we can."

Somehow, in the time it had taken us to inhale two super-size containers of McDonald's fries for dinner, the sun had managed to set completely. Even with a handful of stars and the glow of the golden arches and the lights dotting the pavement, it was dark now, scary dark. There were a few cars scattered across this end of the parking lot, but they were empty.

"B.J.," I whispered. "I mean it. Let's get out of here. *Now*."

She put her hands on her hips. "In your dreams, jerkface," she yelled.

"Please tell me you didn't really just do that," I whispered.

B.J. rummaged in her purse and pulled out her keys, along with a tiny pad of paper with a mini pen attached. "And furthermore," she yelled, "we are going to report you for harassment to whomever it is that governs the big wheel truckers' association."

The door of the eighteen-wheeler swung open.

I screamed.

B.J. threw me her car keys. "I can't see the license plate from here. Drive me by fast and then we'll get the hell away from this loser."

Two large leather boots appeared beneath the door of the truck. The trucker jumped down and hiked his jeans up over a river of white flesh until they met his T-shirt. He was tall and wide with a high round medicine ball of a belly. The baseball hat was casting a shadow over his face, so I couldn't make out his expression from here, but he had a mean tilt to his head.

B.J. was halfway to the Mustang before I realized she'd started to run.

I could feel my whole body freeze, the way it does in a dream when someone is chasing you. The trucker stepped under a light and grinned at me. It was an ugly grin, a bully's grin.

"Run," B.J. yelled.

I ran. She jumped into the passenger side and pushed the driver's door open for me.

I bent over and leaned my head into the car. "You drive."

Behind me I heard a long *woo-hoo* of a whistle, aimed right at my rear end.

I jumped in.

B.J. reached over and turned the key in the ignition.

"Go," she yelled. "Now."

"What an idiot," B.J. said. "We probably should have held our ground—I hope he doesn't think he scared us away. At least we got his license plate number. Can you believe the way he looked running across that parking lot after us? I mean, how about try finding a gym instead of harassing hot women, buddy."

I gripped Mustang Sally's frayed leather steering wheel and focused on trying to breathe. I'd planned to make B.J. drive once we'd made it safely out of the parking lot and had ditched the trucker. But once I started looking for a place to pull over, suddenly the entrance to the highway was my only choice and before I knew it we were on it.

The traffic was much lighter now. All I had to do was make it to the next exit and I'd be fine. It probably wouldn't be a bad idea to get out of the breakdown lane, too, just so I didn't get pulled over for driving in it after seven PM.

"You do realize we're in the breakdown lane, right?" B.J. said.

"Ha," I said. "I guess that guy really rattled me."

I put on my blinker. I checked for cars in the rearview mirror. B.J. half turned in her seat. "You're fine. Nothing's coming."

"Good to go," she added a few seconds later.

As soon as I turned the wheel my mouth went dry. I pulled us into the slow lane as gradually as I could. Then I concentrated on pushing down on the accelerator.

The baby elephant sat right down on my chest and made itself at home once again. I wanted a sip of something, anything, to unstick my tongue from the roof of my mouth, but when I tried to let go of the steering wheel to reach for my water bottle, I was paralyzed.

I had to get off. I couldn't get off.

A whistle blew behind us, long and low, like a train announcing the next stop.

"Don't look now," B.J. said, "but he's ba-ack."

I managed to shift my eyes to the rearview mirror. "Why is he flapping his tongue at us like that?"

B.J. turned the mirror in her direction. "Yuck, that one I know. Trust me, you don't want to think about it. Although on some level I suppose he almost deserves a minuscule amount of credit for acknowledging that sex is not all about the guy."

"Eww."

"Right, I know. It's not about sex. It's about power. Ohmigod, he is right on our ass. You don't think he's actually trying to hit us, do you?"

My right thigh started to shake.

"Don't slow down," B.J. screamed.

"What should I do?" I screamed back.

"Get into the fast lane. I don't think they allow big trucks there."

"I don't think they allow them to hit small cars, either." I glanced over at the passing lane. It was only two lanes away but it seemed like another planet. A big white SUV with headlights a mile high was barreling down it, followed by a long silver sports car slung low to the ground. These were not my people in the fast lane.

The truck's headlights were actually lighting up the interior of the Mustang. When I looked in the rearview mirror again, all I could see was glare.

"Melanie," B.J. said. "Switch lanes. Now."

I tried with all my might to turn the wheel to the left, but it wouldn't seem to go. So I jerked it to the right, into the break-down lane. If the cops stopped us for driving in it, we'd just have to explain. Actually, if the cops stopped us, that might fix every-thing.

The truck pulled up beside us.

"Genius," B.J. said. "Why don't you just invite him over for a drink?"

I turned my head half an inch and looked way up. The trucker made a kissy face down at me. Or maybe it was a fishy face. It was hard to tell.

"Call nine-one-one," I said.

"Where the hell did I put my phone?" B.J. said.

The truck edged over the white line and into our lane.

I thought I'd fantasized every kind of highway death imag-inable, in vivid detail, but never this one. It broke my heart that Trevor and Troy would have to be this traumatized when they identified my mangled body. Unless Kurt could do it, but he'd probably bring *Crissy*, and the last thing I wanted was to give her the satisfaction of seeing me looking like that. And the truck driver probably wouldn't bother to stop, and even if he did, it's not like he'd admit to the real story. He'd probably make it sound like it was all *our* fault, that he'd tried his hardest to swerve out of the way of these two crazy women but it was too late.

And the funeral, the funeral. How many times had I meant to pick out a decent outfit. And burial or cremation, I'd never re-ally crossed that bridge, either. Music was important, too—the song that played at the services was the song Trevor and Troy would associate with me for the rest of their lives. Was the theme song from *Beaches* too over-the-top? Maybe Whitney Houston's "I Will Always Love You" from *her* funeral?

My eyes filled up just thinking about it.

"Scratch my Mustang and I will sue your pants off," B.J. yelled. She lowered her voice. "Sorry, bad word choice. Listen, he's just trying to intimidate us. It's probably not even his truck—his boss will kill him if he hits us."

I stared straight ahead and tried to blink my tears away.

"Holy smokes," B.J. yelled. "He's going to hit us. Floor it."

She might as well have asked me to make the car fly. The harder I tried to push the gas pedal, the more my leg shook.

I jerked the wheel to the right and we bumped off the road.

The truck kept going. We slowed to a stop.

"Wow," B.J. said. "Brilliant maneuver. I knew you had it in you, Thelma. Impressive, really impressive."

I put the Mustang into park and leaned forward against the steering wheel. My whole body was drenched with sweat, and the salt was making my tattoo burn. I focused on my breathing, in through my nose and out through my mouth, and waited for my heart to stop trying to beat out of my chest.

"Uh-oh," B.J. said. "Don't look now."

I raised my weary head and looked.

The eighteen-wheeler was backing down the breakdown lane in our direction.

"Noooo," I said.

"Ohmigod," B.J. said. "This guy is insane. I didn't even know those trucks beep when they go backward. Come on, let's get out of here. Fast."

I reached for my door. "Switch seats with me."

"Melanie, come on, *hurry*."

The truck was getting closer. I had a really creepy feeling it was planning to plow right through us. *Oops*, I could hear the trucker saying when the cops arrived, *I didn't even see the little ladies.*

When I tore my tongue away from the roof of my mouth, it hurt. "I can't," I said. "I can't drive."

"Are you crazy?"

"Yes, I'm crazy," I yelled at the top of my lungs, for the whole wide world to hear. "I'm crazy afraid of highways!"

CHAPTER 21

I kicked open the door and ran around to the passenger side. By the time I managed to yank that door open, B.J. had already crawled over to the driver's side and put the Mustang into drive.

"Whoa," I said as I jumped in. "Wait for *me*."

B.J. floored it before I even finished closing the door.

Ahead of us, the truck had stopped, and the trucker was sliding down from the cab.

He was a lot less scary when he wasn't surrounded by a gazillion-ton fortress of metal. "Hey, Beej," I said, "could he possibly be coming over to ask us out on a date?"

B.J. headed straight for him.

The trucker's feet hit the ground. He turned his back toward us and gave his non-existent butt a little wiggle.

B.J. kept going.

The trucker turned around and grinned. Then his mouth opened into a big O.

I screamed.

The Mustang couldn't have been much more than a foot or two away when he finally jumped out of our path.

"Ch-ch-*chiiiicken*," B.J. yelled. She leaned on the horn, then put on her blinker. We pulled out onto the highway without losing much speed. She navigated expertly into the passing lane. "Call nine-one-one. Tell them we just passed a trucker harassing two women. Give them the mile marker and the license plate."

"Aye aye," I said. "Wow, you were awesome back there, Louise."

She didn't say anything.

I made the call, then I leaned back in my seat and tried to get comfortable. The car reeked of silence.

Across the highway, an SUV with a single headlight heading in our direction reminded me of one of our favorite car games from high school. "Padiddle," I yelled.

B.J. didn't say anything.

"Hey, do you remember what it was that you were supposed to yell when it was the back headlight that was burned out?"

"Don't talk to me," she shouted at the top of her lungs.

One of the two lights on Veronica's front porch had burned out. Moths were circling and diving at the other one, which glowed a soft umber. I watched them crash into the glass barrier repeatedly, the same movement leading to the same result, over and over and over again. How many stupid moves did it take for them to catch on?

Butterflies may have been done to death in metal sculpture, but what about moths? And would it even be possible to differentiate between the two in metal? Maybe if I kept them simple and airy, a fine steel mesh pulled tight over thin wire in a matching tone. The trick would be to make the wings look so ethereal they'd flap in the gentlest breeze, but at the same time construct them sturdily enough to hold up to the elements.

Beside me, B.J. shifted in her seat and let out a quick pissed-off puff of air.

The whole rest of the way to Veronica's house, neither of us had said a word. I wasn't sure it was a record, but if it wasn't the longest we'd ever gone without talking when we were together, it had to be close.

Once she'd made it clear she really wasn't speaking to me, I'd twisted around in the passenger seat until I found just the right position to support my lower back and take the pressure off my tattoo at the same time. Then I'd closed my eyes and pretended to nap while she drove.

It was strange to think that, as close as we'd been for so many years, I'd never picked up on B.J.'s needle phobia. I thought I might have remembered some vague references, but maybe I was only rewriting our history, because now I knew. I couldn't even remember her getting her ears pierced, though I remembered getting mine done in vivid detail. I could picture my sister and me carrying our little fourteen-karat gold studs in their identical beige hard plastic boxes into our dentist's office after our mother had decided that doctor and dentist offices were the only truly sanitary places to get ears pierced. She'd made us wait months until we were due for our yearly cleanings, all in the name of her favorite pastime of killing two birds with one stone. Two daughters who invariably had to do everything together and never quite got over it.

And then when our mother died, her two daughters sprang apart forever, never to be close enough to be killed by the same stone again.

When I'd finally opened my eyes, B.J. was cruising right over the Sagamore Bridge without even hitting the brakes. Relief that I didn't have to be the one to drive over it washed over me. The only thing worse than driving on a highway was driving over a bridge on a highway. From the corner of my eye I could see boat lights and house lights twinkling on the canal way down below. I gripped the armrest and shifted toward the center of the car so I wouldn't fall out.

B.J. let out a long, martyred sigh and brought me back to Veronica's driveway.

"Come on," I said. "Just fish or cut bait."

She didn't say anything.

"Poop or get off the pot?"

She still didn't say anything.

"Put an egg in your shoe and beat it?" It didn't quite fit, but I was running out of stupid expressions.

Even in the dark Mustang, I could tell she was staring straight ahead.

"I mean it," I said. "Either say it or shake it off. I'm not sitting here for the rest of my life. And if Veronica sees us out here, she's going to think we're staking out the place."

B.J. took a long swallow of Tab and put the can back in the console.

"I can't believe," she finally said, "you would do that to me."

"What," I said.

She shifted in her seat. "I can't believe you would let me pour my heart out to you about my deepest, darkest fear and let me think I was completely, histrionically, Looney Tunes insane, and never once, not once, even hint—"

When I rolled down the window, a moth flew into the car.

"Put that window up right now," B.J. yelled.

I ignored her. The coolest thing about non-power windows was that you had total control of the one on your side. Sometimes progress wasn't all it was meant to be. If only I'd brought my own iPod. I could put in my earbuds and listen to anything I wanted to. Or maybe I'd just put in the earbuds as a sound barrier and not even bother to turn on the music.

"Believe it or not," I said, "some things aren't about you. And if you sigh one more time, I might have to kill you."

B.J. let out a sigh, long and loud.

I shook my head. "It's a completely different thing. Mine came out of the blue. It's not like it was a lifelong fear, like I was always afraid of highway driving. At least not really. And I think it's only temporary." The moth flew back out and another one flew in. B.J. rolled her window down, too, maybe to make it go out her window, maybe to catch her own moth. "I hated, *hated* driving with Kurt. So then Kurt leaves and now I hate driving with myself. It's like he jinxed me or something."

B.J. reached for her Tab. "Maybe he's got a Melanie voodoo

doll. You know, you're driving down the highway and he sticks in a pin and says, *Take that*."

"Ha. If Kurt was capable of spending that much time thinking about my feelings, we might still be together."

"That's funny. Either that or really masochistic."

I thought for a moment. "So how come you can handle talking about voodoo dolls? Isn't a pin just like a needle?"

"Don't be ridiculous. They're completely different."

I let out my own sigh. "I know I'm doing it to myself, but I can't figure out why I'd be that self-destructive. It's like I know there's a whole new life out there for me, and the only thing standing between me and it is this stupid barrier. And I can't get past it." I tilted my head back and blinked to keep the tears from spilling out. "It's so embarrassing."

"So what does it feel like?"

"Exactly the way you looked in the tattoo parlor." I closed my eyes. "My mouth gets all dry and it's like I can't swallow. And I get this tingly feeling as if my hands and arms are starting to swell."

"Ooh," B.J. said, "I don't get the tingly thing. I get this queasy feeling in my stomach and I feel like I'm going to pass out. And sometimes my heart feels like it's going to beat right out of my chest."

"I get the heart thing, too." I took a deep breath. "And then this baby elephant crawls onto my chest and sits down."

"Ohmigod, I get the baby elephant, too," B.J. shrieked.

I looked over to see if she was making fun of me. It was hard to tell in the dark. "Are you sure you're not making that up?"

"No, really. It sits right down like it's trying to squeeze all the air out of me. Mine is a girl elephant, and its toenails are painted pink."

"Mine is gender neutral," I said. "And you, my old friend, are insane."

B.J. let out a soft Tab burp. "I would say, based on this conversation, we both are."

I reached for her Tab and took a small sip. "Do you think maybe people just get crazier as they get older? My father had this ancient uncle Kenneth who used to come over for Sunday dinner sometimes. And every once in a while he'd just start to bark."

"Bark?"

"Yeah, bark. At the dinner table. My parents and sister and I all just pretended it was completely normal and kept eating our mashed potatoes. And eventually dinner would be over and my father would take him back to wherever it was he came from."

B.J. snorted. "The kennel?"

It wasn't that funny, but I totally cracked up anyway.

"Did he bark like a Labradoodle?" B.J. said. "Or more like a shih tzu?"

This was even less funny, but we laughed harder.

I wiped my eyes. "I think you're supposed to say *sheet*. You know, like *sheet-zoo*."

"Shit," B.J. said.

"Sheet," I said.

B.J. shifted in her seat. "No, I mean, did you see that?"

"What?"

"Over by that tree. Something just ran across."

"Oh, no," I said. "Not that fruckin' tucker again."

"It was probably just a dog," B.J. said. "Either that or your father's uncle Kenneth."

"Funny," I said.

We heard a branch crack. A chill tickled the back of my newly bare neck.

"Mel," B.J. said. "Maybe—"

Something rained down on the Mustang's canvas top. Pebbles?

It stopped. We waited.

"I think there's something on top of the car," I whispered.

"Roll. Up. Your. Window."

I reached for the handle.

An upside-down head appeared in the windshield.

"OOB," it screamed.

CHAPTER 22

We were still shrieking when Veronica came into view.

B.J. and I flung open Mustang Sally's doors in perfect tandem and jumped out.

Veronica reached up and scooped a little girl off the roof of the car. She buried her head against Veronica's shoulder, then peeked up at us and grinned.

"Well," Veronica said, "what a nice surprise. And it looks like you've already met Fawn."

"Ohmigod," I said. "Ohmigod, ohmigod, ohmigod."

"Wimp," B.J. said. She shut her car door and gave Veronica a big hug, partially enveloping Fawn. "Nice to meet you, honey. I'm B.J."

I shut my car door. "Oh, puh-lease. You were just as terrified as I was." I gave Veronica my own hug as Fawn wiggled to the ground and ran in the direction of the house. "I'm Melanie," I yelled.

"Come on in," Veronica said as she took off after Fawn.

"The kid's adorable," B.J. said once we were settled around the kitchen table, "but she scared the shit out of me."

"Sheet," I said. "She scared the sheet out of you."

"Teehs," a voice said from the other room.

Veronica shook her head. "Little pitchers have big ears," she whispered.

"Srae gib evah srehctip elttil," the voice said, louder this time.

Veronica shook her head again. Judging by the way her frizzy hair looked, she'd been shaking it a lot lately. "Fawn," she yelled in a singsongy voice, "come say good ni-ight."

Fawn appeared in the doorway to the kitchen. She had shiny, saucerlike brown eyes that seemed to take up most of her face. They reminded me of those paintings of big-eyed children everybody had on their walls when we were kids. She was holding a huge laptop, which made her arms and legs look spindly and frail in comparison. "Syad eerht ot pu rof yenom repap no evil nac smreg ulf," she said.

B.J. and I looked at Veronica.

"Flu germs can live on paper money for up to three days," Veronica said. "It's one of her favorite sayings."

"Wow, is that true? They can really live for three days?" I said. "Oh, I get it. It's backward, right?"

"Is she . . ." B.J. hesitated. "D-y-s-l-e-x-i-c?"

Fawn fixed her enormous eyes on B.J. "C-i-x-e-l-s-y-d," she said.

Veronica had that kind of reddish blond hair that just got lighter and whiter as you aged instead of turning gray. It was pulled back into a ponytail and looked like it hadn't been brushed in at least a few days. Her greenish gray eyes had dark circles under them, and she looked like she could use a good nap. She was wearing baggy sweatpants and a faded WHERE THE SIDEWALK ENDS T-shirt with stains on the front.

She took a sip of her Tab and put the can down on the kitchen table. "Wow, I haven't had a Tab in a million years." She grinned. "Still sucks like it always did."

"Isn't it great?" B.J. said. "It's like a direct line to high school. So, is it kind of a *Rain Man* thing? Or is she normal otherwise?"

"Have you had her evaluated?" I asked.

B.J. popped open another Tab for herself. I was busy turning the rest of the six-pack sitting in the center of the table into a centerpiece by circling it with pieces of sea glass I'd found in a mason jar on the counter.

"And not to pry," B.J. said, "but whose kid is she anyway? I mean, is that why you've been blowing me off? She's not yours, is she?"

Veronica grinned some more. "I love you guys." She took another sip of Tab and made a face as she swallowed. "Fawn is my granddaughter. She's my daughter Julia's child. Who is currently in rehab for the third time since Fawn was born."

"Wow," I said, because it was the best I could do.

"I know this isn't the main point," B.J. said. "But I can't believe you're a grandmother."

"Beej," I said.

Veronica smiled. "That's okay. It kind of floored me, too. Especially since Mark and I didn't even find out about her until she was almost two and a half."

"Wow," I said again.

"Where is Mark anyway?" B.J. asked.

"His company restructured so he's working down south right now. Rehab's insanely expensive and money's tight, but he tries to fly home a weekend or two a month." Veronica crossed her arms over her chest. "It's been tough on Fawn. She loves her pop."

"Pop," I said. "It's the same thing frontward and backward."

Veronica reached for the mason jar and poured herself a handful of sea glass. "Yeah, they joke about that all the time. Sometimes she calls him Spop."

"What does she call you?" I'd always wondered what my own grandkids would call me one day. For the first time it occurred to me that they'd probably have to call *Crissy* something, too.

"Mom." Veronica shook her head. "She calls me Mom and she doesn't call her mother anything. She doesn't talk about her, she won't read her letters or let us read them to her, but she carries Julia's laptop around with her everywhere she goes. She even sleeps on it like a pillow."

"Wow," I said. I couldn't seem to stop saying it.

"Well, the good news is you're a teacher," B.J. said. "At least you're plugged into getting her everything she needs. Have you ruled out anything neurological? What about Asperger's?"

"It seems to me," I said, "that if she's smart enough to reverse all those letters, she's probably really, really smart. Maybe she's gifted and just bored. Can you get her into some kind of accelerated program? How old is she anyway?"

Veronica waited until we'd finished. "I have nothing but respect for the fields of education and medicine, but the last thing this kid needs is a diagnosis to follow her around. I've got the whole summer to spend with her, and we should know more about Julia by the fall, too. I'm looking into taking a sabbatical next year if it comes to that—maybe I can homeschool her for a year and tutor on the side to make ends meet. Or something."

The three of us looked at one another across the kitchen table. I tried to think of something to say besides *wow*.

Veronica reached back and pulled her ponytail tighter. "Okay, enough about me. Sorry to hear about you and Kurt, Mel. You were always too good for him."

"Dah-dah-dah-duuuuh," B.J. sang.

I'd taken off my T-shirt and Veronica had given me a beach towel to wrap around me. Veronica and B.J. each held one end of my Band-Aid and pulled it off slowly.

"How's it look?" I said.

"I've had one on my ankle since college," Veronica said. "It'll be pretty puffy and angry looking for the first few weeks or so, but once the scab falls off—"

"Scab?" I said.

"Puffy and angry?" B.J. said. "Really? Mine, too?"

I turned around to look at B.J. "How could you not know that?"

"Don't look at me like that," B.J. said. "You didn't know it, either."

"I wasn't planning on getting a tattoo. You were the master-mind behind the whole thing."

"Oh, please, I didn't make you do anything you didn't want to do. Ha, my first boyfriend used to say that. Okay, wait a min-ute." She reached over and pulled a sheet of paper out of her purse. "Can either of you read this thing without glasses?"

Veronica and I shook our heads.

"Shit," B.J. said. "Where the hell did I put my reading glasses?"

Veronica got up and found a pair in one of her kitchen drawers. She handed them to B.J.

"Your New Tattoo and You," B.J. read.

"Catchy," I said.

B.J. cleared her throat. "'Two hours after your new tattoo is complete, remove the bandage.'"

"Oops," I said. "We're a little late."

"Shh," B.J. said. "'Wash gently with lukewarm water and a mild antibacterial soap.'"

"Got it," Veronica said. I followed her over to the sink, and she went to work on my tattoo.

"'Pat dry,'" B.J. continued, "'being extremely careful not to rub. Then work a thin coat of antibacterial ointment into the skin.

Make sure you don't use too much or it might remove some of the color from the tattoo.'"

"Great," I said. "Just what I need—an angry, scabby, polka-dotted broken heart on the outside to match the one on the inside."

"Almost there," Veronica said behind me. The antibacterial ointment was soothing, and she had a mom's gentle touch.

"Noooo," B.J. said.

"What?" I said.

"Nothing." B.J. folded the paper in half and stuffed it back in her purse. "I think that's pretty much it."

I crossed the room in three big steps and yanked the paper out of B.J.'s purse. I grabbed Veronica's glasses from her.

I hiked up my beach towel and scanned the list. "'Avoid soaking the tattoo in water or letting the shower spray pound directly on it. Avoid the sun.'"

"Too much water dries out your skin anyway," B.J. said. "And we both have more than our share of sun damage."

"Speak for yourself. 'Avoid swimming in both pools and in the sea.' Gee, thanks. I finally see the ocean again—"

"It's not like you even went in when we were at the beach earlier today."

"That's not the point," I said. "The point is that I *could* have. Okay, 'Use ice packs to minimize redness and swelling.' Eww, 'Refrain from picking at scabs.'"

B.J. reached for the paper. "See, it's all pretty much common sense." I turned and blocked her with my good shoulder.

I let out a gasp. "'They will fall off on their own as the tattoo heals, usually in two. To three. Weeks.'"

"I forget," Veronica said. "When *is* the reunion anyway?"

I looked over Veronica's reading glasses at B.J. "Tell her."

B.J. shrugged. "Pretty soon."

I shook my head. "Try the day after tomorrow. You might want to call Macy's and take the hold off those sexy little peasant blouses. Maybe they have some surgical wrap we can wear instead."

"Or," B.J. said, "we could bank on the fact that we're both quick healers."

The only good news I could think of was that it was my turn to take off B.J.'s bandage. I pulled a little bit harder than I had to.

"Ouch," B.J. said.

"Guess what," I said to Veronica as she dabbed on the antibiotic ointment. "B.J. and I have been discussing phobias. She's terrified of nee—"

"Don't say it," B.J. said.

"Needles, needles, needles," I said.

"Highways, highways, highways," she said.

"Oh, grow up."

"You grow up."

Veronica shivered. "Sn . . . uh . . . akes. I can't go near them at the zoo. Or the nature center. I can't look at a picture of one. I even check under the bed for them when I'm traveling." She shivered again. "There is nothing else in the world I am afraid of like that. If you told me there was a snake outside, I would never leave this house for the rest of my natural life. I hate, hate, *hate* sn—"

There was a loud thud in the next room.

We all jumped.

B.J. and I looked at Veronica. She took a step toward the doorway.

We heard a long hiss, low to the ground.

Fawn wiggled into the kitchen on her stomach and hissed again.

"*Supercalifragilisticexpialidocious*," B.J. said.

Fawn looked up from her Frosted Mini-Wheats and rolled her eyes.

"She probably had that one down before she could crawl," I said. "Didn't you, honey?"

"Come on, Fawn," B.J. said. "I double-dog-dare you."

Fawn put her spoon down and wiped her mouth with the back of her hand.

"Suoicodilaipxecitsiligarfilacrepus," she said.

"Good job, sweetie," I said. I wasn't sure if reinforcing this behavior was the way to go, but if there was one thing I'd learned as a parent it was that your kids needed you to tell them how wonderful they are. And if you did, they would rise to the occasion.

Fawn jumped up from the table, put her cereal bowl next to

the sink, and walked backward out of the kitchen. I took a bite of my own Frosted Mini-Wheats.

"I wish these were french fries." B.J. grabbed the Mini-Wheats and started eating them out of the box. "God, I just remembered I had a nightmare about that trucker. He was chasing me around at the reunion and it turned out I went to the prom with him. Terrifying."

"Ha," I said. "I wouldn't worry too much about him showing up. After all, you're going to report him to the big wheel truckers' association."

She reached for another handful. "What's wrong with that?"

"Big Wheels are those toddler cars. Remember? Trevor and Troy had a whole convoy of them."

B.J. stretched. "Well, whatever. We called the cops on him, so they can figure out which association to turn him over to. Do you want the next shower or can I have it?"

"Go ahead," I said.

From the depths of my shoulder bag, my cell phone rang. I took my time walking over to the kitchen counter to get it. Kurt was nothing if not persistent. Even if I'd actually managed to block him after all, he could be calling from his work number, or even from *Crissy's* phone. Maybe I should talk to him, at least to get the credit card thing squared away. But, really, why should I? I mean, I was on vacation, after all, the first vacation I'd had in forever. Not that he knew that, but still, he had absolutely no right to interrupt it. I hadn't seen my old friends in ages, and while I couldn't technically blame him for that, it was my life now and he certainly didn't have the right to intrude on it anymore. Enough was enough.

I found the phone and pushed ACCEPT. "*What?*" I said.

"And a top o' the mornin' to you, too," Ted Brody's voice boomed.

I took a moment to wrap my brain around non-Kurt's voice.

"Me, too," I said.

"Excuse me?"

"I mean, you, too." My caffeine kicked in and fueled a major blush, or possibly a hot flash, or maybe even a hybrid. Sometimes it was hard to tell.

B.J. was watching me with interest. Great. The last thing I needed was for her to find out about Ted Brody and make too big a deal of it. "Let me just step outside so I can hear you," I said a little louder than necessary. "Cell service and beach towns, well, you know."

I pushed the kitchen door open and stepped out onto a wooden deck. Across the backyard, a squirrel perched on the bird feeder was chowing down, and two mourning doves were ground feeding on the seeds it dropped to the pine needles below. Hostas and ferns and daylilies clumped in the shady corners of the yard. Hydrangeas, heavy with blue snowball-size blooms, edged the deck. A Slip'n Slide with a garden hose attached almost knocked me over with nostalgia.

"Hello?"

I looked at the phone in my hand and then put it to my ear.

"Hi," I said. "Sorry, I just walked outside and there was this Slip'n Slide in the yard. My kids used to live on theirs in the summer. I think we must have gone through half a dozen of them— they just wore them right out."

There was dead silence on the other end.

I laughed an odd little laugh. "That's probably not what you called to talk about, huh?"

"I was conjuring up an image of the one we used to have. I think it had car-wash features and the girls would drive through it in their Barbie vehicles, their whole posse of dolls riding shotgun."

"Mine tried pulling a wagon full of their stuffed animals over one of theirs to give them a bath. Which seemed like a good idea until the mildew set in."

"So, before you hang up on me again."

"Right," I said. "Sorry about that." The mourning doves flew off together and then the squirrel scampered across the lawn and up the side of an oak tree. The air was cool and breezy and a little bit salty, or maybe I was just imagining that I could smell the ocean from here.

Ted Brody cleared his throat. "I know you're in reunion mode so I won't take up much of your time. I was wondering, now that you've seen the courtyard, what you think I should do to light up that sculpture of yours at night? I've got all these strands of white lights, but when I tried hanging them on the wall, it looked an awful lot like Christmas."

"Hmm." I took a moment to picture the space. "What if I made you some rusted metal fireflies that attached to the wall, and we strung the lights through those? I could turn them into blinking lights—all I'd have to do is replace the bulb on the end of the light string closest to the electrical outlet with a blinking bulb. They'll blink on and off just like real fireflies and also light up the wall along with *Endless Loop*."

There was silence on the other end.

"Or you could buy a spotlight at Home Depot," I said.

He laughed. "No, it's a great idea. I was just thinking how refreshing it is to talk to someone who's doing her own thing and enjoying it."

"Thanks. And, um, ditto."

"When I decided to open Sprout, my then-wife thought I was single-handedly throwing away everything we'd worked so hard to build together. My way of seeing it was that I'd toed the line my whole life and didn't want to end up rocking away on my front porch one day counting my regrets. I'd dreamed about own-ing a restaurant for years, and I'd imagined every single inch of the place." He cleared his throat. "Anyway, I think those fireflies of yours will be just the thing."

"That must have been a tough time for you," I said.

"It became the Mason-Dixon line of our marriage, and ulti-mately we went our separate ways."

The Mason-Dixon line of our marriage. I loved that. I wanted to make it come alive in metal, maybe huge etched and spat-tered scrap metal profiles, male and female, facing away from each other, and a long jagged copper line separating the two. The line would be studded with bits and pieces of things—tiny sticks and stones and shards of sea glass—the detritus of their time together. A lifeline of their marriage.

"Have you both remarried?" I asked, because it seemed less personal than asking if *he'd* remarried, as if I just happened to be taking a general survey.

"She has. I haven't. I guess the thing about restaurants is that they basically call the shots on your personal life. Romantic din-ners can only happen on Monday nights, when we're closed."

"Romantic breakfasts are nice," I heard myself say. The squirrel was back on top of the bird feeder now, looking over at me as if I'd just said the most ridiculous thing it had ever heard. *Romantic breakfasts are nice*—what an idiot I was. Clearly this was a business call.

"Thank you for the optimism," he said.

"You're welcome," I said, for lack of a better idea.

"And your story, if you don't mind me asking?"

"My husband left me for someone named *Crissy*. For some reason that bothers me far more than if she were a Simone or a Giovanna. Or even a Ruth."

"I can understand that. My ex-wife is married to a Dick."

I burst out laughing.

"Laugh if you will, but it's gotten me through some tough moments."

"I bet. How long did it take you?"

"To what?"

"Get through your tough moments?"

"Hmm." The mourning doves were back now, too, or maybe they were new ones. Ever since I'd found out that mourning doves mated for life, it bothered me whenever I saw one alone. What had happened to its mate? Did mourning doves have tough moments, too? Did one of them want to ground feed in the same yard every day, while the other wanted to move on? Was it my turn to talk, or was it his?

"Someone once told me," he said, "that it takes a month to get over each year you were married."

"I hope that someone was wrong," I said. "I'm not sure I've got that long."

He let out another laugh. He had a great laugh, nothing

mean or measured about it. "But I think in some ways you can start counting from the time you first begin detaching from each other, if that makes sense."

"Oh, yeah," I said. "That does make sense."

"Well, I'll let you get primping for that reunion."

"Well, it's not till tomorrow. And I'm a fast primper. But I should get back to my friends. Anyway, shall I give you a call about the fireflies when I'm back in town?"

"I'd like that."

"Okay, I'm going to let you hang up first this time."

I could still hear Ted Brody's booming laugh after we hung up. He was a nice guy, and for a moment I almost wished I was still back in Atlanta so we could hang out and talk some more.

Then I remembered Finn Miller. I did a quick email check before I headed back inside.

To: Melanie
From: Finn Miller
Subject: playlist

Thought about asking if you wanted to meet for a drink first but I don't want to miss watching you walk through the door.

Here's the whole playlist. Been listening to it for weeks.

Nights in White Satin, The Moody Blues

Stairway to Heaven, Led Zeppelin

You Are So Beautiful, Joe Cocker

The Letter, The Box Tops

More Than a Feeling, Boston

When Will I Be Loved, Linda Ronstadt version of course

Wonderful Tonight, Eric Clapton

Right Now and Not Later, The Marshalls

Love the One You're With, Crosby, Stills, Nash & Young

Brand New Key, Melanie (your namesake)

Let's Get It On, Marvin Gaye

To: Finn Miller
From: Melanie
Subject: Re: playlist

I forgot all about the other Melanie!

Just so we synchronize our arrivals, what time are you groin?

"Hurry up," B.J. yelled. "We're way off schedule."

"I'll be right there," I yelled back. I pulled up Finn's email and double-checked a song. I'd managed to sign into my iTunes account and was downloading Finn's playlist to my phone.

B.J. poked her head into the guest room. "*What* are you doing?"

"Nothing. Just buying a few more songs I remembered."

She crossed her arms over her chest. "I worked really hard on that playlist. I think we have plenty."

I tapped the final BUY link and jumped up. "Of course we do. But when it comes to the old songs, more is more."

I grabbed my purse and my carry-on and followed B.J. down the stairs.

Fawn was wearing a Hello Kitty bathing suit and skidding across the Slip'n Slide, backward of course, when we got outside. Veronica kept one eye on her as the three of us had a group hug.

"Are you sure you two can't come with us?" I said.

"I'm sure," Veronica said. "But thanks for stopping by. It was great hanging out with you."

"What about Mark?" B.J. said. "Will he be home this weekend? You could just drive up by yourself for a few hours for the reunion. I'm on the committee, so I'm sure I can still get you a ticket. If they've already given the numbers to the caterer, I'll just steal someone else's."

"He's not coming home this weekend." Veronica combed her fingers through her hair. "And I have to tell you, I don't think I'd be up for it anyway. Too much I don't feel like talking about."

"Not a problem," B.J. said. "We'll make up a story for you. We could say you've invented a breakfast cereal that entertains kids for hours by making them talk backward."

"Beej," I said.

Veronica looked over at Fawn. "Yeah, and as soon as I come up with the antidote, I'll let you know."

"What about one of your other kids?" B.J. said. "Couldn't they watch her for a few hours?"

Fawn stretched out on the Slip'n Slide facing us. Her eyes were half closed, like a snake sunning itself. Every once in a while, she'd stick her tongue out and pull it back in so quickly, it was as if it had never happened.

Veronica lowered her voice even more. "Neither of them is around this summer. And let's just say that I'm not comfortable leaving her with anyone else right now anyway."

"Fine," B.J. said. "We'll just pack her up and take her with us then. We'll tell everyone at the reunion she's with the band. And Mel and I will help you keep an eye on her."

"If there's one thing this kid doesn't need, it's another party," Veronica said in a flat voice.

She gave us each another hug, carefully avoiding our tattoos, then turned to Fawn. "Say good-bye to Melanie and B.J.," she yelled across the backyard.

Fawn stuck her tongue way out and slowly pulled it back into her mouth. "Eyb-doog," she said.

"Eyb-doog," we said.

"Okay, we're out of here," B.J. said.

"Let me just run back in and go to the bathroom again first," I said.

B.J. shook her head. "Make it fast."

"Are you sure you don't want to drive while you have me as your copilot?" B.J. asked. "I mean, maybe now that you've talked about it openly, driving on the highway won't be as much of an issue."

"Isn't it supposed to be God who's my copilot?" I said.

B.J. rummaged in her shoulder bag for her keys. "Or dog, depending on the bumper sticker."

"Why do I think Fawn may have come up with that bumper sticker? That is one smart kid."

"Scary smart," B.J. said.

I put my suitcase down behind the Mustang. We'd stripped the guest room beds and thrown the sheets and pillowcases into the washing machine when we got up, and loaded the breakfast dishes into the dishwasher before we left. We'd both gone back inside and written our cell phone numbers on the memo pad hanging on the refrigerator, just to be sure Veronica knew where they were. But I was still feeling a little bit guilty that we could breeze right out the door.

B.J. finally pulled out her key ring. "Well, that's a relief—I was starting to think my keys had disappeared. I love Veronica, but I don't think I could have handled five more minutes here. I've paid my dues. My caretaking days are over."

"I don't know," I said. "They say it's completely different when it's your own grandchild."

"Right," B.J. said as she popped the Mustang's trunk open. "And they say cauliflower can taste like mashed potatoes, too." She collapsed the handle of her carry-on and hefted it in. "It's probably a suburban myth fabricated by some ungrateful kid who wants you to babysit her ungrateful kid."

I slid my carry-on into the trunk beside B.J.'s. "Whoa. Where did that come from?"

B.J. shrugged. "I just want to enjoy my fifteen minutes of self-ishness, that's all. I mean, first it's all about your kids, and then it's the dog they left behind and never fed anyway, and then it's your parents. And now we've both got this tiny window to enjoy ourselves before it all starts up again. So let's party on, Romy. And hopefully Veronica will find a way to ditch the kid and meet us at the reunion. And I really think you should drive."

I headed for the passenger side. "Sure, I'll drive. And we'll stop and get you another tattoo while we're out so you can work on your needle phobia. Maybe this one will heal by tomorrow."

Fawn wiggled out from under the Mustang and hissed.

B.J. screamed, long and loud.

I held my phone out so we could both hear the music and rocked my head back and forth to the slow, sexy beat of "You Are So Beautiful."

B.J. turned to look at me. "Okay, what's going on?"

"What do you mean?"

"Well, first of all, Sally's speakers are obviously far superior, so I don't even know why we're listening to your cell phone. But, come on, really? 'When Will I Be Loved,' 'Wonderful Tonight,' and now 'You Are So Beautiful.' Even I think we might have a theme here."

"I have no idea what you're talking about."

B.J. adjusted her scarf. The ride back had been uneventful and truckerless. I had a few early warning twinges riding over the Sagamore Bridge, even with B.J. driving, but nothing after that. Once we got off the highway, we'd pulled over to put Mustang Sally's top down. Then we tied on scarves to protect B.J.'s hair and what was left of mine.

We'd finished Finn Miller's playlist, so we switched back to B.J.'s iPod as we drove along the back roads to Marshbury. Elton John burst into "Bennie and the Jets."

"She's got electric boobs and a new tattoo," B.J. sang.

I burst out laughing. "Well, at least we have one of them now."

B.J. stuck out her chest and wiggled her shoulders. "Speak for yourself."

I shook my head. "Remember when we really thought those were the lyrics? Until my sister Marion made fun of us."

"Marion," B.J. said. She pushed the SHUFFLE button and we sang along with Crosby, Stills, Nash & Young about loving the one you're with and living with cinnamon girls and finding the cost of freedom.

"So gentle and pure," I said. "It was a different time back then."

"It sure was," B.J. said. "We are lucky to be alive. Remember that time when we told our parents we were sleeping over at each other's houses and we hitchhiked all the way up to that concert in Maine?"

"No," I said. "I think we talked about it, but we chickened out."

B.J. turned and looked over her sunglasses at me. "No offense, but you're such a buzz crusher."

We stopped at Satuit Saloon to pick up fish-and-chips. The second we got back out to the Mustang, we tore open the brown paper take-out bag. The scent of fried fish filled the car. We took turns reaching into the bag to sample french fries as we headed for the beach.

"Thank you for treating," I said.

"What are friends for," B.J. said. "When my husband cancels my credit cards on me, you can pay me back."

We circled around and around and around the block, hoping one of the rare parking spaces that overlooked the beach would open up for us like a clamshell.

"There," I yelled.

The car in front of us, which had driven just beyond the car that was pulling out, put on its blinker and started backing up.

"As if," B.J. yelled. She put on her blinker and leaned forward like a racecar driver. The instant the space was mostly empty, she hit the gas.

The other car beeped, long and loud.

B.J. shook her head. "What an idiot. Everybody knows that once you've passed it, you can't go back. Ohmigod, that sounds like a metaphor. Good thing I don't believe in those, either."

I laughed and reached for what was left of our fries.

Directly across from us was the seawall, topped with a simple barrier made of galvanized-steel posts and railings. It did the trick in terms of function, but if I were in charge of the beach I'd redesign the whole thing. It would have to stay as open as possible, of course, because the point was to be able to see through to the ocean. But why couldn't the posts be bent to form fish standing on their fins, with the crosspieces curving up and down like waves breaking?

I'd search the architectural supply catalogs until I found the perfect materials—I was pretty sure eight-inch steel spirals would work for the waves, and dotting the fish scales with two-inch ball bearings would make them pop. The trick would be lots and lots of edge grinding so that the barrier would be safe for pedestrians. But it would be worth every bit of effort, and when it was finished it would be spectacular.

Beneath the seawall, a thirty-foot drop ended at the beach. People of all shapes and sizes and ages filled almost every available inch of sand as they crisscrossed between the water and a patchwork of beach blankets and towels and chairs and coolers and toys. There were so many things to look at it was like trying to navigate an old *Where's Waldo?* picture book.

As I scanned the crowd, I had the oddest feeling that I was looking for myself. I found a mom and two sons who could almost be Trevor and Troy as toddlers if I squinted. A youngish couple shared a blanket, and the man was putting sunscreen on the woman's back, the way Kurt had once done for me so long ago it felt like another lifetime.

I looked slowly across the entire expanse of beach. Who would I be next? That solitary woman in a big floppy hat and sunglasses and a long-sleeved cover-up huddled under an umbrella with a book? One half of the older couple sitting so far apart on the sand that their matching plaid beach chairs were the only clue they were together?

Another couple, Boomer-aged and both in rolled-up jeans, held hands as they walked along the water's edge, laughing as they dodged the people they passed. When two little girls ran through the water in their direction, they lifted up their hands like a bridge and the girls ran right under. My eyes teared up.

"I lost my virginity on this beach," B.J. said. She reached her hand into the take-out bag, then picked up the bag and looked inside. "Tell me you didn't just eat the last french fry."

"Please don't make me listen to that story again," I said. "And I'm pretty sure it was you who ate the last one."

"I don't think so. And what's wrong with that story?"

"I think losing-your-virginity stories are only interesting if you were there."

"Hmm, I never thought of it that way. Do you want another Tab?"

I shook my head. Minot's Light, the locally famous light that blinked 1–4–3 to signify "I love you," a number standing for the number of letters in each word, was directly in front of us, way out in the ocean.

"I forgot all about Minot's Light," I said.

"Do you think it was a siren thing?" B.J. asked. "You know, blink I love you, and the sailors got all flustered and crashed into the rocks?"

"I don't think so," I said. "At least that's not the story the historical society puts out there."

"Well," B.J. said. "You know how those hysterical types are. I mean, historical."

I sighed.

B.J. sighed.

I sighed again.

"Shit," B.J. said. "I think we've passed it by. The last wild thing that's ever going to happen to us was that disgusting trucker wiggling his pitiful butt at us. That's it. That's as good as it's going to get. When we're ninety-nine and a half, that's the story we're going to be telling each other as we sit in our wheelchairs in the solarium of the nursing home doing shots of prune juice."

CHAPTER 25

A mint-green-and-white car was parked in Jan's driveway.

"Wow," I said. "What *is* that? The color is gorgeous."

"Big deal," B.J. said. "So it's a vintage Jaguar. I completely forgot how competitive Jan is. And I'd much rather have Mustang Sally any day."

"Maybe she rented it for the week," I said. "Maybe her profile says she's independently wealthy after a series of savvy investments and has a fourteen-car garage to house her collection of vintage cars. But the truth is she shops at Marshalls like the rest of us and still drives a mini van."

"Thank you," B.J. said. "You're a good friend, Thelma."

"Why aren't there more cars here?" I asked. "Do you think the partying got so wild last night that everyone went home for a nap?"

B.J. tilted her head to get a better look. "Maybe. I hope the cops didn't have to come and break things up. It would be a total bummer if we missed that, too."

I unbuckled my seat belt and twisted around to take the pressure off my tattoo. It didn't burn as much anymore, but my skin was starting to feel itchy and tight. "You don't think they all took off and went to another party, do you? Maybe someone left their Jaguar here where it would be safe."

B.J. untied her scarf and shook out her hair. "They'd better not have. I will kill Jan when I get my hands on her if she didn't at least leave us a note telling us where they all went."

I untied my scarf, too, and tossed my short hair like a salad. "Does my hair look okay?"

B.J. looked. "Of course it does. You look about twelve. Well, except for around the eyes. And the jawline."

"So, are we going to go inside or are we just going to sit out here while you insult me?"

"Okay, let me find a safe place to park in case it turns into a mob scene. If any of our classmates so much as scratches my Sally, I will take them out."

B.J. finished pulling Sally off the road and onto the edge of Jan's lawn. Then she leaned her head back and drained her Tab.

I picked up my water bottle from the console and took a long gulp, as if I were hydrating before a marathon.

B.J. let out a soft Tab burp. "Okay, just promise me that if somebody obnoxious gets my ear, you'll come rescue me."

"Sure," I said, "but how will I know if somebody I think is obnoxious isn't somebody you're crazy about?"

B.J. reached for her lip gloss. "That's a really good point. Okay, we need a signal. How about if I need you to rescue me, I'll roll my eyes."

I rolled my eyes. "Perfect. They'll be so insulted you're rolling your eyes at them that you won't even need me to rescue you. And by the way, if we're going to do it, this rescue thing needs to work both ways. I can't spend my whole night saving you."

"Okay, how about whoever needs to be rescued points their index finger at their tattoo and then taps it up and down on their shoulder three times?"

"Right, let's just call attention to our scabbing broken hearts."

"Okay, fine. You pick the signal."

"How about I just give you a look like I'm going to kill you if you don't rescue me?"

"Genius," B.J. said. "Now let's get in there while there's still room. Should I bring a six-pack of Tab in with us now, or should we wait and make sure the party's Tab-worthy?"

Jan opened the door on the first knock. "Come in! Come in!" She looked so different from the Jan I semi-remembered from high school that I was pretty sure I wouldn't have been able to pick her out in a police lineup. Her hair was platinum blond and her eyes were an odd emerald green, like a cat's. I searched her face for a single wrinkle and came up empty.

"You two haven't changed a bit," she said.

"You haven't changed a bit, either," B.J. said. "You've changed completely."

"You look great," I said. It wasn't quite true, but you could look at it like the hostess gift we'd forgotten to bring. When I smiled at her, the corners of her mouth may have lifted in return. It was hard to be sure.

B.J. and I stepped into a foyer with high beadboard wainscoting and a perfectly refinished old hardwood floor with a compass rose inlaid in the center. I wanted the house, the floor, the compass rose. I wanted to move right in and stay.

"Sorry we're a day late," B.J. said. "We got a little bit sidetracked."

Jan gave B.J. a hug. B.J. kept her tattooed shoulder angled back, just out of reach.

When it was my turn, I did the same thing. "Sorry to hear about you and Kurt," Jan whispered. "You were always too good for him."

I tried to give B.J. a dirty look for apparently informing the entire world about the breakup of my marriage, but she was too busy checking out the house. "Cool place," she said.

"It's my mother-in-law's," Jan said. "And I should probably tell you that she's not supposed to be—"

A tiny woman with a cane walked into the foyer. She was wearing a pink Chanel suit and a matching pink pillbox hat. I couldn't see from where I was standing but I just knew her stockings had seams running up the back. Her black orthopedic shoes were freshly polished and she had two little pink circles of rouge on her papery cheeks.

The rings on her gnarled fingers twinkled with jewels the size of small countries.

She lifted her cane high in the air and pointed it at B.J. and me.

"Whose thieving bastard children are you?" she roared.

"Put your money in real estate," Jan's mother-in-law said. She owned all of Marvin Gardens already and was plunking houses down as fast as she could buy them up.

"Well, sure," B.J. said, "if the location will hold its value. But what about all those poor people whose mortgages went upside down?"

Jan's mother-in-law adjusted her row of little yellow houses until they were all lined up neatly on the curb. "Apple," she said.

B.J. leaned forward. "Do you mean put your money in the computer or in the fruit?"

I reached for the dice. "I forgot how much fun Monopoly is," I lied politely. "It was one of my sons' favorite games when they were growing up."

Jan's mother-in-law reached for her cane, which was hooked over the back of her chair. "Whose thieving bastard children are you?"

"Mom," Jan said. She leaned across the kitchen table and put her hand on her mother-in-law's forearm. "Remember? B.J. and Melanie, my two friends from high school?"

Her mother-in-law yanked her arm away. "Whose thieving bastard child are *you*?"

Jan made a tiny movement with her lips that was like a mini frown.

B.J. rolled her eyes at me. Then she pointed to her tattoo and tapped her finger on her shoulder three times. Then she glared, long and hard.

I ignored her and took my move. I drew a card. *Do not pass go. Do not collect $200.* Apparently even Monopoly couldn't cut me a break. Maybe Kurt had shut off my Monopoly credit, too. I buried the card at the bottom of the pile and hoped we wouldn't still be here by the time it rose to the top again.

Jan's mother-in-law pushed herself up and hobbled over to the sink. She opened a drawer. She looked over her shoulder at us and moved to block our view.

B.J. rolled the dice and counted seven spaces. "Woo-hoo. Free parking." She held out her hand. "Okay, cough it up, everybody. I forget, how much do you all have to give me?"

"Nothing," I said. "It's just free parking."

"I think Melanie's right," Jan said.

"Great," B.J. said. "We've been playing the longest game in the world for, like, two centuries, and now you two are going to start cheating."

"Do you want me to Google the rules?" I said.

B.J. glared at me. "No, I don't want you to Google the rules. I want you to play by them."

Jan's mother-in-law came back and sat down again. Next to her houses on Marvin Gardens she placed a candle, a pencil, and a tampon. She picked up the tampon and pointed it at the little television on the kitchen counter and made a clicking sound.

She put the tampon back down next to the pencil and adjusted her pink hat. Then she picked up the dice. "Whose thieving bastard children are *you*?" she asked them.

B.J. and I sat on the front steps, pretending we were taking a cigarette break.

"Isn't Jan going to not smell the smoke?" I asked.

B.J. shrugged. "Whatever. One more minute in there and I was going to start trying to turn on the TV with a tampon, too."

I sighed. "That poor thing."

B.J. lit the candle. She held it like a cigarette and pretended to take a drag.

I shook my head. "I hope Jan's mother-in-law doesn't notice her candle is missing."

"She'll just think those thieving bastard dice took it."

"Can you imagine ending up like that?"

B.J. blew some imaginary smoke rings. "Like Jan? I think her face will be fine once it loosens up a little."

"I meant her mother-in-law."

"We've both been there. It sucks. I've already told my kids to just take me out and shoot me when my quality of life starts to slip."

"But what if you don't realize your quality of life has started to slip? I mean, did you see how happy Jan's mother-in-law was when she rolled those double sixes?"

B.J. started crisscrossing her candle in front of her like a sparkler, and I looked up at the stars twinkling away in the sky on this crisp summer night. Sitting there on the rough wooden steps, leaning back on my elbows, I had a moment of clarity about my own life. Sure, Kurt had left me, but I had so many more choices than either Veronica or Jan did, sandwiched as they were between two needier generations. For the first time in a long time, I felt almost lucky.

B.J. sighed. "I'm just so glad we didn't waste any Tab on this night. How much longer do you think we have to stay?"

I sighed, too. "Weren't we supposed to stay here the whole time? And we're already a day late. And where else would we stay anyway?" I thought it through while I took a deep, candle-scented breath. "Another hour?"

B.J. took one more drag and then blew out her candle. "Forty-five minutes tops. And I don't care if we have to sleep on the beach."

CHAPTER 26

"The sunrise would have been worth the sore muscles," B.J. said, "and the mosquito bites. And those awful midgies, or no-see-ums, or whatever it is they're called."

"Right," I said, "until the cops came."

"I didn't even think of that. We should have done it just for the cops. It would have been a great story to tell at the reunion. Bummer, we definitely should have slept on the beach."

"Right," I said, "and then our tattoos would have gotten sandy and then they would have become infected and then we would have had to go to the doctor, who would've had to give you a—"

B.J. threw her pillow at me. "Highway, highway, highway."

I threw mine back.

"Oh, grow up," we said at the same time.

"Jinx," we both yelled.

"I'm glad we stayed last night," I said. "Well, not glad-glad, but happy-we-did-the-right-thing glad."

"It's tragic. An entire generation has gone from hovering over their kids to hovering over their parents and grandchildren without any time off for good behavior. It's our civic duty to have some fun for Veronica and Jan and all the rest of the shut-ins in our class who can't get out to do it on their own. You and I are the last wild girls standing, Thelma."

I yawned. When I stretched the full length of my bed, the old springs creaked and my feet hit the iron posts of the footboard.

B.J. sat up and gave her bed a bounce. "These beds are right out of the asylum scenes in *One Flew Over the Cuckoo's Nest*. One more night in them and we'd both be stark raving nuts. Good thing I was still able to get us a hotel room for tonight. I think it's probably for the best anyway. I mean, if it gets really wild at the reunion, it might be safer to stay within crawling distance."

"Thank you," I said, "but we'll have to break it to Jan gently. And I promise I'll pay you back for everything as soon as I straighten things out with Kurt."

There was a knock on the door. "Good morning," Jan said. She came in holding a tray loaded with coffee and scones.

"Wow," B.J. said. "You could almost talk me into staying another night with that."

"Smooth, Beej." I pushed myself up to a sitting position.

Jan put the tray on the foot of B.J.'s bed and then opened the tiny closet. She pulled out a luggage rack and settled the tray on top of it. She handed us each a folded cloth napkin and a mug. She reached for the coffeepot.

B.J. and I jumped up before she could start serving us our scones and cutting them into bite-size pieces.

"Wow," I said. "You didn't have to do all that."

Jan leaned back against the wall. "And you didn't have to stay last night. Thank you. It meant a lot."

B.J. grabbed a scone. "Where is she now?"

"Downstairs arranging her Cheerios on the kitchen table side by side with every round thing she can find in the house. I think it's her way of trying to order a world that no longer makes sense."

"Oh, that's so sad," I said. "How long have you, uh, had her?"

Jan shrugged. "I shouldn't have her at all. She walked right out of her first nursing home and hit a nurse with her cane at the second one."

B.J. opened her mouth to make a crack and then shut it again.

"So," Jan continued, "we hired a companion to live with her in her year-round house, then we hired another companion after she ran away from that companion. And that companion just quit two days ago."

"Where's your husband?" B.J. asked. "I mean, after all, isn't it *his* mother?"

Jan shrugged. "On a business trip—what else is new. I'll tell you, if he doesn't find a way to get his butt back in time for me to make it to the reunion—"

"Can you get some kind of respite care?" I said. "You know, just for the night?"

Jan tried to get her mouth to smile. "I've got some calls in."

B.J. and I nodded encouragingly.

"And if that doesn't work, I might just have to take her with me. You have no idea what I went through to get myself ready for this reunion."

While B.J. took the first shower, I stripped the beds in Jan's guest room and then took a walk on the beach, hoping to get enough cell service to check my email.

To: Melanie
From: Finn Miller
Subject: Re: Re: playlist

Whoa, baby. I'll be the first one in the door.

To: Finn Miller
From: Melanie
Subject: Re: Re: playlist

You knew groin was a typo, right?

Remember my friend B.J.? Well, I'm staying with herd and she's on the committee, so I'll be there early, too. I can't believe it's almost here. I have this crazy feeling, as if this, as if *we* were meant to pee.

I've been listening to your playlist over and over again. Today's fa-vorite song: "You Are Ho Beautiful."

The tide was out. A long expanse of sand stretched before me, like a life filled with possibility. I stepped over the jumble of pebbles and seaweed at the high-tide line and then turned back. A perfect piece of sea glass I'd almost missed sparkled up at me.

I reached down to pick it up. I turned it over in my hand a few times, and then I called Ted Brody.

He answered his phone on the second ring. "Well, isn't this a nice surprise. Unless you accidentally called the wrong number and you're about to yell at me."

I laughed. "Nope, I just thought it was my turn to call you."

"I'm glad you did. So, what's up?"

"I have an idea for the cement walkway that leads up to your restaurant."

"And to think I wasn't even aware that ideas for cement walk-ways were a possibility."

"Okay, picture this. We mix up a batch of cement and spread just a thin coat on top of the existing walkway. We sprinkle some sea glass over it, and smooth it down with a board. And once it's dry, Sprout has a sparkling, beckoning entrance that's not only unique and beautiful, but impossible to resist. Customers will be lined up out to the street."

"I like the sound of that."

I bent down and picked up another piece of sea glass. "They've done it down by the waterfront here, and it's spectacular. I'll take some pictures for you."

"Sounds great. But in case you've forgotten, Atlanta isn't on the ocean, so finding sea glass here can be surprisingly tricky."

I laughed. "Don't worry, I'm on it. The Christmas Tree Shop sells it by the bag, really cheap."

"Christmas Tree Shop? I'm not sure that's exactly the look I'm going for. The sea glass isn't red and green, is it?"

I laughed some more. "No, they sell tons of beachy stuff, too. I don't even know how to explain it. It's so hard for me to imagine someone not knowing what the Christmas Tree Shop is."

I looked out at the ocean while I waited for him to say something. The tide had turned and water was eating up the beach again, wave by wave.

"Um," I finally said. "I just meant that everyone here has the same frame of reference."

"Yeah, it's amazing that we can even converse without an interpreter."

"That's not what—"

"Listen, I hate to cut you short, but there's a delivery I've got to check up on. I'll leave you to your tribe."

I was still looking at my cell phone when B.J. yelled down from the edge of the beach that it was my turn to take a shower.

CHAPTER 27

B.J. and I were parked outside the mall waiting for Macy's to open.

We took a sip of our coffee at the exact same moment.

"Jinx," B.J. said.

"Owe me a Tab," I said at the same time.

"So," B.J. said. "Ask me who I was talking to on the phone while you ran into Starbucks."

"Who?"

B.J. sighed and took another sip of Tab. "My. Husband."

"Lovely," I said in my best British accent. "It's heartening beyond all measure to come upon this empirical evidence that functional marriages still exist, isn't it?"

B.J. burped. "That's a really bad British accent. Do me a favor and don't use it tonight, okay? Do you want to know why that romantic husband of mine left me three messages last night while my phone was out in the car?"

I sighed. "Because he was worried about you?"

B.J. shook her head.

I hoped this wasn't going to be too gaggable. "Because he missed you?"

B.J. shook her head again. A woman with a key on a lanyard was just unlocking Macy's front door and getting ready to push it open.

I grabbed my door handle. "I give up," I said. "Why *did* that romantic husband of yours leave you three messages?"

B.J. tilted her head back and drained the rest of her Tab. Then she made the pink metal crumple between the heels of both hands. There was a sculpture in there somewhere, but I couldn't quite wrap my brain around it.

She threw her crushed Tab can over her shoulder into the backseat.

She reached for her door. "He couldn't find the ketchup."

B.J. and I stepped out of our dressing rooms and looked at each other. Then we pivoted like twin Midlife Barbies to face the three-panel mirror. My peasant blouse was coral and B.J.'s was turquoise, and they were billowy enough to cover everything that went south at our age. Our white skinny jeans even had some kind of magic stretch in them that made us look, well, practically skinny.

"Oh, Louise," B.J. said. "Look at us. I knew we were still gorgeous."

I couldn't take my eyes off us. "You're only letting me be Louise to talk me into this."

B.J. turned sideways and pulled in her stomach. "We'll be the hit of the reunion, Romy. Big hoop earrings. High strappy sandals. Well, not high-high, but maybe the highest we can find with good arch support. And we can always bring flip-flops with us for backup."

I turned sideways and pulled in my stomach, too. I let my stomach back out. The good news was that in this top, you couldn't really see much difference.

"You don't think it would be weird to show up dressed alike?"

B.J. dropped her head forward and flipped it back. Her hair defied gravity and floated around her face like a *Flashdance* flashback. "Are you kidding? Everybody else will wish they'd thought of it first."

I gave my hair a quick toss. Then I lowered the elastic at the top of my peasant blouse so that the big ruffle that circled the whole thing dropped below my shoulders the way it was supposed to.

"See," B.J. said. "Total sexitude with full upper-arm coverage."

I turned my back to the mirror and looked over my shoulder. My tattoo, puffy and angry and scabby and itchy, was fully exposed. Just looking at it made me want to scratch. Carefully.

I looked at B.J. She wiggled her ruffle down to match mine.

"It'll be fine," she said. "I mean, I'm on the committee, so I'll just make sure they keep the lights down low. Nobody will be able to see anything this small without their reading glasses anyway, but they won't want to put them on, because they won't want everyone else to know they can't see anything without them."

"It terrifies me that I can follow that." I turned my head and looked over my other shoulder. Even squinting, my tattoo was not a pretty sight.

"How about this," B.J. said. She lifted the ruffle up on my tattoo side and hooked it over my shoulder. The angry tattoo was gone and my other shoulder didn't look half bad.

"I guess it could work," I said. "I just had such a vision of you and me and our badass tattoos."

B.J. pulled the shoulder of her blouse down a little lower. "Oh, don't worry. We'll still be badass. Trust me."

B.J. dropped me off at my sister's house on her way to meet the rest of the reunion committee.

"Maybe I should go with you," I said. "I could help decorate."

"We have plenty of people," B.J. said. "And if you don't stop by to see her now, you'll run out of time, and she'll be pissed and then things will be awkward the next time you see each other."

"Yeah, that'll be different." I gazed at my sister's perfect house. "Okay, an hour and a half tops. And keep your cell with you in case I need an early rescue. And don't leave until we're sure she's home."

I should have called first. I wouldn't even stop by B.J.'s if she lived down the street from me without at least sending her a quick text on the way over. But somehow, even though I knew I should have, I didn't.

When I rang it, my sister's doorbell played a loud rendition of "The William Tell Overture." No wonder I had sister issues.

I was just about to turn and run back to the safety of the

car when the heavy oak door finally opened. Marion's hair was chin-length and tawny this time, and she didn't have even a hint of regrowth at the roots. Her posture was still exactly like our mother's had been. Her back screamed *I'm standing up straight* and then her shoulders curved forward as if she'd forgotten to take them along for the ride. The vertical lines between the outsides of her nose and the corners of her mouth had deepened. Now they looked just like the ones our father used to have.

"I wondered when you'd show your face," she said. "That big box you sent is taking up half the garage."

I'd almost forgotten about my box spring ladies. It seemed like such a long, long time ago that I'd packed them up and shipped them off. I couldn't wait to put them in Mustang Sally's rear seat so we could all ride around together like we were back in high school. And it would be so great if one of Marshbury's high-end tourist shops would take them on consignment. Nothing would give me more satisfaction than having Kurt think I hadn't even noticed he canceled that credit card. That I didn't need a thing from him, ever again.

I faked a smile. "Sorry. I should have called to tell you."

She just looked at me.

"Good to see you," I said. I leaned in for an awkward hug.

Marion patted me once on the back of the shoulder and pulled away.

"Ouch," I said.

"What's wrong?" she said. Not with any real concern, but as if she couldn't wait to tell me she was healthy as a horse.

"Nothing," I said. "Actually, B.J. talked me into getting a tattoo with her."

She shook her head. "Why does that not surprise me."

I bit my tongue so I wouldn't say, *What do you mean by that?* Because then she'd say, *What do you think I mean by that?* And then we'd be fighting already.

"Kurt moved out," I said instead.

"You were always too good for him," she said.

"Really?" I'd always thought she liked Kurt better than she liked me. Maybe I did like my sister a little bit after all.

She twisted her big fat diamond ring around on her finger. "Marriages take work. Jonathan still sends me flowers once a month."

I reminded myself that I was decades too old to kick my sister in the shins. Or pull her hair.

"Well," she said. "You'll get through it." She brushed her hands together like cymbals, her ever-aggravating signal for a change of subject. "Brittany and her family are summering in Provence, and Tiffany just got a promotion."

"Trevor lost an arm and Troy joined a cult," I said.

My sister looked at me. Then she turned and walked away.

I followed her out to the garage. The box was bigger than I remembered it.

Marion crossed her arms over her chest. "Jonathan thought maybe we should open it, as if it might be a present for us. I told him not to hold his breath."

"It was addressed to me," I said.

"You should have asked," she said.

"I said I was sorry."

There was so much outrage flashing between us you could almost see it like an aura. I wanted her to be my big sister again—to braid my hair and push me on the swing and make me a peanut-butter-and-grape-jelly sandwich because they always tasted better when she made them.

I tried another smile. "Does this mean we're not going to have cookies and milk?"

Marion looked at me like I had three heads. "I'm gluten-free."

"Hey," I said. "Remember how right before Mom died she always wanted us to be in the room together? How every time we tried to take shifts with her, she would freak out?"

Marion's arms were still crossed over her chest. "She got like that as soon as Dad died. You just didn't have to hear it because you weren't around. I waited on her hand and foot and all she ever said was, 'Where's my Melanie?'"

My eyes filled. "I was twelve hundred miles away. I did the best I could."

"Sure," Marion said. "When it was too late to make a difference."

I'd flown up practically every weekend those last few months. I'd talked to doctors, made funeral arrangements, sorted through her things at the assisted-living apartment, the whole time knowing that nothing would ever be enough, just as it hadn't been when our father had died three years before.

And maybe it wasn't. Maybe nothing I did would ever be enough to get past this logjam between my sister and me.

But maybe if I could just find a way to pretend she was someone I actually liked, even almost a friend, she'd rise to the occasion and be likable.

I found some garden clippers on a shelf and used one of the blades to slice the tape holding the top of the box closed. I removed the tissue paper and unloaded my box spring ladies.

I peeled off their bubble wrap and lined them up on the garage floor.

One by one I twirled them around and inspected them for damages. They were perfect, and even more beautiful than I remembered them.

It took everything I had to turn to my sister and smile. "I'd really like you to have one," I said. "Take your pick."

She gave them a quick once-over. "Cute, but thanks anyway. Not that there's anything wrong with them—they're just not my style."

CHAPTER 28

The box spring ladies and I were standing at the end of my sister's driveway.

When I saw the Mustang coming, I stuck out my thumb.

B.J. pulled up beside us. "Wanna go for a ride, little girls?"

She put the car into park and jumped out. "Ohmigod, they're amazing. I love, love the parasols. Did you make them? Of course you did. Wow, you've come a long way, baby."

I sniffed. "Thank you."

B.J. shook her head. "Oh, no. What did that bitch say to you this time?"

I bent over and picked up one of the box spring ladies. "Come on, let's just get out of here."

The top was down so we lowered all three box spring ladies into the backseat.

"Do you think they'll be okay," B.J. asked, "or should I put the top up for them?"

"They're pretty heavy, so I think they'll be fine," I said, "but we'd better buckle them in just to be sure."

After we got them squared away, B.J. handed me a scarf and I found my sunglasses. B.J. gunned the motor a little louder than necessary and burned some rubber as we peeled out of my sister's perfect neighborhood.

I tried to focus on the fact that it was a spectacular summer day, sunny and breezy and dry.

When we stopped at a red light, B.J. turned to me. "Spill it."

I reached up under my sunglasses and wiped a few stupid tears from my eyes. I tilted my head back and blinked the rest away. There was no way in hell my sister deserved the satisfaction of giving me puffy eyes for my reunion.

"I offered her one." I pointed over my shoulder at the box spring ladies. "Just to be nice." I sniffed. "And maybe, well, so we'd get along for a few minutes."

The light changed and B.J. took a right toward the beach. "Are you crazy? You could get a lot of money for those. And in case you've forgotten, you don't seem to have any at the moment. What did she say?"

I swallowed back a sob. "She told me they. Weren't." I cleared my throat. "Her. Style." I tilted my head back again, but it was too late. Tears rolled down my cheeks like a waterfall.

"Oh, please," B.J. said. "Her style is early Stepford Wives." She reached one hand over and patted my knee. "I'd hug you, but I don't want to crack up my car. Or bruise your tattoo."

I sniffed.

She handed me a tissue. "Here. Blow."

I blew.

"She's not worth it, Mel. And she's totally, totally jealous of you. She always has been. You have more talent in your little finger than she has in that entire overplucked body of hers."

"Really? She's overplucked?"

"Oh, please, those eyebrows of hers, are you kidding me? And they'll never grow back at this point, you know, even if she smartens up and realizes how ridiculous they look. She'll be drawing them on with crayons for the rest of her ugly natural life."

"Thank you," I said. "You're a good friend, Romy."

"Damn right I am, Thelma. Okay, so we've got three options here. One, we can toilet paper your stupid sister's house after the reunion. Two, we can go online and give your stupid sister's email to every annoying politician we can think of. Or three, we can go find a ridiculously overpriced tourist trap and see if we can get them to take these gorgeous sculptures of yours."

"Hmm. That's a tough one."

B.J. stopped at another red light. She popped the trunk. I ran around and got us each a can of Tab. I made it back to my seat just before the light changed.

"Well done," B.J. said. "Good to see you haven't lost your touch."

"Thank you," I said. I clicked open one of the Tabs and handed it to B.J. Then I opened the other one. I leaned over the seat to give each of the box spring ladies a pretend sip, then I buckled myself back in and took a real sip. It wasn't sweet tea, but I had to admit the tinny, chemical taste was starting to grow on me.

I burped, long and loud. "Take that, my stupid perfect sister."

B.J. burped, too. "And this one's from me, Marion. Special delivery."

I scrolled through B.J.'s playlist until I found Gloria Gaynor's "I Will Survive."

"That's the spirit," B.J. said. She reached over and cranked it up and we sang along at the top of our lungs.

"Evivrus Lliw I," I yelled when we finished.

B.J. reached for her lip gloss. "Wow, that's so weird. I was just thinking about Fawn, too. I wonder if Veronica will find a way to make it to the reunion."

"No way," I said. "We both know that. Maybe the next one, though. Hey, you know what I was just thinking? What if we brought my box spring ladies over to the reunion? They could be part of the decorations. You never know, one of our classmates might turn out to be a collector."

"That's a good idea. You'd think at least one person we graduated with would have to have money *and* taste."

"Maybe Finn Miller will want them," I said, mostly because I was dying to say his name out loud again.

"Of course he will." B.J. checked the rearview mirror and then made a U-turn. "And they'll definitely be a step up from all those crepe-paper streamers and those tacky Best Class Evah balloons. Plus, it wouldn't hurt for me to show my face one more time before tonight to drop them off. You know how those committees are—blah, blah, blah about who's doing all the work, like I didn't do most of the early stuff. But I don't want to get stuck there forever, so why don't you let me just run them in? You can keep Mustang Sally idling by the curb."

"Fine, Louise," I said. "You run them in and I'll be the getaway driver. Just make sure you put them somewhere safe."

B.J. reached over and hit the SHUFFLE button on her iPod.

"'Itchycoo Park'? I said. "Are you kidding me? That song was way before our time."

"No way." B.J. turned it up. "We were young, but my first words were 'It's all too bootiful.'"

The Small Faces were impossible to resist, so we both sang along to the rest of the song.

"I'm not sure you should have included songs from before high school," I said when we finished. "I think it might make us feel older than we actually are."

"Incense and Peppermints" by the Strawberry Alarm Clock came on next. I reached over and turned the iPod up even louder. "Aww," I yelled over the music. "I forgot how much I loved this." I turned it down a little. "Okay, you were right. Pre-high-school songs are fine as long as they're special enough."

"Thank you," B.J. said. "I was waiting for your permission."

We pulled into the Marshbury Marine Park, which was tucked into a corner of the inner harbor on a narrow causeway that connected two oceanside cliffs. Across the harbor the main downtown area bustled with tourists. The last time I'd been here, it had looked like a boat junkyard, not that there was anything wrong with that.

Now it was upscale and amazing, with fancy new docks bobbing up and down on the water, sea-glass-studded walking trails spiraling through the whole property, and picnic tables everywhere. There was a great big building in the center with silvery white cedar shingles and whitewashed trim. And a huge deck with horizontal steel cable railings framed harbor views that went on forever.

"Wow," I said. "*This* is where we're having the reunion?"

The Mustang's tires crunched over clamshells bleached snow white by the sun. B.J. pulled up right in front of the main entrance. "Only the best for you, Romy. They just finished it about a year ago. Wait till you see the sunset from that deck—the committee had our first meeting here just to check it out. And the price was right—the marine center is a nonprofit and part of their mission is to make the building available to community groups at a nominal price."

I clicked my door open. "I can't wait to see it. I'll just run in with you for a second and then run right back out before anyone catches my ear. It's not like you can carry all three of them in by yourself anyway."

B.J. put the Mustang into park and jumped out. "Okay, fine. You can run one of them to the door for me and peek in the window. But that's it. I'm not kidding you, once those committee vultures smell fresh meat they'll be all over you and we'll never get out of here."

Resisting B.J. was a lot like trying to swim against a tsunami, so I carried the first box spring lady I'd made, the one with the big floppy hat of chicken wire mesh, to the front door. Her hat looked a little bit plain without anything growing in it, so I pinched off some hot pink petunias from the two overflowing boat-shaped planter boxes that flanked the front steps and tucked them into the hat's sphagnum moss.

I looked around for a hose to wet down the hat.

"*What* are you doing?" B.J. said. "We don't have time for that.

Do you have any idea how much work we have ahead of us if we're going to look dazzling by tonight?"

I picked up a half-full watering can tucked behind one of the planters. "I just have to water this sphagnum moss. I don't want the petunias to wilt before the reunion."

"Fine," B.J. said. "But I have to tell you that your priorities are way off."

I held the door open for B.J. and the other two box spring ladies. I kept it open long enough to see a huge room with dark wood floors, high white beadboard ceilings, and a gorgeous beach stone fireplace.

As soon as I finished watering the first box spring lady, B.J. was back to grab her. "Just give me half a second to find a good place for them."

Mustang Sally was still running so I kept one eye on her as I peeked around the building. The water sparkled a placid blue in the late-afternoon sun. A family was pulling up to one of the docks in their cabin cruiser, two little boys in bright orange life jackets sitting on the bow. The older boy was holding a rope, getting ready to jump to the dock and tie up the boat when they got close enough.

For the gazillionth time, I wondered what it would have been like if my family and I had never left Marshbury. Would Trevor and Troy have been happier? Would my sister hate me less? Would Kurt and I still be together?

It took me a minute to realize that B.J. was standing behind me.

I turned around. "Did you find a good place for them?"

She gave me a funny look. "Who?"

"My box spring ladies. Tell me you didn't just put them down anywhere."

"Of course I didn't. I found this big niche next to the fireplace. There was all this marine stuff in it so I just stuck that in the kitchen. Anyway, your box spring ladies will be the stars of the reunion."

"Are you okay?" I asked. "You don't look right."

B.J. slid her sunglasses down from the top of her head and over her eyes. "Of course I am. Come on, let's get out of here."

CHAPTER 29

We were taking a quick walk on the beach before we started getting ready for the reunion.

"Even without that high school reunion diet, we'll look ten years younger than the rest of those tramps in our class," B.J. said. "It's all about the endorphins, Thelma."

I decided there wasn't really a point in mentioning that we possibly should have started walking before today. I just kept swinging my arms and tried to keep up with her. We navigated our way around a couple coming in our direction, and then dodged a gang of preschoolers and their sand-castles-in-progress.

"This is ridiculous," B.J. said. "They have bike lanes on the streets—why can't they have right-of-way lanes on the beach?"

"Wouldn't the tide just wash them away?" I asked.

B.J. hurdled over a small cooler. "So what. The first person who walks the next day just draws the lines back in the sand again."

After we finished walking, we stretched and bought french fries. We took turns reaching into the take-out bag as we strolled our way back to the hotel.

"Wouldn't it be amazing," B.J. said, "if we could walk and eat fries together every day for the rest of our lives?"

Half an hour or so later we were both freshly showered and sitting out on the balcony of our hotel room in matching white terry-cloth bathrobes.

I slid my white plastic chair back as far as it would go so I could put my bare feet up on the black wrought-iron balcony railing. B.J. did the same thing.

"Well," I said. "I think the robes almost make up for the size of the balcony."

"No way. It's not like they let you keep them." B.J. blew out a puff of air. "Do you believe they told me this room had an ocean view?"

I leaned way over to the left. "It sort of does, if you look between those two buildings. And at least you can smell the salt air."

"What I smell is mildew. And that water pressure is ridiculous—I probably still have soap in my ears."

"What? I can't hear you. I have soap in my ears."

"Funny." B.J. uncrossed her ankles and crossed them again so that the other foot was on top. "So funny I forgot to laugh."

I recrossed my ankles, too. "At least we've got music. You have to admit that iPod dock on the bedside alarm was a nice touch."

"I can't even hear the music over the sound of these stupid seagulls."

I swung my feet off the railing. "Fine, I'll turn it up."

"Grab that bottle of wine I bought while you're in there, okay?"

I found the right button and cranked up the volume on the iPod dock as far as it would go without getting us arrested. Then I grabbed the wine and two plastic-wrapped cups from the bathroom.

Barry White serenaded me back out to the balcony with "Can't Get Enough of Your Love, Babe." I stopped for a moment and pretended I was dancing with Finn Miller.

I sighed. "Hey, Beej, you didn't happen to bring a corkscrew, did you?"

A gull swooped low, maybe to see if we had any french fries left, and then glided away with a disappointed squawk. B.J. swung her feet off the railing. "Here, give it to me. I'll open it with my teeth."

I shrugged. "It's your dental work."

The bottle top made a little click-click-click sound as B.J. twisted it off.

"Classy," I said. I held out the plastic cups.

B.J. poured. "They make good wines like this now." She screwed the top back on and put the bottle down on the cement floor of the balcony.

She held up her cup. "To the three of us. You, me, and Barry White."

I touched my cup to hers. "Good-bye Yellow Brick Road" came on and we sang along with Elton.

"It's a great song," I said. "I'm not sure I really understood what it meant back then."

B.J. put her feet back up on the railing. "You mean that it's about returning to who you really are?"

I put my feet up, too, and took a long sip of Chardonnay. It was dry and oaky and I didn't miss the cork at all.

I sighed. "Yeah. I guess I keep expecting to feel that way about being back here, you know, like I'm home again."

"And you don't?"

"Maybe a little. But mostly it feels like I'm still missing it the way I always do, even though I'm actually here."

B.J. pulled her lip gloss out of the pocket of her bathrobe. "I think I know what you mean. I feel like that sometimes, and I only live a couple of hours away. It's not like I can't drive here anytime I want to."

I could feel my tattoo starting to ooze a little from the shower, so I adjusted my bathrobe to keep it from getting stuck to it. "Yeah, I think maybe it's more about the fantasy of place than the actual place. And I think it's also that the memory evokes another time, too, when everything seemed simpler."

"Heavy." B.J. leaned back in her white plastic chair. "Write that down so we can Tweet it to Elton. I think we might have another hit for him."

We sipped our wine and watched two people kissing in a window across the courtyard from us.

"Get a room," B.J. yelled.

"Ha," I said. "I think they already did."

The song changed and Bonnie Raitt broke into "Longing in Their Hearts."

"Wow," I said. I rolled back the sleeve of my bathrobe and looked at my forearm. "That just gave me goose bumps. Do you believe this song came on at this exact moment?"

"That's our Bonnie," B.J. said. "She's been there. She gets it."

B. J. ran into the hotel room to play it again. "I don't know why they don't just make all the electronics the same," she said when she came out. "And could they possibly make those digital displays any smaller?"

I leaned back and closed my eyes. "It's not that there aren't newer songs that I like, but they just don't get to me in such a punched-in-the-gut, visceral way as the old ones, you know?"

B.J. finished belting out the chorus before she answered. "Yeah, it's like there's still this sixteen-year-old girl trapped inside of me, and this is the music that lets her come out."

I ran my finger around the lip of my plastic bathroom cup. "I know. It's like is he ever going to look at me, and will he ask me to dance, and who will I become and how will I survive until I get there all rolled into one."

"Sometimes I feel that longing-in-my-heart thing about my marriage," B.J. said. "I mean, Tom and I love each other and he's a perfectly good husband and everything." She recrossed her ankles on the railing. "I know this, because as you might remember my first husband was a perfectly bad husband."

"I remember." I recrossed my ankles, too.

B.J. sighed. "But what I wouldn't give to be back in that happy horseshit stage with someone, just one more time. You know, before you start to aggravate each other every time you turn around. Which is when, eighteen months in—if you're lucky?"

"I don't remember," I said. "I don't remember dating. I don't remember how you're supposed to act. I don't remember what you're supposed to say."

"Anyway, there's a part of me that's a little bit jealous that you have all that ahead of you. Not Marion-jealous, but more like I wish I could take a sabbatical from my marriage—just a month or two. So we could double-date."

"I don't think I remember who I am," I said.

B.J. shook her head. "Are you even listening to me?"

Then she let out a scream, long and loud.

"Can you believe that seagull shit all over me?" B.J. said. "Is it *shit* or *shat*?"

"I'm not sure," I said. "It might even be *shitted*."

"No way." B.J. dropped her head forward and dabbed her hair with a towel. "I didn't need Honors English to tell you it's not *shitted*. I just hope that wasn't a bad omen for the reunion. Geez Louise, my hair is never going to survive this second washing."

"Your hair will be fine," I said. I held up my Skin Skribe permanent sterile marker. "Come on, you'll feel much better once I get your fake tattoo drawn on."

"Purple?" B.J. said. "I think that might be a little bit much with my turquoise blouse. I don't want to look gaudy."

I uncapped the marker. "I don't think we have a choice. Unless you want me to use lipstick."

"Nah, that'll never hold up. I can't even keep it on my lips for more than five minutes. Okay, fine, purple broken heart it is."

She dropped her bathrobe down over one shoulder. I took a deep breath and tried to get into the zone. I knew the trick was not to try to be too perfect, but to loosen up and remember that whatever you started with could be tweaked until you got it just the way you wanted it.

"Whoa," B.J. said when she saw it in the bathroom mirror. "I think that might be even better than Ariel's heart."

"Thank you," I said. "Maybe if the box spring ladies don't sell, I could look into becoming a faux tattoo artist on the side."

"And it doesn't even look like a fake tattoo. I have to tell you, we could have saved ourselves a lot of aggravation if we'd just gone Sharpie shopping."

I handed B.J. the marker. "Come on, we should probably pick up the pace. I'd like to get to the reunion as early as possible."

I dropped my robe down over my shoulder.

"I'm not sure I can do this," B.J. said. "Especially on half a glass of wine. Maybe we should go get some more french fries first."

"Of course you can. Just stay relaxed and copy this." I held up the heart I'd drawn for practice on the back of a receipt. "You can always adjust it afterward if you need to."

"Gotcha. Okay, here goes nothing."

"Ouch," I said. "Not so hard. It's supposed to be a tattoo, not a piercing."

"Don't," B.J. said.

"What?" I said. "I didn't say nee—"

"Watch it. Come on, I'm trying to focus here."

I felt the pressure of the marker on the back of my shoulder. Then I didn't. Then I did. Then I didn't. It might have been my imagination, but it sure felt like my fake tattoo was taking a lot longer than B.J.'s had.

"Okey-dokey," B.J. said. "I think it's done now."

I twisted around to look over my shoulder at the mirror.

I gasped. "Ohmigod, I can't believe you did that to me. It looks like a purple pumpkin."

"It most certainly does *not* look like a purple pumpkin," B.J. said. "It's just a slightly different style of heart from the ones you and Ariel made. I would think you, of all people, would want to encourage my freedom to express myself artistically."

"I'm all about your artistic freedom. Just not on the back of my shoulder."

"That's an awfully narrow way of looking at things, Romy."

My phone rang. I ignored it. "Oh, please. You totally screwed up my fake tattoo and you know it. You're going to sashay into the reunion with a sexy broken heart. I'm the one who has to walk in there wearing a purple pumpkin."

"I keep telling you, without their reading glasses, nobody's even going to be able to tell them apart. They'll see a blur of tattoo and go immediately to being completely impressed."

B.J.'s phone rang.

She reached for it. "Hey, what's up? Are you sure? How long? Okay, okay. Hang tight, we'll be right there."

B.J. poured the rest of her glass of wine down the bathroom sink. "Come on, throw your clothes on. Fast. Veronica can't find Fawn."

CHAPTER 30

I took a long skip to catch up with B.J. We were both wearing flip-flops and carrying our high strappy sandals.

B.J. unlocked Mustang Sally and climbed in. She leaned across the seats and unlocked my door for me.

I jumped in and buckled my seat belt carefully so I wouldn't wrinkle my peasant blouse. "She's probably just playing a game. Listen, how about if we give it a little more time. We can go to the reunion early and give Veronica a call from there to check in with her."

B.J. gave me a look. "Do you really think she would have called us right before the reunion if she didn't need us?"

"Has she called the police?"

B.J. put her blinker on and took a right toward the highway. "She's afraid to. Apparently Fawn was taken away from Veronica's daughter at one point, and Veronica's afraid it'll look like she wasn't watching her, either."

"Of course the police won't think that," I said.

"Can you guarantee that?"

I shook my head. "It's a crazy world."

"That's for shit sure," B.J. said.

Most of the crazy world must have been heading to the Cape. We crawled along so slowly I barely felt any anxiety. When we finally pulled up to Veronica's house almost two hours later, it was dusk and the outside lights were already on. The burned-out light on the porch had been replaced.

B.J. turned off the car and looked at me. "I've been trying so hard not to think about this. But what if Fawn heard me talking about her right before we left?"

I reached for my door handle. "Let's hope not."

Veronica met us at the door, gripping a mug of coffee. Her hair was a mess and she looked exhausted. She looked like a grandmother.

B.J. and I both leaned in to hug her at once.

Veronica took a step back. "Don't. I'm trying to keep it together."

"Is Mark here yet?" I asked.

Veronica pursed her lips together and shook her head. "I haven't called him yet. I just kept thinking she'd show up and there's nothing he can do from there except worry and by the time he got a flight . . . So I called you."

B.J. closed her eyes. "I think this might be my fault. I said some stupid things in front of Fawn. I'm really sorry."

Veronica crossed her arms over her chest. "Like what?"

"Ugh," B.J. said. "I think I said something about how my caretaking days are over and I couldn't have handled five more minutes here. Damn my stupid smart-ass mouth—I didn't even really mean it. And Mel and I had no idea she was hiding under my car."

I closed my eyes and tried to picture us standing out in the driveway. "And then I said something about how they say it's different when it's your own grandchild."

"And then I said something about hoping you could find a way to ditch the kid and meet us at the reunion." B.J. hit her forehead with the heel of her hand. "I'm an idiot."

Veronica turned and walked away from us.

B.J. and I looked at each other. Then we followed Veronica across the kitchen and into the family room. We climbed the narrow wooden staircase behind her up to the second floor.

She pushed open the door to a small bathroom. We all walked in and stood elbow-to-elbow. A Hello Kitty shower curtain had been pulled all the way over to one side. A message was scrawled across the bottom of the white porcelain tub in a child's handwriting.

> ᴎo pʃɒγ ʍiƚɥ γonɿ ʇɿiǝnbƨ

"Is it backward?" B.J. said.

"It's mirror writing," I said. "If you hold the words up to a mirror you can read them, so I guess that makes it reversed but not really backward. I used to spend hours and hours practicing mirror writing when I was a kid."

"Go play with your friends," B.J. read.

Veronica shook her head. "I've called the family of every single child she's ever played with around here, not that there have been many of them. Plus her swimming instructor, the bookstore where we go for story hour, her favorite ice cream place. I don't know what else to do but keep looking."

I shook my head. "What if she was telling you she was leaving so you could go play with *your* friends?"

B.J. and I were crisscrossing the yard with the rays of our flashlights.

"Ally ally in free," I yelled.

"Yrros os m'i," B.J. yelled. "Please come here so I can apologize to you, Fawn. And after that I'm going to buy you your weight in ice cream."

We walked to the end of the driveway and yelled Fawn's name.

"Fawn," Veronica yelled from the other side of the house.

"Listen," I whispered to B.J. "I think we have to convince Veronica to call the police. We can tell them how responsible she is. I mean, it's not like she's a drug dealer. She's a *teacher*."

"You heard what she told us," B.J. whispered. "The last time the police came here, it was to arrest Fawn's mom. What if Fawn's out there and she sees them drive up and thinks they're coming for *her*?"

I sighed. "But we're going to miss the whole reunion. Do you have any idea how long it's been since I—"

"Mel, it's a freakin' reunion."

"I know, I know, but I really . . ."

Even in the dark I couldn't miss the look B.J. gave me before she walked away.

I stood at the edge of Veronica's driveway by myself for the longest time. Like B.J. had never been selfish before. Like it hadn't been a zillion years since I'd had any fun. Like Finn Miller might not be the last guy who ever waited for me to walk into a room.

"Have you ever taken her to see Minot's Light?" B.J. was saying when I found them on the front steps. "You know, the one that flashes one–four–three for 'I love you'?"

Under the soft glow of the front light Veronica nodded. "It's one of her favorite places to visit when we go up to Marshbury. She and her pop even have this little ritual when he puts her to bed. Mark flashes one–four–three with her bedroom light on the way out the door."

Veronica let out a little sob, then coughed to cover it up.

"I can't shake the feeling she's right around here," B.J. whispered. "Maybe she's watching our every move and just needs to be sure you really want her back."

Veronica nodded. "Maybe I just want it to be true, but that sounds like her."

"So," B.J. whispered, "let's go put on the biggest lovefest anybody has seen since Woodstock. Not that we're old enough to remember Woodstock."

Veronica and B.J. went into the house to get all the candles they could find. I felt left out, excluded in that awful junior high way when two friends align and leave you out in the cold. I wondered if that was how we'd made Fawn feel.

I followed the beam of my flashlight out to the backyard. The drone of the cicadas was loud and eerie. A mosquito bit the side of my neck, and I swatted it hard. I knew Veronica and B.J. were a quick scream away, but I was still afraid—afraid of the dark, afraid of what I might find just around the corner. I could only imagine how alone and afraid Fawn must feel right now.

I found the Slip'n Slide. I unscrewed the hose from the back of the house, juggling the flashlight from one hand to the other and finally tucking it under my arm. I dragged the whole thing around to the front yard, stretched out the Slip'n Slide under the lights in front of Veronica's house, and attached the hose to another water spigot. I turned it on so that the water trickled across the slippery blue plastic like an invitation.

I looked up at the pitch-black sky and wished on the first star I saw that Fawn was out there in the dark somewhere watching my every move. Veronica came out carrying a big tray of candles, mostly plain white votives and big fat hurricane candles. B.J. followed her with a black wrought-iron candelabra filled with long tapered candles. Crystals dangled from it like a throwback to romantic dinners of long ago.

I took the candelabra from B.J. and set it up on the highest step. Then Veronica and I arranged the rest of the candles on the steps. When we finished, it looked so much like a shrine that it was creepy. A shiver ran across my back.

"This is just her kind of thing," Veronica whispered. "Oh, please, let her be out there."

Veronica and I started lighting the candles with long fireplace matches. B.J. came out carrying her iPod. She held up a hot pink iPod dock. "I found this in Fawn's room. Okay if I use it?"

Veronica looked up from lighting the last candle and nodded.

B.J. started scrolling through songs. "Ooh, ooh here it is. I knew I had it on here."

B.J. turned up the volume full blast, and the night filled with the sound of seagulls. A wooden flute chimed in, followed by a rich, acoustic guitar and a soothing voice singing about sand dunes and sea grass and foghorns in the distance. And a guardian angel giving a blind ship back its sight with a lighthouse that flashes 1–4–3.

We did our best to flash the numbers with our flashlights to the gentle beat of the song, over and over again. By the time David Ogden had finished singing his "1–4–3 (Lighthouse Song)" all the way through, Fawn had walked up to the edge of the yard and stood there hugging her mother's laptop to her like a blanket.

CHAPTER 31

"Faster," I screamed.

B.J. leaned forward over the steering wheel. Mustang Sally roared.

"Stop!" I yelled.

We slowed down.

"Don't listen to me," I shrieked.

We sped up again. My heart started to beat right out of my chest. The skin on my arms prickled and my hands started to swell. The baby elephant sat down and tried to squeeze the life out of me.

"I don't want to die," I whispered. My tongue stuck to the roof of my mouth on every syllable. "I don't want to die. I don't want to die."

"Knock it off with the death talk," B.J. said. "You're killing me. I've never even had an accident that was my fault."

"I don't want to miss the reunion, I don't want to miss the reunion, I don't want to miss the reunion," I whispered.

"That's the spirit."

I started tapping alternating feet as if the galloping sound might help get us there sooner. The rhythm was almost soothing.

"Hurry!" I yelled.

"If I go any faster, we're going to get stopped for speeding and then we really will miss the reunion."

I'd done my best to pretend I wasn't watching the clock in Veronica's kitchen while we waited around to make sure Fawn was okay. She was curled up on Veronica's lap sucking on a Popsicle while Veronica dabbed the mosquito bites on her back with ointment. They were angry and swollen, but they appeared to be her only physical damage.

Finally Veronica set us free. "Go," she'd said. "You still have time to make it."

"Are you sure?" B.J. and I both said at once. Neither of us took the time to say *jinx*.

Veronica blew us a kiss. "Love you both. Now get the hell out of here."

B.J. passed a sports car cruising up the highway in front of us. "Do you believe Fawn had that laptop with her the whole time? Veronica probably could have just emailed her. It's a whole new world, Louise."

"Shit, shit, shit," I said. "We are soooo going to miss the reunion."

B.J. took a long swig of her Tab. "We're not going to miss it. We're going to get there just in time to make an entrance. We'll be the hit of the party, Romy."

We passed an SUV and I closed my eyes so I wouldn't have to

look. Then I opened them again so I wouldn't have to die without any warning. My stomach growled, long and loud. I was gripping the sides of my seat as hard as I could, but I risked letting go long enough to take a quick sip of my Tab. "The food will be all gone, too. I knew we should have gotten two orders of french fries earlier."

"Think how flat our stomachs are going to be when we get there. It'll be like we went on the high school reunion diet after all. Just remember not to touch the Goldfish until we make sure they've finished all the dorky reunion games."

I didn't say anything. I just went back to tapping my feet. Maybe I could tap a hole right through the floor of the Mustang and jog us along a little faster, like the Flintstones used to do.

Flintstones made me remember B.J.'s and my fantasy about Finn Miller creating a daily vitamin that reverses gray hair. Which made me remember the sculpture I'd imagined he was going to commission me to make for his Maui estate. Did they have estates in Maui, or just big beach houses? I could always scale the size of the sculpture up or down accordingly.

"You know," B.J. said, interrupting my pipeless pipe dream, "even if we miss it, Fawn's okay and we were there for Veronica when she needed us. That's all that really matters."

"Yeah, right." I mean, easy for B.J. to be so generous. Her husband hadn't just pulled her life out from under her. I leaned over to turn up the music.

B.J. reached over and turned it down again. "You know, the whole time we were growing up, all I ever heard was how nice that Melanie was. Even my own mother would say, 'Why can't you be a good girl like Melanie?' I might not always show it, but at least I'm there when you need me."

It was a direct hit. B.J. didn't get mad often, but she had a knack for it when she did. I searched for a get-out-of-jail-free card.

"So, guess what? Finn Miller emailed me. And I emailed back. And well, we've emailed a few times."

"*What?* And you didn't tell me?" B.J. forgot all about the guilt trip she was laying on me and pressed down on the accelerator.

"Don't!" I yelled.

She slowed down.

"Don't!" I yelled again.

She sped up. "How could you not tell me that?"

"I don't know. I guess I didn't want to jinx it."

We pulled around another car and I tried not to scream. We stayed in the passing lane.

B.J. glanced over at me. "I guess I can understand that. Okay, so fill me in. You've Googled him and checked out his Facebook profile, right?"

"No."

"Are you kidding me? What kind of a crush is that?"

"Sorry. I'm a couple of decades out of practice."

"It'll come back. It's like being Nancy Drew, only without all the legwork. And with a red Mustang instead of a blue roadster. Come on, Facebook. Now."

I gripped my seat with one hand while I opened the Facebook app Troy had installed on my cell phone and tracked down Finn Miller.

"What's it say under relationship?" B.J. asked.

"Divorced."

"Good sign. See, you're compatible already. What does he look like?"

I squinted at my phone. "Little. And square."

B.J. shook her head. "Somebody needs to make bigger cell phone screens. You know, like those big phones with numbers that look like alphabet blocks."

I rummaged around unsuccessfully in the depths of my shoulder bag for my reading glasses.

B.J. shook her head. "Somebody also needs to make reading glasses that come when you call them. I think I left mine back at the hotel. Oh, well, we'll find out soon enough. Wow, Finn Miller—I'm trying to picture him from high school . . . Ooh, I know."

She leaned over and reached under my seat. The car swerved.

I screamed. "B.J., knock it off." My heart skipped a beat. I waited to see if I'd go into full-blown panic mode.

"Sorry. Listen, reach under your seat and see if you can find my yearbook."

"You brought your yearbook?" I fumbled under my seat carefully with one hand. And to think I'd been too embarrassed to pack mine. Maybe I should have brought my Spin-the-Bottle bottle for backup, too.

"Of course I brought my yearbook. I figured we could look at it right before we went in, so we'd have a better chance of recognizing people. Do you know that you can download age progression software now? I thought about uploading my senior picture to see if I turned out even better than I was supposed to."

After I finally managed to find the glasses and open the yearbook, I realized it was too dark in the car to see a thing. Life was just too damn complicated. "Hey, you don't happen to have a flashlight, do you?"

B.J. reached for the glove compartment. Mustang Sally swerved over the line and the SUV beside us leaned on the horn. B.J. gave it the finger.

"Please, B.J.," I whispered. I closed my eyes and tried to make my just-returned dry mouth go away.

B.J. handed me the flashlight. "Come on, start with Derrick Donohue."

"Derrick Donohue?"

"Remember? He's the one who's going to take one look at me and eat his heart out that he never gave me the time of day in high school when he still had a chance."

"Right. Okay, here he is. What do you want to know? And don't you dare take your eyes off the road."

"Do you think he was as cute as I think he was?"

"I guess he was pretty cute. In a bad-haircut kind of way. He looks a little bit out of it in this picture, though. And his yearbook quote is *Don't drink the bong water*."

"Hey, give him a break. It was a different time back then. Okay, find me."

I flipped through until I found B.J.'s picture. "You were gorgeous, Barb. That orange mock turtleneck was so becoming on you."

"I know, I know. And how about my quote: *Her eyelashes would sweep the cobwebs from any man's heart*."

"No wonder you got most conceited."

"Hey, I *resemble* that remark. What was your quote again?"

"I'm afraid to look."

"Do it."

I took a deep breath and finally faced my own picture. As

soon as I saw it—frizzy hair, bad eyebrows, tentative smile—all
the insecurity of the time came back as if it were yesterday. Or
even today.

B.J. turned her head.

"Keep your eyes on the road!"

"Relax. Come on, what does it say?"

"*You only live once, but if you do it right, once is enough.* Mae
West. Ugh. So much for yearbook quotes as prophecy."

"Hey, Thelma, chill, you've got plenty of time to get it right.
Okay, Finn Miller." B.J. put on her blinker, and I could actually
see the off-ramp up ahead. I hoped it wasn't a mirage.

I opened to Finn's page on the first try. Apparently practice really did make perfect. "*School's out,*" I read, as if I hadn't
already memorized it. "*Memories past. Don't ever doubt. The fun
will last.*"

"Not bad."

"Where did you say he lives now?"

B.J. reached for her Tab. "As I remember, he divides his time
between the Hamptons and the south of France."

"No, I think he'd need a ski house. And maybe an urban loft,
too."

B.J. sighed. "What if this was the movie of our lives and we
were just getting to the good part?"

"What would we call it?"

"Hmm, excellent question, Louise." B.J. pulled off the highway and took a right.

My breathing slowed down and the elephant climbed off my
chest. I twisted to the left to take the pressure off my real tattoo.

B.J. hit the steering wheel with the palm of one hand. "Oh, oh, I know. What about *B.J. and Melanie's Midlife Adventure?*"

"See, you always do that. Why can't it be *Melanie and B.J.'s Midlife Adventure?*"

"It's not about top billing, Mel. It just has a better ring to it that way, that's all."

I drained the rest of my Tab. I crunched the can with the heels of both hands and threw it over my shoulder. It made a pleasing metallic sound when it hit the others in the backseat.

We wove our way through the back roads to Marshbury, an occasional glimpse of the stars breaking through the tall trees. I tried to imagine this movie of my life having a happy ending.

I reached over and turned the music on again and hit SHUF- FLE. The first orchestral strains of "Nights in White Satin" filled the car. Maybe it was a good omen. Maybe it was just the luck of the shuffle. My heart filled with yearning anyway.

We circled the harbor and found the road that led to the reunion.

"Hey," B.J. said. "Remember how they always made one chaperone at each dance the designated tapper? Whoever it was had to walk around during the slow dances and tap you on the shoulder if any hands started to roam, or if you were getting 'too cozy,' and you'd have to separate."

"I kid you not," I said, "if you tap me on the shoulder while I'm dancing with Finn Miller, I will never, ever speak to you again."

CHAPTER 32

I grabbed my door handle.

"Wait. I just want to sit here for a second."

"Are you crazy? We've only got seventeen minutes left."

"Eighteen." B.J. sighed. "It's just that this has always been my favorite part. You know, right before you get somewhere, when it's all potential and the night can be anything. Derrick Donohue could be standing right by the front door hoping to catch a glimpse of me."

"And 'Nights in White Satin' could be playing and Finn Miller's eyes could light up the moment he sees me. Okay, time's up—let's *go*."

"How does my hair look?"

"Great," I said. I jumped out and gave my hair a quick fluff. I slid one side of my off-the-shoulder peasant blouse back down to where it was supposed to be. My white jeans had been whiter a few hours ago, but hopefully it would be dark enough inside that nobody would notice. We'd put our strappy sandals on in Veronica's driveway. I had to admit mine were a lot less comfortable than my flip-flops had been.

A middle-aged man wearing only a pair of striped boxer shorts ran out the front door of the marine center and streaked around the building. A crowd of middle-aged people holding drinks followed him. He climbed the steel cable railing, wobbled, then pounded his chest and let out a Tarzan yell before he flopped forward into the water.

It was enough to get B.J. out of the Mustang. "Who do you think *that* was?"

The spectators, most of them dressed, peered over the railing and cheered.

I shrugged. "I don't know. He just looked like somebody's father to me. Come on. I can't wait any longer. And I really need to find a bathroom."

"Fine. But before we go in I should probably give you a heads-up—"

A thunderous roar came from the deck, followed by a big splash.

"B.J., I mean it. Hurry. We're down to fourteen minutes."

The first thing I saw was my trio of box spring ladies. They were perched side by side in a softly lit niche set into the wall on one side of the huge beach stone fireplace. Their metal hoop skirts sparkled like jewels. The petunias in the hat of the first box spring lady were still perky, and her parasol was tilted like she was shading them from the sun. The second box spring lady held her parasol out in front of her like a weapon, as though she were protecting her friends. The boat propeller hat tied under the chin of the third lady gave her just the right nautical touch, as if I'd somehow known all along that she'd end up on display by the side of the sea.

A long rectangular table blocked our entrance. Two women with freshly frosted hair and no-nonsense looks on their faces sat behind it like bouncers. There was a sign on one side of the table that said A–L, and on the other, one that said M–Z. There were exactly two name tags left on the beachy blue tablecloth.

"It's about time, Barb," one of the women said to B.J. "You know you were supposed to be here at six thirty sharp to get ready for the committee receiving line."

B.J. pretended to stick her index finger down her throat and kept walking.

The other woman stood up to block her. "Wait," she said, "you forgot your name tag. We made special ones for the committee members." She pointed to her own tag, which said ALICE ADAMS WARRICK! in royal blue Sharpie next to a black-and-white copy of her yearbook picture. "See, we get little gold stars next to our names . . ."

B.J. rolled her eyes. "Adorable. But I don't need a name tag. Everyone will know who I am. And if not, oh, well, their loss."

ALICE ADAMS WARRICK! crossed her arms over her chest. "I can't let you in without one, Barb. You were at the meeting when we voted on it."

"Fine," B.J. said. She grabbed her name tag, peeled off the back, and stuck it onto her forehead upside down.

The first woman shrugged. She took a sip of her drink and then handed me my name tag. "Hi, Melanie," she said. She pointed to her own name tag, where her senior picture showed a person from an entirely different lifetime. "Bev Braxton. I know, you never would have recognized me. Sorry to hear about you and Kurt." She lowered her voice. "You were always too good for him."

B.J. grabbed me by the arm and yanked. She peeled her name tag off her forehead as we worked our way through the crowd.

Off to our right, a guy in a suit was leaning over a table dipping a shrimp into some cocktail sauce. B.J. tiptoed over and pressed her name tag to his butt.

He turned around and smiled boozily at her.

"Oops," she said. "Thought you were someone else." She reached past him for a shrimp.

"Classy," I said. We worked our way through the crowded room. B.J. stopped to talk to someone and I kept going, on a mission to find the restroom. As much as I couldn't wait to get here, now I couldn't shake the feeling that I didn't belong, that I was impersonating someone who had gone to high school with all these strangers.

B.J. caught up to me. "Should I Stay or Should I Go" blasted out at a deafening volume, heavy on the bass, from two enormous speakers that seemed to have weathered as many decades as the people in the room.

"What?" B.J. yelled. "Are you kidding me? This isn't one of our high school songs. I was practically a *homeowner* when this song came out."

"So?" I yelled. "It's a good song."

"Some idiot on the committee had the crazy idea that if they played the music that came after us, it would make us feel younger, but I know we voted it down. Wait till I get my hands on that music subcommittee."

B.J. stomped off into the crowd. I found the door to the restroom and pushed it open.

I took my place behind five or six women already in line. Two other women looked up from the sinks. "Melanieeeee," one of them screamed.

"Hiii," I said as I tried frantically to remember her name. I knew it began with a *J*, but was it Janie or Jeannie. Janet? I squinted at her nametag, trying to decipher it. Wouldn't you think they could have at least made the font a little bigger?

"Kitteeee," she said. She shook her hands dry as she lurched over to give me a hug.

"Ouch," I said.

"Are you okaaaay?" she said. Her breath was strong and retro. Kahlúa Sombrero? White Russian?

"Fine," I said. "Nice to see you again." A stall opened and someone else I didn't recognize emerged. The line inched forward.

Kitty Kahlúa Breath stepped behind me. "Ohmigod," she screamed. "Ohmigod, ohmigod, ohmigod. Did Kurt do that to you?"

The line disbanded and re-formed behind my back. I thought about making a run for it, but my Tab-filled bladder wouldn't let me.

A gasp filled the air.

"Relax," I said. "It's just purple marker." I heard another gasp. "Really. Skin Skribe surgical marker."

"You were always too good for Kurt," somebody behind me said.

I peed as quickly as I could and managed to escape the restroom. B.J. was nowhere in sight, so I decided my game plan would be to cover every square inch of the room to make it easy for Finn to find me. Casually, so it wouldn't look like I was trying too hard to be found.

The Beastie Boys were singing "Fight for Your Right to Party." The après-swim crowd was just coming in, carrying their clothes and dripping water everywhere. The guy in his boxer shorts gave another Tarzan yell. He ran over and pretended to belly-flop on one of the tables.

"Pig pile," somebody bellowed.

CHAPTER 33

Blue and white crepe-paper streamers zigzagged overhead. Bouquets of Best Class Evah helium balloons rose from flowerpots on each table. A few balloons had managed to break free and slip past the crepe paper to roll around on the wooden ceiling.

My stomach growled again. I grabbed a handful of Goldfish from a fish-shaped dish on a table and ate them fast, before anyone could tell me not to.

Mobiles made from actual vinyl record albums dangled from the ceiling around the DJ station on one side of the room. On the other side, big rectangles of fluorescent yellow and green poster board, already starting to curl at the edges from the seaside humidity, decorated the wall behind the bar with retro drink recipes written in huge, Boomer-friendly letters.

TEQUILA SUNRISE

2 oz. tequila

4 oz. orange juice

¾ oz. grenadine syrup

Pour tequila and orange juice over ice in tall glass and stir.
Tilt glass and pour grenadine down side. It will go straight
to the bottom and rise up through the drink like a sunrise.
Garnish with maraschino cherry and orange slice.

LONG SLOW COMFORTABLE SCREW
UP AGAINST THE WALL

1 oz. sloe gin

1 oz. vodka

1 oz. Southern Comfort

1 oz. Galliano

orange juice

Mix all ingredients in tall glass filled with ice. Find a wall.

SEX ON THE BEACH

1 ½ oz. vodka

1 ½ oz. peach schnapps

2 oz. cranberry juice

2 oz. orange juice

Mix all ingredients in tall glass filled with ice. Find a beach.

I walked the outskirts of the room counterclockwise, hoping I'd recognize Finn if I saw him. Maybe casually waiting for him to find me wasn't the way to go after all. Would it be totally embarrassing to have him paged?

Madonna's voice joined the party with a rousing rendition of "Vogue." The dance floor filled with people who were old enough to know better. The boxer short brigade had decided to air-dry and piled their clothes on an empty chair. They surged onto the dance floor en masse, and the dry people gave them their space. One of the swimmers was wearing only her very nice animal print bra and underpants set with strands of blue and white crepe paper knotted around her waist like a beach wrap. She looked amazingly good for our age. I wondered whether she'd had a pre-reunion tune-up.

I watched as the sea of dancers framed their aging faces and threw their hands behind their balding heads, remembering that short window of time when the whole world was striking poses and vogue-ing it all day long. It was definitely post-high-school, probably post-college, too, and that realization made me feel not younger, the way the music subcommittee intended, but practically ancient. Like so much of life, "Vogue" had passed me right by. Was I married already? Had Trevor and Troy been born yet? What was I *doing* when I could have been vogue-ing away?

A group of women were dancing together in a circle near the edge of the dance floor, flipping their expensive hair and flashing their freshly painted nails as they vogued. One of them caught my eye and motioned for me to join them. I smiled and backed away.

I turned and started walking in the other direction, narrowing my circles to make sure I'd casually covered every square inch where Finn could be waiting. I had a horrible feeling I'd eventually end up in the exact center of the room, twirling in a circle like the cheese who stands alone in "The Farmer in the Dell."

Even with all the windows open and big ceiling fans circling frantically, I was starting to sweat. I worked my way up to the bar. First I'd have some water. Then I'd get a drink before it was too late. Would Sex on the Beach be too obvious? Finn would find me sitting at the bar and ask me what I was drinking. I'd look at him and smile and tell him to ask the bartender.

Years from now, he'd still be telling the story. *So there I was, looking for the love of my life everywhere, and I finally find her up at the bar. And what do you think she's drinking? So what could we do— we headed for the beach and stayed there till the sun came up.*

Of course, we wouldn't really have had actual sex on the beach. You had to be young and foolish to put up with all that sand, not to mention the fact that you'd be lucky to get a blanket, let alone a sexy top sheet to drape strategically over the body parts that had started to show some wear and tear. But we'd have sat on the beach and talked about old times, and planned some new ones, and kissed the night away.

Halfway to the bar, I spotted a woman I was pretty sure had been in Finn's and my Algebra class. She still wore her hair long and parted in the middle. I wove my way over to her.

I squinted at her name tag. "You look great, Carrie," I said.

"Connie." She squinted at mine. "You, too, Melody," she said.

"Hey, you haven't seen Finn Miller, have you? There's a quadratic equation I need to ask him about."

"Let's Dance" blasted out, burying her answer.

"What?" I yelled.

"Gone," she yelled.

I made a final loop of the room, mortified to realize I was fighting back tears like a lovesick teenager. I heard B.J. yell my name from across the room somewhere, but I ignored her.

Finn Miller was gone. GONE. We'd passed each other like ships in the night, and now he was probably back in his hotel room, wondering how I could have done this to him. How I could have broken his heart twice in one lifetime.

The bar area was packed, no surprise, but there was a vacant chair down toward one end. I worked my way over, saying excuse me again and again. Finally, I wiggled my way up to the empty space.

David Bowie finished singing and the room burst into applause.

The bartender put a cocktail napkin in front of me. "Last call," she said.

I looked at the clock on the wall behind her. In three minutes, I'd turn into a pumpkin to match the one on my back. I'd return to my hotel room and sit out on the pathetic little balcony and pout until the sun came up.

"I'll have a Long Slow Comfortable Screw Up Against the Wall," I said. "Or a Sex on the Beach. Whichever is better. You decide."

The bartender grinned. "I've had pretty good luck with both of them."

"Surprise me."

She walked away. I tapped the guy sitting next to the empty chair on the shoulder. "Is this seat taken?" I yelled.

Kurt turned around and looked me right in the eyes.

CHAPTER 34

Kurt and I went out in high school for about five minutes. We had a study hall together senior year, both cut off from the friends we usually traveled in a pack with by the randomness of scheduling. The holiday break had come and gone, and snow covered everything like a big white cocoon. College essays were in, and there was nothing to do but wait, and try not to let our grades slip too much in the final stretch before freedom.

"We have to make every single second count," B.J. would say at least twice a day. She alternated this with "I am counting the seconds till we leave this hellhole behind." Three can be a dangerous number for friendships, but for B.J., Veronica, and me, it worked. We were the kind of girls who only had boyfriends once in a while, and rarely at the same time. So the other two held the fort while one of us, usually B.J., was off dating.

My turn had come and gone junior year, and my lack of dating since then felt like a drought that might never end. "Don't sweat it, Mel," B.J. said, after three seniors in a row I had crushes on went off to date cute, perky sophomores. "It's just that guys our age are actually three years younger in maturity. Developmentally, they have nothing to offer us. College is where it will all be happening."

And then, after all that math, Finn Miller finally asked me out. He carried my books to my classes. He called me every night. He took me out on actual dates, to the movies, even to a concert.

"It's just," I said to B.J. and Veronica, "he kind of gets on my nerves."

"I think he's cute," Veronica said as she flipped through the latest issue of *Rolling Stone*.

"So give him to Veronica," B.J. said.

"I meant Art Garfunkel," Veronica said.

B.J. held her place in her magazine with an index finger and slid over to get a look. "Get real," she said. "His hair is way too frizzy."

When I got up to sharpen a pencil in study hall one day, I could feel Kurt watching me walk across the room. I held in my stomach and was glad I'd worn my good dungarees that day, the ones with bell-bottoms so wide they almost looked like a skirt. I even had on my favorite turtleneck bodysuit that snapped at the crotch. I had to sit just right for it to be comfortable, but it was worth every pinch for the long sleek line it gave me.

I took a roundabout way back to my seat, and when I passed Kurt's chair I could feel the force field between us. I'd chosen this route so I could happen to look at him and smile, but I chickened out at the last minute.

We ignored each other for another week or two.

"I don't like him," B.J. said. "He thinks he's way too cool for school. *And* he has a girlfriend."

"Uh-uh," Veronica said. "They broke up. She's in my French class."

"What's she like?" I asked.

"You're much prettier," Veronica said, because she knew this was what I was really asking. "I think *she* dumped *him*. For one of her older brother's friends."

That weekend I called Finn and told him I needed to spend some time with my friends. The three of us tracked Kurt down at a party. It wasn't that hard. The town was small, and only a limited number of parental units went away and left their high school seniors in charge of the house on any given weekend. Like maybe one. If we were lucky.

By this point in our senior year, you could feel the hard edges of the high school cliques softening, an early warning flash of the nostalgia to come. The freaks and the jocks and the band geeks could all coexist at the same party, as long as the music was loud.

We worked our way through the grass-filled haze, stopping to join a circle of kids passing a joint around long enough to take a toke to show how cool we were. Someone handed me a bottle of Boone's Farm Apple Wine, and I wiped the top of it with my hand before I took a sip.

B.J. was the first to spot Kurt. "The eagle has landed," she whispered. He was standing off by himself, lighting his cigarette with his hands cupped around a Zippo lighter like the Marlboro Man. Once he got the cigarette going, he took a long drag in and blew it out expertly, managing to bounce his head more or less to the beat of Aerosmith's "Dream On" at the same time.

As I watched him from across the room, my crush grew to epic proportions. "What a stone fox," I whispered.

"A total stud muffin," Veronica said.

"Far freakin' out," B.J. added as the grass kicked in.

We giggled our way across the room. We stopped when we got to Kurt, and I waited to see what would happen next.

A record scratched on a turntable somewhere and Alice Cooper broke into "School's Out."

"Wicked pissa song," Kurt said.

There was nothing all that funny about it, since pretty much everybody in Marshbury talked that way, but that didn't stop us. We dissolved into fits of laughter.

B.J. pushed me into Kurt. By the time "School's Out" was over, B.J. and Veronica had disappeared. Kurt and I looked at each other. He held his cigarette off to one side and we started making out.

When I looked up, Finn was standing across the room, looking like a puppy that had just been kicked.

By Monday, Kurt and I were a couple. We sat together in study hall, doodling on each other's book covers, our thighs pressed together, our dungaree-clad ankles intertwined under the long cafeteria table. The next weekend we skipped the party and went straight to the beach parking lot and watched Minot's Light blink 1–4–3 for "I love you."

"You know what that means, don't you?" he said.

I nodded, speechless, one part of my brain hovering over us, planning the way I was going to tell this to B.J. and Veronica later. *And so then we looked through the windshield and he said . . .*

With the motor running to keep us from frostbite, we climbed into the backseat of his parents' station wagon with a blanket that just happened to be there. We split a beer Kurt had stolen from his father's stash, and then we had sex. After that we drew pictures in the fogged-up windows and then he took me home.

By the following Monday he was back with his ex-girlfriend. Veronica found out before I did, in their French class. By last period, it was all over school.

He never broke up with me. We just started ignoring each other in study hall, and everywhere else our paths happened to cross. Finn and I also ignored each other. All this ignoring was exhausting, but I limped my way through the rest of senior year and then we graduated.

Eventually Kurt apologized. It was summertime and we'd both just finished two years of college in different states. I'd gone to the beach with B.J. and Veronica, because we'd all finally managed to get the same day off from our summer waitressing jobs. I walked up to buy us Popsicles from Seaside Market and saw him standing there.

I slowed my pace to give him a chance to pretend he didn't see me. Instead he waited just outside the door.

"I was a total jerk," he said, as if it had happened just last week and not two and a half years before. "You were too good for me."

"This is true," I said. I tossed my hair back and then adjusted the Celestial Wheel Signs zodiac beach towel I'd wrapped around my wet two-piece bathing suit.

He watched my every move.

I smiled sweetly. "But you did me a favor. You helped me appreciate my next boyfriend when I met him."

When I pushed past him to go into the store, sparks flew between us like fireworks.

"Catch you later," he said. I ignored him.

I let him chase me for the rest of the summer.

And then for decades I never let him go.

CHAPTER 35

The music had stopped, but the roar of conversation and laughter rose up to fill the silence.

Kurt took a long drink of his scotch on the rocks.

I put my purse down on the bar. The bartender came over with my drink.

"Last call," she said to Kurt.

"I'll have another one. Why don't you make that a double. And whatever she wants."

The bartender looked at me.

"Whatever you got me before, get me the other one," I said. "Please."

She shrugged and walked away.

"It's not my fault," Kurt said.

"It never is," I said.

"I tried to call you repeatedly. If I'd known you were coming, then I wouldn't have. Obviously."

"You canceled my credit card."

"Only to get you to take your head out of the clouds. You can't keep pretending none of this is happening, Melanie."

I picked up my drink and considered pouring it over his head. I decided I needed it more.

I took a long gulp. "My head is not in the clouds, *Kurt.* But yours, by the way, is up your— Oh, never mind. What are you even doing here? How many times did I try to get you to come to one of our reunions? You didn't want any part of them." It had never once occurred to me that he'd actually come to this one.

Kurt began tearing his cocktail napkin into long even strips. In the scheme of his annoying habits, this one barely registered, and it almost made me feel nostalgic.

He saw me watching him and stopped.

"Knock yourself out," I said. "I don't have to clean it up anymore."

He laughed. "Like you ever did."

"Hey, it was your mess."

He drained the rest of his scotch. I resisted a knee-jerk urge to ask him how many he'd had. Kurt was a creature of habit and control—a drink or two and then he'd stop. Rarely did he venture into third-drink zone, and when he did the results were unpredictable. But this was not my problem anymore. He could drink himself into oblivion for all I cared.

In the dim light, his eyes were barely blue. The lines around them were deeper than I remembered, and he was wearing a soft summer-weight buttondown shirt I'd bought for him last year.

Part of me was oddly touched and another part of me wanted to say *How dare you?*

He shrugged. "So, I guess we won't get the award for the couple who lasted the longest, huh?"

I bit my tongue so I wouldn't say *Whose fault is that?*

I shrugged. "I guess not."

He tilted his empty glass back to get the mostly melted ice cubes, then picked up his new drink. The couple seated beside us turned to stare.

"So," I said. "Why didn't you bring her?"

He looked straight ahead. "I did."

I tried not to react, but it hurt so much it was embarrassing. Or maybe it was so embarrassing it actually hurt.

I started to push myself off the bar stool, just so I wouldn't have to do it in front of her when she came back from the bathroom, or wherever she was.

"She's gone," he said.

"Gone-gone?" I heard myself say. Like maybe she'd only been a hallucination.

"She took the rental car and went back to the hotel. Apparently someone in the ladies' room told her she wasn't welcome here. And then somebody else told her to get away from me while she still could, and something about she should see what I did to my wife."

I slid the ruffle on my fake tattoo side up over my shoulder. "And you didn't go with her?"

"We've been fighting since we got here." Kurt sighed. "I don't know what's going on. She used to be so much fun."

"Don't," I said. "I don't want to hear—"

B.J. poked her head between us. "Hey, Kurt. News flash: Mel's not your dating coach."

Kurt and B.J. stared at each other.

"B.J.," Kurt finally said. "Nice to see you. Is Tom here?"

"He's home where he belongs." B.J. picked up one of my drinks. She threw her purse on top of mine on the bar. "Keep an eye on these—we'll be right back."

She gave Kurt her most dazzling smile. "Touch my credit cards and I'll cut your balls off."

I followed B.J. out to the parking lot. "I really think the balls part was unnecessary," I said. "And now Kurt will know I've been talking about him."

"Of course you've been talking about him. I'm your best friend."

"He brought her with him. *Crissy*."

B.J. stopped walking. "I know. I found out when I brought the box spring ladies in today. It must have been a last-minute thing. His name was definitely not on the list the last time I saw it."

I crossed my arms over my chest. "And you didn't tell me?"

B.J. put one hand on her hip. "It was a tough call. I didn't want you to get all worked up about it. So I figured I'd tell you just before we went in, but by then you were all about the bathroom."

"It's just such an invasion. But there's also this part of me that really wanted to check her—*Crissy*—out. Did you see her?"

B.J. shook her head. "Nope, but I heard from several reliable sources that she's a huge step down from you. Oh, and everybody loves your new haircut."

I smiled. "You're a good friend, Louise. But if one more person tells me I was always too good for Kurt . . ."

"I think you're the only one left who still has to believe it, Romy."

I pointed to where my fake tattoo was hiding under my ruffle. "Everybody thinks he gave me this."

B.J. grinned. "I know. And I'm proud to say I started that rumor." She reached for my ruffle. "Here, get that down over your shoulder. No offense, but it makes you look a little bit matronly like that."

"Thanks," I said. "I needed that right about now. And I bet you only started that rumor because you knew the fake tattoo you drew couldn't even pass for a purple pumpkin. Your only hope was a serious bruise."

"Hey, watch it. That's my artistic self-esteem you're shattering."

"I just don't want you to get all conceited."

"Ha. Too late for that."

"Can I ask you a question?"

"Sure."

"Why are we standing out here in the parking lot?"

"Oh, shit. Come on. I finally tracked down the music sub-committee and told them the eighties called and wants its bad music back. I think we might still have time to get one good song in."

B.J. unlocked Mustang Sally and reached in for her iPod. I put my drink on the hood, opened the other door, and found my flip-flops.

"*What* do you think you're doing?" B.J. said. "Oh, never mind. My feet are freakin' killing me."

After we'd both taken off our strappy sandals as fast as we could and slid into our flip-flops, B.J. locked up again and took a quick sip of my drink. "Wow, I haven't had Sex on the Beach in forever. So get this, Derrick Donohue has a new wife who looks about twelve and has breast implants. So much for eating his heart out."

I looked up at the stars sparkling over the water and wiggled my toes in the cool night air. "Finn Miller didn't even wait for me." I took a slug of my Long Slow Comfortable Screw Up Against the Wall. "Bummer."

"Okay, here's my plan," B.J. said as we headed for the front door of the Marine Center. "I think we should go get the rest of the Tab and set up a little stand to catch people on their way out. We'll say it's vintage Tab and charge twenty bucks a pop for it. Your money issues will be over in no time."

"Let's not and say we did," I said.

"Aww, I totally forgot about that expression."

"Maybe we should rent out cots and sleeping bags instead. I'm worried about some of these people driving home. Actually most of them. They definitely shouldn't be on the road, that's for sure."

"Don't worry, we have a designated driver subcommittee. They've been going around collecting car keys. Mostly everyone is staying at the same hotel anyway, so they'll just herd them over there like cattle. And five years from now their hangovers will be a distant memory and they can do it all over again."

"Wow, even though this night still sucks, I have to say, that reunion committee of yours is amazingly thorough."

"The thing about committees is that you can't live without them, but they're so anal you can't stand being around them. Never again, Thelma, never again. And if I forget, don't forget to remind me in five years, okay?"

A really bad and extremely loud version of the Macarena greeted us at the door.

B.J. shook her head. "Oh, no, it's come to this. We'd better get my iPod in there fast. This simply cannot be the last song of the night."

My breath caught. In front of the fireplace, three members of the boxer shorts brigade were doing the Macarena with the box spring ladies balanced on top of their heads. It was like a clash of cultures—boxer shorts below, hoop skirts and parasols above. Too late, I wanted to cover the eyes of my beautiful box spring ladies so their sensibilities wouldn't be offended.

"And we thought someone we graduated with might have money *and* class," B.J. said. "Apparently it was too much to expect."

I put up my hand like a crossing guard. "Stop," I yelled. "Right this minute."

The boxer shorts brigade kept dancing.

I turned to B.J. "Hurry. Stop the music. You know drunks can never resist the Macarena."

I tried to assess the damage. So far all three ladies looked okay, at least physically. Not for the first time I was glad I worked in metal and not glass.

My hand was still out in front of me. "Stop," I said again in my best mom-voice.

They kept dancing.

"Freeze," I yelled.

They all froze. The three guys in their boxer shorts wobbled a bit. They looked like midlife Weebles, those egg-shaped toys from our childhood. *Weebles wobble but they don't fall down* popped into my head randomly.

Their audience froze, too, and I noticed the classmate wearing her underwear now had a man's T-shirt over it. Her blue and white streamers had come untied and stuck to her legs like strands of seaweed. When she froze she held one leg out to the side with her toe pointed.

She put her hand up. "Mother, may I—"

"No, you may not," I said.

CHAPTER 36

When we got back inside the reunion after locking the box spring ladies safely in Mustang Sally's backseat, Marvin Gaye was crooning a low and sexy "Let's Get It On."

"My work here is done," B.J. said. She took a moment to close her eyes and sway to the music.

The lights came on and everybody started groaning and covering their faces. Several committee members began walking around the room with trays of hot coffee. Another circulated a towering plate of what looked like Famous Amos chocolate chip cookies, and still another a big heaping tray of brownies. "Let's just hope somebody had the good sense to add aspirin and flaxseed to those brownies," B.J. said. "Hey, look. Do you see Jan and her mother-in-law over there in the corner?"

I followed her gaze to a group of classmates sitting at a big round table playing Monopoly. Jan's mother-in-law threw the dice and everybody cheered. We waved and Jan waved back.

When we reached the bar, my purse was open and Kurt was talking on my cell phone.

I blinked my eyes and squinted to be sure it was mine. My first thought was that it might be Trevor or Troy, and maybe I should be glad one of them was talking to his father. But my second thought was that Kurt wouldn't have known that until he reached into my purse and looked at my phone.

"How dare you," I said.

Perhaps a little too loudly. It might have been my imagination, but it felt like the whole room stopped talking and turned to us, like that old *When E. F. Hutton talks, people listen!* commercial. The refreshments subcommittee member carrying the Famous Amos cookies stopped in her tracks next to us. The people on the bar stools on either side of Kurt turned around and reached for a cookie as if they were grabbing a handful of popcorn to go with their movie.

Kurt held up one finger, telling me to wait a minute. I could tell by the red, white, and blue of his patriotic eyes that a double scotch had been consumed since B.J. and I had left him in charge of our purses.

"Nah, really," he said. "Hang on, she's back now. What? Sorry I'm talking so loud—Mel and I are at our high school reunion and, well, things are a little bit wild around here. And cell service near the beach, what can I say, it sucks big-time. Didja know we were high school sweethearts, Mel and me?"

Even in his inebriated state, Kurt must have seen my jaw drop. "Well, briefly," he added. "Long story short—"

I lunged for my phone.

Kurt twisted his bar stool away. "—but at least I smartened up in college. You know how it goes, young and foolish and all that razzmatazz. What did you say your name was again, pal?"

I lunged for my phone again.

Kurt twisted his bar stool the other way. "Hey, wait just a minute, hon. I'm talking to my pal Tom Brady here. What? Sorry, Brody. Tim Brody."

"Give me that phone right this instant," I yelled with every bit of rage that had accumulated over the long tenure of our marriage. I grabbed Kurt by the shirt I'd bought him last summer and turned him around to face me.

Kurt looked at me with boozy shock, as if I'd just morphed into someone else right before his blurry eyes.

I managed to get one hand around my phone. Then I pulled as hard as I could.

Kurt let go at the same time.

I slid backward across the wood floor, practically moonwalking for the first time in my life. Somebody screamed.

Somebody else must have put out his hands to stop me. When I felt large palms connect with my healing tattoo, I screamed.

"Oww," I yelled. "Oww, oww, oww."

"Melanieeee," Kitty Kahlúa Breath yelled. "Are you all riiiiight?"

Finn Miller appeared out of nowhere and put his hands on my shoulders.

"Ouch," I said again. It takes a fresh tattoo to find out the world is full of shoulder-touchers.

"I'll. Kill. Him," my former math crush said. He turned and swaggered in Kurt's direction like a gunslinger in an old Western.

Kurt tilted his head as Finn approached. "Hey, buddy. How's it goin'? History class, right? Junior year? Third period? Or was it four—"

Finn grabbed two handfuls of Kurt's shirt. "Don't you evah," he said, "touch my Melanie again."

Kurt slid off the bar stool and managed to plant both feet on the floor. He pushed Finn's hands away. The two of them wobbled a bit, then came back to center.

"Don't you evah," Kurt said, "call her your Melanie again."

B.J. sidled up to me. "So, is this the most fun you've had in decades or what?"

I ignored her and put my phone to my ear. "Hello," I said. "This is Melanie."

"Listen," Ted Brody said. "I don't know what's going on between you and your husband, but I completely misunderstood the situation."

Finn swung at Kurt, a big right hook that went wide.

The drunken crowd let out a cheer.

"There is no situation," I yelled.

"I just had a minute to breathe before we closed up for the night . . ."

Kurt swung at Finn. Finn stepped back and Kurt's fist sailed right past him.

The crowd roared.

"Cheater," Kurt said. "Cheater, cheater, pumpkin eater."

"Look who's talking, you cheese weasel," Finn said. He closed one eye and tried to line up his next punch. "Cheater, cheater, wife beater."

Ted Brody was still talking in my ear. ". . . high school reunions can be. So I just thought I'd leave you a message to call me if you felt like it. But again, clearly I mis . . ."

Kurt decided not to wait his turn. He pulled his fist back, too.

My former current crush and my almost former husband let their punches go at once.

Their fists cruised past each other but their arms somehow managed to link at the elbows. Finn's must have had more heft behind it, because they circled around in his direction.

"Hi-ho, the derrrrryyyy-oooohhhh," Kitty Kahlúa Breath sang.

Jan's mother-in-law stood up at her table and raised her cane. "Who's thieving bastard children are you?" she yelled.

Kurt and Finn were laughing now, do-si-do-ing in one direction and then the other, an aging flashback to our square dance unit in senior gym class.

Now that my sons no longer seemed to be in danger of becoming fatherless, I turned away to find a quieter place to talk.

"Let me explain," I said as I took a step toward the door.

But Ted Brody was gone.

Somebody I didn't remember pointed at me and whispered something to her friend.

"Take a picture, it lasts longer," B.J. yelled.

"Ooh, I almost forgot about Facebook," somebody else said. Cell phone cameras began to flash at an alarming rate.

B.J. grabbed my arm and pulled. "Come on, let's get out of here. Once the lights come on it never gets any prettier."

"Don't forget you're on the cleanup subcommittee, Barb," ALICE ADAMS WARRICK! said as we passed her.

"Clean this," B.J. said.

"Giving her the finger when you said that was completely unnecessary," I said as we pushed the double doors open. "A simple wave would have been sufficient."

The first heartbreaking strains of "Nights in White Satin" followed us out of the building.

CHAPTER 37

B.J. and I were back in our white bathrobes, sitting out on our pathetic little balcony with our flip-flop-clad feet up on the railing.

B.J. had grabbed a bowl of Goldfish when she ran back into the Marshbury Marine Center for her iPod. We both reached for a handful at the same time.

"Jinx," we said.

"Stealing is so tacky," I added after I finished chewing.

"Fine, so don't eat any. And I didn't steal it. It was a five-finger discount."

I reached for some more. "What I'd really like to know," I said, "is who stole my Long Slow Comfortable Screw Up Against the Wall while we were carrying the box spring ladies out to the car. I only got about three sips."

B.J. swallowed a mouthful of Goldfish. "My Sex on the Beach disappeared, too."

"Ha. Well, *my* sex on the beach sure disappeared. Along with my chances for sex in a bed or anywhere else for the rest of my natural life."

B.J. swung her legs off the railing and disappeared into our room.

She came back and handed me a plastic bathroom cup filled with wine. "I just remembered we still had some slow comfortable screw-top wine left."

"Perfect." I held up my cup. "To a really crappy night."

B.J. tapped hers to mine. "An evening that starts with seagull poop rarely ends well."

We sat there silently for a few moments. A sea breeze was keeping the mosquitoes away, and it was nice to smell the salt air again.

B.J. sighed. "I spent most of my eighteen minutes wandering around feeling like I was still sixteen and possibly not quite as cool as I hoped I was. And worried about whether someone would ask me to the prom."

"I felt the same way."

"And when I finally got through that ridiculously long line and into the ladies' room, I looked in the mirror. And I was stunned. Stunned. I mean, how the hell did we get to be so old, Romy?"

"Speak for yourself." I yawned. "I wonder who won the awards."

B.J. yawned, too. "Let's see. I think Kurt won for the most sensitivity-impaired husband."

"Almost former husband," I said.

"It was a combined category."

"That makes sense. One so often leads to the other, I would imagine."

"Did you notice he couldn't take his eyes off you tonight?"

"Kurt? Then he must have been seeing two of me. Boyohboy, I haven't seen him that drunk since the last time the Red Sox won the World Series."

"My point is that I don't think it's going to last between him and what's her name. Prissy."

"*Crissy.* But I think I like Prissy better. Maybe we can get her to change it."

"Do you think you'd give it another try? You know, if Kurt dumps her and says he wants to?"

I sighed. "You know, it was the weirdest thing tonight. I kept looking at Kurt and thinking *You stole my life. And I let you.*"

"So that would be a no."

"I don't think I would have had the guts to have done it myself, but I can almost imagine someday in the not-so-distant future being really glad he left me."

"That's good. Wait a minute. You know when Kurt answered your phone and you went ballistic?"

"Don't remind me. I still can't believe he did that."

"It was probably just force of habit."

"More like force of scotch. I don't think he ever once answered my phone when we were together."

B.J. took a sip of her wine and recrossed her ankles on the railing. "So, who was it?"

"Who was what?" I tried.

"Come on, Louise, spill it."

I was too tired to make something up. "His name is Ted Brody and he bought one of my pieces for his restaurant court-yard in Atlanta. And then he had some problems with it so I went to his restaurant and fixed it for him."

"And?"

"And then he called to talk about me making some firefly lights for the courtyard."

"Right, he picked up his phone after last call on a Saturday night to ask you about firefly lights."

"No, that was a different call. And he owns a restaurant, so he works late."

"How old is he? What does he look like? What kind of rat-ings does his restaurant have?"

"What kind of ratings does his restaurant have?"

"It's secondary to the first two, but it's still an important question."

"Of course it is. You can tell a lot about a man by his restau-rant ratings."

"You most certainly can." B.J. poured the rest of the wine into our cups. "Think about it. If the service is slow and there are spots on the silverware, and heaven forbid there's a fly in your soup, it has to say something about his slovenly personality. And if the food is average and unimaginative, you've gotta figure that's going to carry over into the bedroom, Romy."

"The slow service might factor in, too," I said.

"Exactly."

"You're certifiable."

"You just hate it when I'm right. Okay, how old is he and what does he look like?"

I thought about it. "He's about our age, I think, though how can you even tell anymore?"

"It's simple. If he says 'no problem' instead of 'you're welcome,' that's a dead giveaway that he's too young for you."

"Ha, and if he reads you the obituaries out loud, and starts every sentence with 'Nowadays,' you know he's too old for you."

B.J. yawned. "Or he keeps telling you what he had for dinner last night. And then repeating it ten minutes later."

I yawned, too. "Well, we might have to cut him some slack on that, since he owns a restaurant."

"Fine. But just the first part. I'm going to have to insist that the repeating part is a deal-breaker. Okay, up next: looks."

"He's good-looking, I guess. He has a nice smile."

"Married or single?"

"Divorced."

"And you're not having sex on the beach with him yet because?"

I swung my legs off the railing. "Back off, B.J., okay? I don't even know him. Okay, let's see, where were we? Awards. Kitty What's Her Name got the award for strongest Kahlúa breath."

"Ha. Did you see those cheerleaders knocking back all those Tequila Sunrises? Okay, and Finn Miller won for drunkest and for carrying a torch the longest. And worst right hook. I have to say, he really didn't live up to his profile. No offense. But maybe he'll show better once he sobers up."

"I'm not holding my breath."

We heard splashing and the distant roar of drunken laughter.

"Hubba Bubba called tonight," B.J. said.

"Looking for the mustard?"

"Funny. He said he missed me and wished he had come to the reunion. And the weird thing is I kind of felt that way, too. Though I think reunions are one of those grass-is-always-greener situations. If he'd come with me, he would have spent the whole time checking his watch and I would have spent the whole time wishing I'd left him at home with the ketchup."

"The worst thing about tonight," I said, "was that I was so sure it would help me figure out who I'm supposed to be now that Kurt's gone. But nothing. No sign, no hint, no clue."

B.J. crunched her empty plastic cup in one hand. "Just because Kurt changed doesn't mean you have to become another person, Mel. If anything, I think it might mean you get to go back to being who you really were all along."

CHAPTER 38

I hadn't realized just how many hopes I'd pinned on the reunion until the bubble burst. It was ridiculous, but it still left me feeling lost and rudderless. I tossed and turned all night, my head swimming with so many random thoughts I was afraid it might burst, too.

When I woke up, B.J. was sitting up in her bed with her laptop.

I groaned. "Don't tell me you've gone back to work already."

"Nope. I said I wouldn't check a single email all week and even though reentry will be hell, I'm holding to it. But I've compiled a list of potential galleries and overpriced tourist shops for your box spring ladies, and now I'm deep into Googling phobias."

I rubbed my eyes. "My, aren't we a morning person."

B.J. focused on the screen. "It's really fascinating. Apparently forty percent of women experience a full-blown phobia at some point in their lives. That's twice as many as men."

"Men," I said.

She shrugged. "It probably has some correlation to superior intelligence. Or increased sensitivity. Anyway, part of what makes a phobia a phobia is that the sufferer will do anything she can to avoid the terror of those phobic feelings. And because phobias are so irrational, they're often really embarrassing, so the sufferer tries to hide them from the people around her, which only intensifies the whole thing."

"Exactly," I said. "Wow, that's amazing."

"I know," B.J. said. "How did any of us survive before Wikipedia?"

"So what's the answer?" I asked. "I mean, can you get rid of them?"

"Hmm, so essentially specific phobias can be cured with cognitive behavior therapy. First you have to replace your catastrophic thinking with correct risk assumptions and then you kind of gradually desensitize yourself."

"English, please," I said.

"Well, for me, I suppose first I'd learn to say nee—, the n word, and then—"

"Ooh, I know." I hauled myself into a sitting position. "You could work up to poking a sewing needle just under the skin on your index finger so one end is sticking out on each side. Remember, we used to do that back in elementary school?"

"Not helping, Mel. And for you, I guess you look up all the statistics of who dies where and then you'll realize you're more likely to croak in your sleep or in a parking lot than on the highway, and even if you do die on one, at least you'll be on your way somewhere. Instead of going nowhere." She shook her head. "I'm pretty damn insightful, if I do say so myself."

I stretched both arms up over my head. "You're a good friend, Louise, but I think I need caffeine for this conversation."

B.J. closed her laptop and swung her legs off the bed. "Coming right up."

I looked at her. She was wearing a great sundress, and her makeup was flawless.

"What's up?" I said.

She grinned. "I can't wait to make an entrance at the hotel coffee shop. I'm going to look so much better than the people who had fun last night."

As soon as B.J. left the room, I reached for my phone and called Ted Brody. His phone rang on and on and then went to voicemail. "Hi," I said. "This is Melanie and I just wanted to say that even if you've never been to the Christmas Tree Shop I think we have a lot in common and I really like talking to you. Oh, and if you ever need a recipe for chalkboard paint, I have a good one. I could even help you paint wine bottles for each table and you could write the day's specials on them. Okay, well, have a nice day."

I'd just finished brushing my teeth when my phone rang. I put on my reading glasses and checked the number.

"Hi, honey," I said. I walked across the tiny hotel room and stepped out on the balcony.

Trevor yawned. "Hey, Mom. Dad just called. Apparently he forgot there's a three-hour time difference."

I started to apologize for Kurt, then caught myself when I

realized I didn't have to do that anymore. "Well. I'm glad you two talked. I'm sure he . . ." I stopped myself again. "So, how did it go?"

"Fine. He's Dad, what can I say?" He yawned again. "So how's your trip going? Do you need anything?"

"I'm having a great time, and thanks, I'm all set. How about you—everything okay?"

Trevor made a sound that was a cross between a yawn and a yup.

I smiled. "Why don't you just go back to sleep, honey. We can catch up next week."

"Yeah, good idea. Oh, Dad wanted me to tell you he can't get through to you and he wants you to call him."

I waited until I finished a long, hot shower and took my time getting dressed before dialing Kurt's number. He answered on the second ring. "I'm glad you finally called Trevor," I said, "but don't you ever put him in the middle to try to get to me again."

"Unblock my number and I won't have to." Kurt sighed. "I've talked to both of them a few times. It took me a while to work up to it, that's all. It's bound to be awkward—"

"Speaking of awkward," I said. "Why am I calling you?"

Kurt sighed again. "I was hoping we could meet for lunch today, or at least a cup of coffee."

I held the phone away from my ear and shook my head at it. "What, you, me, and *Crissy*? You're kidding, right?"

"She's going off to spend the day with a friend from college. Or maybe it was a cousin." He lowered his voice. "I think it's over. We didn't even sleep in the same bed last night."

"Too much information, Kurt."

"Sorry. Sorry. It's just that you know what I miss the most? Every time something happens I find myself wanting to ask you what it means, how I should feel about it. It's like ever since we've been apart, half my brain is missing."

I thought for a moment. "It's probably more than half."

"Touché." Kurt laughed his old laugh, the one I'd almost forgotten about.

I ran one finger along the edge of the metal railing. The sun was bright, and a warm breeze carried the scent of the ocean right to my nose. I took a deep breath, inhaling it like a magic potion.

"I miss you," he said.

"It's too late, Kurt. I think there was a point before this all happened when we both should have tried harder, but—"

"Come on, Mel, it's water under the bridge. Let me pick you up for lunch. Where are you staying anyway?"

"Where I'm staying is no longer your business," I said. And then I hung up.

I was still standing on the balcony, watching the seagulls swoop and soar so effortlessly it could almost bring tears to your eyes, when B.J. came back with coffee and breakfast sandwiches.

"Bless you," I said as I reached for my coffee.

"Don't bless me yet. I just gave Finn Miller your number. He wants to take you to lunch."

CHAPTER 39

Finn Miller and I were gazing at each other across a waterfront picnic table topped with iced coffee and red-and-white-checked cardboard platters of fish-and-chips. Seagulls screeched overhead, and sailboats tacked and jibed in the distance.

B.J. and I had spent the morning making a tour of galleries and gift shops. We'd hit potential pay dirt at one, a funky little store right near the main fishing docks. The owner took the box spring ladies on consignment, and even said she'd do her best to keep them together.

"Good french fries," I said.

Finn nodded and popped another Advil. His golf shirt collar was sticking up on one side. He had little marks under the thinning hair on his head that looked like they'd been made by a sewing machine. *Hair Plugs in Sunlight* popped into my head, as if he were a sculpture.

I watched him wash the Advil down with a loud gulp of iced coffee.

He cleared his throat. "So then I told him if you're going to jerk me around like that, forget about it. You can take your friggin' promotion and put it where the sun don't shine."

I reached for another french fry. "Wow, just like that, huh."

"You bet your sweet bippy."

"Aww. I forgot about that expression. *Laugh-In*, right? Not that we're old enough to remember that show."

He shrugged.

"I know it's a long time ago," I said, "but I'm sorry I hurt you back in high school. You were really nice to me and you didn't deserve it."

"Yeah, you were a total bitch. Those Leon Russell tickets weren't cheap, you know. Hey, so what was it you do again? Didn't I read something about Dubai? How's the weather over there?"

I smiled. "I've never actually been to Dubai. I think B.J. may have embellished my profile. I'm a metal sculptor."

"Huh. Where do you get the metal?"

"Well," I said, "sometimes I buy it, but as often as I can I try to work with metal that I find. Junkyards and metal yards and even yard sales. I guess the buzzword is *upcycle*. You know, recycle into something more valuable."

"Good money in that?"

"Well, it has its moments, but I'd have to say the rewards are more creative than monetary."

He leaned forward over the table. "Copper."

I waited for the rest of the sentence to arrive.

Finn chewed a piece of fried fish and grinned at the same time, not the sexiest of combinations.

"Excuse me?" I finally said.

He washed down his fish and swallowed. "Copper. It's gone through the roof. So this is what you do: You hire a bunch of high school kids for cheap and get them to pick through the junkyards for the copper. Or maybe even get your hands on some free college interns."

He shook the bottle of Advil and grinned.

"And?" I finally said, mostly to get him to stop shaking the Advil.

He looked over his shoulder. Apparently satisfied that there were no spies around, he leaned forward again.

"And then you sell it. You'll make a bundle. And feel free to drop my ten percent in the mail."

My cell phone rang and I grabbed for it like a life preserver.

"Good news or bad news?" B.J. said.

"Good would be nice," I said. I aimed a fake smile at Finn, but he was busy spearing some more fish.

"I just grabbed Maria's subs with a bunch of classmates who wouldn't give us the time of day in high school, and now we're on our way to play miniature golf. The good news is I left you the car keys in case you want to join us. Unless Finn turns into an overnight.'"

"Not a snowball's chance in hell," I said. "But thanks for the first part."

"Okay, and Kurt called Tom at home to find out where we were staying, and I'd just talked to Tom and happened to mention where you were meeting your old friend Finn and I know, I know, it's none of his business but he is my husband and we used to go to that fish-and-chips place together all the time when we were dating. And anyway, long story short—"

"Thanks for the heads-up." I clicked the OFF button, tucked my phone back in my purse, and slung it over my shoulder.

I stood up as Kurt wove his way toward us through the picnic tables.

"Look who's here," I said. "What a nice surprise."

Kurt stopped and looked over his shoulder.

I smiled at him encouragingly.

"Sit, sit," I said when he got to the table. "Listen, why don't you boys catch up while I hit the little girls' room to powder my nose."

Kurt gave me a funny look, as if he thought he might remember that I didn't really talk like this, but couldn't be sure.

I walked back into the restaurant and made a quick stop in the ladies' room. Like everything else lately, the graffiti-covered stall brought me back to high school. WHO TOOK THE CHARMIN? I'M TOO SEXY FOR THIS PLACE. K.L. & B.H. FOREVER. FOR A GOOD TIME, CALL 1-800-CRISSY. WIPE FRONT TO BACK. HERE I SIT, BROKENHEARTED.

Here I sat, brokenhearted, too.

Wait. Actually, I was kind of relieved.

I'd foolishly pinned my hopes on a guy I had nothing in common with but high school math class a gazillion years ago. It would have been a great story if it had worked out, but the truth was I didn't even like math. And I didn't like Finn Miller any more the second time around.

I left the graffiti behind and gazed at myself in the mirror as I washed my hands. Under the harsh fluorescent lights, even with makeup I looked every bit my age. My eyes had crinkles around them and my face was heading south, along with the rest of me.

But I was too good for Kurt and I was too good for Finn Miller. B.J. was right—I'd been the only one who still had to believe it.

I believed it.

I found our waitress. "Excuse me," I said, "but once I'm out of sight, would you mind telling those two guys over there that I got a better offer? On second thought, that's kind of mean—maybe you should just say that something came up."

She tilted her head to look, then grinned. "Are you telling me they're both available?"

I grinned back, as if we'd gone to high school together. "They're all yours, honey—take your pick. Oh, wait, neither of them lives around here."

She rolled her eyes. "Tourists."

As soon as I got back to the hotel room I called Veronica.

"Hey," she said. "How was the reunion?"

"It totally sucked. Well, actually, ask me again in a few months. How's Fawn?"

"She's doing okay. Thanks for asking, and thanks again for last night. It meant a lot."

I closed my eyes. "Listen, I'm sorry I've been a crappy friend all these years."

"Life gets busy."

"Yeah, but what would it have taken? I never even called you back the last time you called."

"Don't worry about it, Melanie. I get it."

"Where in the South is Mark working?"

"Birmingham."

"Seriously? That's only about two and a half hours from my house. Well, with Atlanta traffic, you never know, but still. Anyway, maybe you and Fawn could come stay with me for a while. Mark is welcome, too—I have plenty of room. I was just thinking it might be good for you to have a change of pace, and for Fawn to have something to look forward to."

"Are you sure? As you may have noticed, Fawn can be a little bit of a handful."

"Of course I'm sure. I was thinking I could help her make some sculptures. Nothing dangerous—I'm thinking soda cans and a glue gun. Remember that awesome table I made with Tab cans junior year?"

"Like it was yesterday. Glass top with an empty space in the middle to hide things? I tried to copy you and make one, too, but it collapsed midway."

"I'll let you in on all my soda can sculpture secrets. And I think I might still have one of Trevor and Troy's old Slip'n Slides, if it hasn't sprung a leak yet. Maybe we could make a soda can obstacle course for Fawn to slide through."

"She'd love that."

"And I'd love to show you guys Atlanta. I actually kind of miss being there."

After Veronica and I hung up, I called Marion right away, before I could chicken out.

Four rings later she finally answered.

"Hello," she said, as if Caller ID had never been invented and she had absolutely no idea who was calling.

"Hi," I said. "It's Melanie. Can I come over and talk to you for a few minutes?"

"Why? It's not like I won't see you in another ten years."

"Please," I said.

CHAPTER 40

Marion and I sat across the coffee table from each other in her stupid, stuffy formal living room, our hands folded in our laps. She didn't even offer me a glass of water.

I cleared my throat. "I'm sorry that I flaked," I said, the expression coming back to me across the years. "I'm sorry I bailed on you. I should have helped you more with Mom and Dad. I should have been a better sister. I should have been there for all of you. I put Kurt before everything and now I see that I screwed up."

Marion looked at the empty space over my shoulder and shrugged.

"I can't undo what I did," I said.

"Or didn't do," she said.

"Or didn't do. I understand that you might not forgive me

and that's your choice, but I apologize from the bottom of my heart."

She made eye contact for the first time. "That's it?"

I shrugged. "Well, unless you want to do a few shots of tequila."

Her eyes teared up. "You think you can just apologize and it'll all go away like it never happened?"

I bit my tongue so I wouldn't take the bait. "I have no expectations. I just want you to know I'm sorry."

We sat there, looking at each other.

"Was Mom afraid of driving on the highway when we were little?" I finally asked.

Marion shook her head. "Don't you remember? She was afraid of everything. Highways, spiders, the basement. Sometimes it wouldn't be that bad, but I remember once she barely left her room for almost a month. Dad and I had to do everything."

"Wow. I mean, I kind of remember it, but I didn't realize it was that bad."

Marion leaned forward. "Why? Are you having symptoms?"

I shrugged. "They say the biggest thing to watch out for is the pattern of avoidance. Funny, kind of the story of my life."

Marion didn't say anything.

"How about you?" I finally said.

"Nothing. Not a thing." She brushed her hands together and stood up. "Well, Jonathan and I have dinner plans tonight, so I need to jump in the shower."

I stood up, too. "Well, thanks for letting me come over. And give my love to Jonathan and the girls."

I reached over and gave her a hug. She may have hugged me back a little bit.

She didn't walk me to the door, so I opened it myself.

"I love you," I yelled.

I closed the door without waiting around to find out if she answered. Whether she did or not, I was going to call her in a week or two. And maybe some day I'd even cop to switching our jewelry boxes all those years ago.

It was a dorky thing to do, but I drove Mustang Sally to the beach and circled around a few times until I lucked out and scored a parking spot right across from the lighthouse that blinked 1–4–3.

Then I called Ted Brody again. He answered on the first ring.

"Hi," I said, "it's Melanie again. First of all, I want you to know that it is completely, one hundred percent over between my husband and me. That doesn't guarantee that he won't be a pain in the neck, but it's the best I can do."

"My daughters," he said, "are a little bit overprotective."

I rolled my window down so I could hear the sound of the waves breaking on the beach.

"The second thing is," I said, "that I get lost in my work, a lot, but you could look at that as a good thing in a way, because half the time I don't even notice when it's the weekend anyway. But I have this weird highway driving phobia, and I'm working on it, but I feel that it's only fair that I warn you I've got some issues."

"I put garlic in everything I cook. Lots of it. So if you don't love garlic, that could be a big issue. But you could look at it that it's a good thing, because if you hang out with me, you will never, ever be bothered by vampires."

"Are you making fun of me?"

"Wait. Sometimes I wake up with recipe ideas in the middle of the night. I can also be a little bit too obsessed with the Cooking Channel, but I learn something new every damn time I watch. And just to be upfront, if I ever get a chance to be on one of those shows, I'm going. It's not that I don't watch the occasional movie, but I have to admit I spend far too much time checking out the set design in the restaurant scenes and I've been known to miss the occasional plot point. And I have to tell you, I'm really digging the idea of those chalkboard bottles."

I smiled. "The only thing I remember from the opening ceremonies of the London Olympics was how cool it was that they actually forged the first Olympic ring to show the industrial revolution, and then the other four rings dropped down from the sky. Oh, and all those lighted copper petals that rose up to become the Olympic flame. I stayed up half the night making my own petals."

"Maybe we could work a few in with the fireflies."

"And finally, what I need right now is a guy who has Mondays off and might be able to pick me up at the airport tomorrow afternoon."

He had a great laugh, a laugh I could get used to. "I could do that. I might even be able to rustle us up a nice Monday early-bird dinner, too."

"Thank you, I'd like that. I'll text you my flight info."

"I'll look for it."

"Great, I'll look for you when I get to the airport."

"I'll look forward to you looking for me."

"Ha. Thanks. Okay, I have to go now. I have some driving to do."

"You know that last scene in *Thelma and Louise*, when they drive off the cliff? Well, it's always bothered me. I mean, I get that they choose their ending, that they *decide* to hold hands and go out in a blaze of glory. But think about it. Men go out in a blaze of glory; women are smarter than that. They don't need the drama."

B.J. looked up from trying to poke her finger with a needle from the sewing kit I'd found in my suitcase. "Do you remember back in elementary school when if you had a good friend you pricked holes in your fingers and pressed them together and became blood brothers? I spent half my time faking sick just to get out of it."

I took a deep breath and started up Mustang Sally.

"Wait," B.J. said. She opened the glove compartment and took out two scarves.

When I tied mine on, my hands were shaking.

"Come on, Thelma, you can do this."

"Louise," I said. "It's my turn to be Louise."

I worked my way out through the tree-lined back roads until we got to the highway. I put the blinker on. I placed my hands carefully at ten and two o'clock.

My mouth made a dry popping sound when I opened it. I cleared my throat. "Okay, let's do it."

The traffic roared. I tried to pretend it was the sound of the waves breaking on the beach just a couple of miles away. It didn't really work, but at least it distracted me from the anxiety that swam through my veins, invading every part of me.

As the ramp fed me to the highway, I tried to breathe my way through it. I looked in the rearview mirror, put on my blinker again, eased my way over into the next-to-slowest lane.

"Hang in there," B.J. said. "You can do this."

In front of us, the highway stretched out endlessly, flanked by marshes and scrub pines and the occasional glimpse of a fast-food restaurant. If I didn't think about having to get off again, it wasn't so bad. Entrances and exits were always the worst.

Life was like that, too. It was the transitions that wreaked havoc on your nerves, your heart, your home. But once you made it through to the open stretches, it was pretty smooth sailing, at least for a while. So maybe the trick was to make the most of those times. Maybe The Rolling Stones were right and you had to get it while you can.

Time flies. Time flies faster every year. Time flies whether you're having fun or not, whether you're living your life big or small, whether you surround yourself with fear or with laughter. It might have been just a dream, but Corita Kent and Sister Bertrille were right—there were only two choices, afraid and boring.

I wasn't going to play it safe anymore.

It seemed to me that maybe I'd needed to dabble in my past to recognize my future, and who didn't love a good stroll down memory lane, but life was way too short to get stuck there.

My heart filled with hope and promise. Okay, and a little bit of anxiety.

I took a deep breath and pressed my foot down on the accelerator until I was actually going the speed limit. Maybe I was a little bit better. Or maybe the baby elephant would show up any minute. But, easy or hard, I wasn't going to let it get in the way of having a life anymore. A totally amazing life. I was going to lick this thing, and someday I'd be so comfortable driving I'd even name my own car. Ellie the Element? Eleanor Rigby? Ooh, maybe Elenore, from that old song by The Turtles. I couldn't wait to download it. I couldn't wait to get on with my life.

"Where do you think we should go?" I asked B.J.

"Don't think about it," my best friend said. "Just drive."

ACKNOWLEDGMENTS

First and foremost, I thank you for reading *Time Flies*. If you enjoyed it, I hope you'll take a moment to tell a friend or write a nice review—truly the biggest gifts you can give an author.

Whenever I needed a detail for this novel, it was only a Facebook post or a Tweet away. A huge thank-you to my fabulous readers for taking a stroll down memory lane and helping me remember feelings, songs, clothes, bad makeup, and more. Thanks for always making me feel that I'm writing my books for all of us.

I Skyped and chatted with lots of book clubs while writing and rewriting this book, and I thank you all for choosing my books and for never failing to surprise me with fresh insight. And, of course, for the many laughs.

Alphabetical, but no less heartfelt, thanks to Karin Beyer,

Jackie Blem, Joanne and Caitlin Doggart, Beth Hoffman, Robin Kall, Joan Lang, Allie Larkin, Mary Marken, Jill Miner, Karen Vail, and Wendy Wax for support and inspiration. Thanks to the artists kind enough to chat with me at fairs and shows and festivals. Thanks to the friends who shared fears and phobias. Thanks to the bloggers, booksellers, librarians, and members of the media who continue to give me the gift of this midlife career of mine. You all rock.

Thanks to Jake, Garet, Kaden, and the rest of my family for always being there, and to Daisy Mei for literally always being there with the steady sound of her snoring while I work.

Thank you once again to my incomparable literary agent, Lisa Bankoff, and to ICM's Dan Kirschen, Josie Freedman, Lisa Farrell, and Katie O'Connor, as well as to Helen Manders and Sheila Crowley at Curtis Brown, UK. You're simply the best.

Many thanks to the fabulous Sally Kim, editorial director at Touchstone, for her insight and energy, and to her wonderful assistant, Allegra Ben-Amotz. A big thank-you to my terrific publicist, Ashley Hewlett—it's so nice to hear raves about you from everyone you reach out to—and to marketing dynamic duo Ana Paula De Lima and Meredith Vilarello for your creativity and talent. Thanks to Cherlynne Li for all your hard work and another brilliant cover design. A big thank-you to Stacy Creamer, David Falk, Shida Carr, Linda Sawicki, and the rest of Team Touchstone. More thanks to Simon & Schuster's director of marketing, the amazing Wendy Sheanin, to Joy O'Meara and Claudia Martinez for interior-design perfection, and to Kristy Ojala for blog support.

Another big alphabetical thank-you to high school classmates Susan Baize, Eileen Casey, Liz Giacomozzi, Anna Holmes, Polly Kimmitt, Carol Donkin Lareau, Hollis Mac-Arthur, Joni Padduck, Pamela Padley, Susan Priestman Perry, Barbara Rhind, Diane Ridley, Deb Stelzer, Lee Terzis, and Sheryl Trainor for sharing memories and photos, and thank you to all of my SHS classmates who've stayed in my life, as well as those I've been lucky enough to reconnect with. See you at the reunion!

ABOUT THE AUTHOR

Claire Cook wrote her first novel in her minivan when she was forty-five. At fifty, she walked the red carpet at the Hollywood premiere of the adaptation of her second novel, *Must Love Dogs*, starring Diane Lane and John Cusack. She is now the critically acclaimed and bestselling author of ten novels, and divides her time between the suburbs of Atlanta and Boston. She shares writing and reinvention tips at Facebook.com/ClaireCookauthorpage and Twitter (@ClaireCookwrite), and at www.ClaireCook.com.